Olivia Gèroux knew her king was reluctant to marry her, whatever the negotiations had arranged. But she never expected to find handsome, arrogant King Rowan obsessed with his stepsister instead. And before she can determine what course to take, she overhears her greatest ally plotting to murder the princess.

Olivia must act quickly—and live with whatever chaos results. As the assassin hunts his prey, a magic mirror appears to show Olivia the three paths that open before her...

~ If she hesitates only a moment, the princess will die—and she will become queen.

~ If she calls for help, she will gain great power—but she must also thrust away her own happiness.

~ If she runs to stop the murder herself, she will know love and contentment—but her whole country will suffer.

As she lives out each path, her wits and courage will be tested as she fights to protect her people, her friends, and her heart. And deciding which to follow will be far from easy...

A CHOICE OF CROWNS

New York Times *bestselling author Barb Hendee reveals a world of ruthless desire, courtly intrigue, and compassion as one woman shapes the fate of a nation...*

Visit us at www.kensingtonbooks.com

First Electronic Edition: February 2018
eISBN-13: 978-1-63573-002-9
eISBN-10: 1-63573-002-3

First Print Edition: February 2018
ISBN-13: 978-1-63573-003-6
ISBN-10: 1-63573-003-1

Printed in the United States of America

A Choice of Crowns
Dark Glass

Barb Hendee

REBEL BASE BOOKS
Kensington Publishing Corp.
www.kensingtonbooks.com

Prologue

There's a story sometimes told on dark nights by families sitting near their hearths seeking ways to entertain one another...

Long ago, a vain lord enslaved a young witch so that he might use her powers to keep him handsome and young. His most valued possession was an ornate three-paneled mirror in which he could see himself from several angles. Each day, he'd look into its panels and admire his own beauty.

Seeking revenge on him, the young witch began secretly imbuing the mirror with power, planning to trap him in the reflection of the three panels, where he might view different outcomes of his useless life over and over, and he would suffer to see himself growing old and unwanted.

Though the young witch had once been kind and generous, her thirst for vengeance twisted her nature into something else. But unknown to her, as she continued to cast power into the mirror, it gained a will and awareness of its own.

One night, the lord caught her as she worked her magic, and he realized she was attempting to enchant his beloved mirror. In a rage, he drew a dagger and killed her. But her spirit fled into the mirror. Though she had been seeking escape, she was once again enslaved...this time by the mirror itself.

It whispered to her that it would protect her, and use the power she'd given it for tasks more important than punishing a vain lord. Together they would seek out those facing difficult decisions and show them outcomes of their choices.

"Wait!" she cried, inside the mirror. "What does that mean?"

The mirror vanished from the lord's room, taking her with it.

And no one knew where it might appear again.

Chapter One

I've heard it said the most important moments in one's life pass more swiftly than others. Perhaps it's true.

I only know that all my senses were on alert as soon as my father sent for me, asking me to come to his private rooms. Eighteen years old, I'd never once been invited to his rooms. In the past several weeks, he'd been closeted away much of the time, sending and receiving messages, but I had no idea what this was about—as he didn't see fit to share such intelligence with me.

Now...he wanted to see me, in his rooms?

I could hardly refuse, nor in fact did I want to. I was curious.

Gathering my long green skirt, I nodded curtly to the servant who'd delivered the message and made my way to the base of the east tower of our family keep. I knew exactly where his rooms were located, even if I'd never been inside.

Upon arriving, I stood with my back straight and knocked on the door. "Father? You sent for me."

"Come," he said from the other side.

With my hand shaking only slightly, I opened the door. Inside, I found a somewhat austere main room that appeared to be a study, with a large desk and chair. There were tapestries of forest scenes on the walls, and an interior door led to a bedroom.

My father, Hugh Géroux, sat behind his desk working on what appeared to be a letter, but he stood as I entered. In his early fifties, he still cut a striking figure, with a smooth-shaven face, dark hair with a sprinkling of gray, and dark eyes.

"Olivia," he said, as if meeting me for the first time.

We didn't know each other well, as I was the fifth and youngest of his children. I had two older brothers and two older sisters, and my father had used all four of them carefully to enhance his own wealth and prestige. My mother died of a fever when I was only seven, so my father raised us alone in a manner that was both distant and overbearing at the same time.

My family, the line of Géroux, was among the old nobility of the kingdom. While past famines and civil wars had destroyed several of the ancient families, ours survived. We were survivors. My father respected strength and nothing else.

His eyes moved dispassionately from my feet to my face, as if assessing me.

I knew only too well what he saw. I was tall for a woman. He was tall, and I could almost look him directly in the eyes. Unfortunately, the current fashion for women was petite and fragile. My hair was long and thick, but it was a shade of burnished red, and again, red hair was not currently in fashion.

Still, I'd been raised to remain sharply aware of everything going on around me, and it was no secret that most men found me desirable. My face had often been called pretty, with clear skin and slanted eyes of green.

I looked best in green velvet.

Though I was not vain, I had also been raised to understand that survival was based on value, and at some point, I'd be given a chance to prove myself valuable.

Had that chance finally come?

"You'll need to pack tonight," he said. "You leave for Partheney in the morning."

In spite of my careful awareness of self-control, I nearly gasped. "Partheney?"

This was the king's city. My family's lands were in the southeast corner of the kingdom. Partheney was in the northwest, near the coast of the sea. I had never been there.

"You're to marry King Rowan," my father said flatly. "His mother, the dowager queen, and I have arranged it."

I stood still as his words began to sink in, but I still couldn't quite follow what he was trying to convey. "King Rowan...the dowager queen...is this why you've been receiving so many messages?"

His eyes flashed, and I dropped my gaze, cursing myself.

Father did not brook questions from his children. He expected only two things from us: strength and obedience. But the slight shaking in my hands grew to a tremble. Had I heard him correctly? I was to marry the king?

Stepping around the desk, he approached me. "Do you know anything of the rumors surrounding King Rowan?"

Unfortunately, I did, hence the reason my hands trembled. Even here, in the isolated southeast, rumors still reached us. In his late twenties, Rowan de Blaise was a young king and had held the throne for only two years. But over those two years, four betrothals with foreign princesses had been arranged via proxy. Envoys had been sent to Partheney to finalize negotiations. In all four cases, when the envoys arrived, Rowan refused to even see them. He'd sent them away.

"I know some of the stories," I answered my father. "I know betrothals have been arranged, and he's sent the envoys packing."

"Yes." My father nodded. "His mother, the dowager, was the one who arranged the betrothals. She is anxious to see him married and founding a line of heirs."

"Why will he not marry?"

My father waved one hand in the air. "That is of no matter. What matters is, the dowager has decided to stop seeking a foreign princess and marry him into one of our own noble families. She's wise and has chosen the line of Géroux. We'll be linked to royalty, and I'll be the grandfather of kings."

The truth of all this hit me, and my hands ceased trembling.

I would be queen.

Clearly there were obstacles, but I allowed my initial worries to vanish and let my mind flow. Father expected complete success from himself and would expect nothing less of me. This thought made me brave.

"If Rowan has refused to even see the envoys," I began, "what makes you and the dowager think he will agree to entertain negotiations this time?"

My question was bold, but instead of growing angry, Father only looked at me as if I were simple—which I was not.

"Because as I said, you will leave in the morning," he answered. "I'm not sending envoys. I have no faith in envoys. I'm sending you. You'll go to the castle, meet the king, and handle negotiations yourself. You are a daughter of the Géroux. He cannot turn you away."

"You'll not come with me?"

"No. That was my first instinct, but the dowager believes it best if the king is given no choice in facing you directly. It will force him to be... polite." His expression darkened. "And you will not fail to secure him. Do you understand? You will not fail."

I met his eyes without flinching.

"I understand."

* * * *

Dinner that night was both strained and exciting. We sat in elegant clothes around a long table while our servants poured wine.

I allowed Father to deliver the news to my siblings—after the first course had been served. Silence followed for a long moment.

Inwardly, I triumphed at my sisters' mouths falling open.

"Olivia?" Margareta asked. "To marry King Rowan?"

She herself was married to a minor baron who'd not only forgone a dowry but also paid a fortune for the privilege of the marriage—in land. My father had long wanted a forty-square-league territory at the bottom of our own lands that boasted fine vineyards. Margareta was a shrewish woman who didn't care for her husband, but she'd married him all the same, as Father had ordered it. Unfortunately, her husband soon grew tired of her and began bringing his mistresses to live at the family manor.

Margareta now spent much of her time here, citing that Father "needed her." He did not need her, but he didn't mind her presence so long she played the dutiful wife and gave the baron no reason to demand his land back.

Raising a goblet to his mouth, Father offered her a measured stare. "Why not Olivia?"

"Because...because..." interrupted my other sister, Eleanor, "she is so young."

Eighteen was hardly considered young for noblewomen. I'd had female cousins married off as early as sixteen.

But—I shamefully admit—with some glee, I knew this news would come as a particular blow to Eleanor. At the age of twenty, she was engaged to marry a silver merchant. Father had arranged it. The man had no title, but his family was obscenely wealthy. Over the past months, Eleanor had been boasting to Margareta and me about the upcoming luxuries she would enjoy for the rest of her life.

As she stared daggers at me across the table, I could see the quiet fury in her face, and her thoughts were so open.

Why her and not me?

Both my sisters had inherited our father's dark hair and our mother's small size. They were considered fashionable and beautiful. I had inherited our mother's coloring and our father's height.

My brother George—the eldest—had also inherited our father's coloring. He swallowed a bite of roast beef. "Do you think Olivia can manage this?" George would inherit our lands and my father's title. He was calm and calculating, all mental gears and wheels and little heart. "I've met Rowan twice, and he struck me as rather intractable."

Father nodded. "She'll manage."

This turn in the conversation caused both my sisters' faces to light up. "I've heard King Rowan prefers men," Margareta said, not bothering to hide her spite. "That may prove challenging."

I shrugged, speaking for the first time. "He'll still need to marry. The people expect it. The nobles expect it."

Her brown eyes flashed hatred at my cavalier reaction.

Eleanor leaned forward. "I've heard he's so possessive of his throne that he won't share it with anyone, not even a queen."

"That's not true," George answered without an ounce of passion. "He works well with the Council of Nobles. He's no tyrant. So long as Olivia makes no mistakes, she'll secure him. She'll have the support of the council and the dowager queen. They all want to see him wed. Olivia just needs to act wisely."

As these words left his mouth, a fraction of my confidence wavered. He and my father would both view any failure here as *my* failure, that *I* had made mistakes. Without meaning to, my gaze shifted to the empty chair at the table. This had belonged to my other brother, Henri. Of all my siblings, he might have been the only one to show me support, to perhaps offer comfort. But he wasn't here. Father had wanted him to rise high in the military, and he expressed a preference to study the arts of healing abroad. They'd argued.

In a cold rage, my father had purchased him a lieutenant's commission in the far north, in the cold, along the border, and sent him away. Henri hated the cold, but Father believed in punishing any act he viewed as dissent.

I could not forget this.

I could never forget this.

"She will succeed," Father said.

I nodded. "Of course."

Eleanor's jealous anger glowed on her face, but I met her eyes evenly. I couldn't wait to be queen and force her to kneel and kiss my skirts.

* * * *

The following morning, as the sun crested the horizon, I stood in the courtyard of our keep watching my trunks being packed into a wagon. I'd packed everything that mattered to me, as I had no plans to return.

No one from my family was present to see me off, but I hadn't expected anyone to rise early. There was no love lost between any of us, and it was pointless to pretend otherwise.

"We're almost ready, my lady," said Captain Reynaud, the head of my family's guard. He was in his late forties, of medium height and a solid build. His beard had gone gray, but his hair was still brown. He wore a wool shirt, chain armor, and the forest-green tabard of the house of Géroux. He was loyal and steady, and I trusted him with my safety.

Father assigned him and nine other guards to escort me to Partheney. Captain Reynaud had made the journey several times with my father or George, and he knew the best routes for each time of the year. Thankfully, we were now in early summer and the roads should be dry.

I watched two of the men tying down my final trunk.

Another guard led my horse, Meesha, from the stable. She was a lovely creature of dappled gray. I'd decided that I would prefer to ride than to sit on the wagon's bench.

Walking over, I reached out to take her reins, and then I stroked her nose. The guard walked away to check the lashings on the back of the wagon.

"We have quite a journey ahead," I whispered to Meesha.

Yes, a long journey with an uncertain ending. I'd stayed up late in the night, talking to my brother, George, as I oversaw the packing of my belongings. Though he and I had seldom had reason to speak outside of the dinner table, he'd been only too willing to help prepare me.

Linking our family to royalty would open doors for him.

Still, he'd told me little that I hadn't known before. Father expected us all to be well informed.

George didn't know any more than anyone else as to why the young king was so reluctant to marry. A man in his position should have a legitimate child in the cradle by now. But Rowan's path to our throne had been unusual. When he was a boy, his father had been king of a small territory off our eastern border, known as the kingdom of Tircelan. His father died, leaving the queen, Genève, and their son, Rowan, at the mercy of a pack of ambitious nobles all vying for power.

Our own king, Eduard, was a widower with a small daughter named Ashton. Upon hearing of the death of the neighboring king, he rode to Tircelan to personally offer any needed assistance—as he feared possible upheaval or civil war so close to his own border.

But upon meeting Genève, Eduard fell in love. They married, and Tircelan was absorbed into our own, much larger kingdom. Any initial resistance was stamped out quickly. This all occurred when Rowan was twelve and Ashton was two. Not long after, King Eduard formally adopted Rowan as his son.

Over the next fifteen years, the blended royal family became admired and loved by the people. Eduard was a good king, respected by the noble families for his attention to securing our borders while not overtaxing the commoners.

Then one night at dinner, he grabbed at his chest and died.

By right of blood and birth, Ashton should have taken the crown, but she was only seventeen—and a woman—and our council of twelve noblemen held a vote to crown Rowan as king. This vote passed unanimously. There was some surprise among the common people, but Rowan and Ashton had long been viewed as brother and sister...and he was the elder brother.

He was crowned without incident two years ago.

Now, he needed a queen. He needed to secure the line with heirs.

I had no intention of letting this chance slip through my fingers, not for any reason. No matter the obstacles, I would overcome them.

Footsteps sounded behind me, and I blinked at the sight of my father walking across the courtyard. Had he come to see me off? To kiss me good-bye?

The absurdity of either reason almost made me laugh.

What did he want?

Stopping a few paces away, he studied me. This morning, I wore a gray cloak over a simple traveling gown. Even in summer, the nights and mornings could be cool.

"Daughter," he said.

"Yes, Father?" I responded dutifully.

"Lord Arullian has asked for your hand again."

Of all the things he might have said, this was not what I expected. Lord Arullian was a corrupt earl in his late fifties—rumored to be sadistic. He'd already had three wives. Two of them died under suspicious circumstances, and the last one killed herself by drinking poison.

Watching my father carefully, I said nothing.

"It would sadden me to see you in his hands," Father went on, "but the connection would be good for the family. Should you come home in failure, I see little choice but to accept his offer."

Though the morning was not overly cool, I shivered.

His threat was clear. I would succeed or he would make me suffer as Arullian's next wife.

"Yes, Father," I answered. "But I won't fail. The next time you see me will be to attend my wedding to King Rowan."

He smiled. "Of course. I have no doubt."

"We're all set, my lord," Captain Reynaud called. "Is Lady Olivia ready to leave?"

Stepping toward me, my father reached out. I took his hand, put my foot in the stirrup, and let him help me settle into Meesha's saddle. I could not remember him ever having touched me before.

"Good-bye, daughter," he said.

"Good-bye."

I looked around the courtyard at the keep. I would not miss this place. I hoped to never see it again.

My new home was the castle in Partheney.

Chapter Two

Four days later, I'd begun to question my decision to ride Meesha rather than riding on the wagon's bench next to our driver. Though Meesha was a gentle creature, I'd never in my life spent four straight days in a sidesaddle. My back ached, and the pain in my right hip, where most of my weight was supported, had become nearly unbearable. I envied the men riding astride.

Still, I was determined to show no weakness, and had been gratified to see so much of the kingdom. Though we entertained frequently at the keep, and I was skilled in the arts of polite society, I'd never been off my family's lands. Today, as the sky grew continually darker and the air more damp and cool, I knew we neared the west coast.

"How much farther?" I asked Captain Reynaud, who rode beside me.

"We'll need to stop for the night soon, my lady," he answered, "but we should reach Partheney by tomorrow afternoon."

This came as a relief. Every day, I'd grown more grateful for his steady presence. He was a bit coarse in his speech and manner, but I cared nothing about that. So far, he'd managed to find shelter for me each night. Twice, he'd found me an inn and arranged quarters in local stables for the men. Last night, when there was no town or village along our path, he'd set up a tent for me and piled blankets for a makeshift bed.

The men slept on the open ground.

Now, we were nearing the end of the fourth day, and we'd not seen a village for hours, but I wasn't worried. I could always sleep in the tent again.

Then…a raindrop hit my shoulder.

Another followed, this one striking my head.

The captain looked up in alarm. As the rain fell harder, I pulled up the hood of my cloak. In the southeast, summer rainstorms were not uncommon, but the sky didn't open quite like this, and I wasn't sure the tent would prove waterproof.

"There, my lady!" Reynaud called, pointing ahead.

Squinting through the falling water, I saw a barn in the distance.

Nudging his horse forward, he led the way. I kept my head down, but Meesha knew enough to follow his horse. Through the sudden storm, I could barely see the men all around us, and I was relieved when we stopped.

"It appears to be abandoned, my lady," Reynaud said. "Shall I go in first and check?"

As the barn indeed appeared abandoned, I didn't care to sit in the rain while he made an inspection. "No, let us just take shelter inside."

Before I could move, he was off his horse and on the ground.

"Put your hands on my shoulders before I lift you."

Though it was hardly acceptable for him to speak to me in such a frank manner, I didn't offer censure. No matter how well I'd hidden my discomfort, he *knew*. Following his instructions, I braced my hands on his shoulders. Grasping my waist, he lifted me down. I could barely feel my legs, and he did not let go.

The rain beat down harder, and I finally nodded to him when I believed I could stand on my feet.

Men around me were hopping down off their horses, and we hurried for the barn. A young guardsman named Talon opened the doors. Captain Reynaud and I stepped inside first.

The first things I noticed were two glowing candle lanterns sitting on crates. Then my eyes scanned the rest of the large interior of the barn, and it took a moment for the scene before me to register.

Five men were already inside, crouched in a circle, and one of them was digging through a burlap bag. Their clothes were tattered and filthy. A small, young woman, perhaps not yet twenty, sat on a crate between them with her eyes down. She wore a fine wool cloak. Her hands were bound in the front, and her expression was that of someone lost to herself.

Beside me, Captain Reynaud breathed in sharply. "My lady...that is Princess Ashton."

"What?"

He never had a chance to answer, as all five men sprang to their feet, and one of them drew the short sword on his hip.

That action alone probably killed him, as Guardsman Talon immediately dodged in front of me and rushed. I never saw him draw his own sword, but he slammed the man's short sword aside and then ran him through with a long blade.

All of my guards were coming in the doors, but instead of turning to fight, the other four strangers bolted in panic, fleeing for the back door. Captain Reynaud gave chase.

Though no longer in his prime, he could still run.

Unfortunately, the young woman stood in panic, staring at my guards in terrified confusion, and then she too turned to run. But she didn't follow the others. There was a window to her left, and even with her hands still tied, she scrambled up onto a crate, trying to get out that window.

"Captain!" I called.

Turning his head, he saw her and veered off in his chase. His men were awaiting orders. Their job was to protect me, and without orders, none of them would leave my side.

In a matter of seconds, he was up on the crate and had the woman in his arms, pulling her back up against his chest.

She cried out with a frightened, anguished sound.

"Princess," he said. "It's all right. I'm from the house of Géroux."

She didn't seem to hear him and struggled in his arms. With little idea what to do—or what was happening here—I walked forward, letting her see me.

As I reached them and took a closer look at her, she struck me as more of a girl than a woman, small and slender with silky black hair, pale skin, and blue eyes. Even in her current state, she was pretty. But she was also hysterical, and no noblewoman worth her weight should ever give in to hysteria.

"Princess," I said, reaching out to untie her hands. "You are all right. These are my guards. Who were those men holding you captive?"

Reynaud looked around in frustration. One of her captors was dead, and due to the distraction Ashton had caused, the other four had escaped. We'd get no answers from anyone but her.

Her eyes locked onto my face, and some of the panic faded. "I want to go home," she whispered. "I want my brother."

Then she fainted in Reynaud's arms.

It was difficult to hold back my disgust. Useless girl. I couldn't imagine any situation in which I might ask for one of my brothers and then faint.

Sighing, I looked to Reynaud. "We'll need to make her comfortable until she wakes."

* * * *

She didn't wake until morning.

We spent a somewhat uncomfortable night in the barn, but at least we'd remained dry. As soon as the sun crested, Reynaud sent a few men outside to see if they could build a fire from straw and a broken crate—so that we might at least boil water for tea.

Two horses had been found outside. We assumed one had been for the princess and the other for the man Guardsman Talon killed. The other men must have escaped on horseback.

As soon as the princess stirred, I sent a guard to see if the tea was ready. A hot drink might do her good.

Kneeling beside her, I heard Reynaud's heavy bootsteps coming up behind me. As Ashton's eyes opened, they widened at the sight of me and then moved swiftly up to Reynaud, but she immediately took in his green tabard. This was a good sign to suggest she might be more coherent.

"Géroux?" she whispered.

I nodded. "I am Olivia Géroux. We are on our way to Partheney."

Her eyes returned to my face. "Olivia? Then you will be our queen." She grasped my hand. "You will be my sister."

While these words caught me off guard, I was beyond glad to hear them. Rowan's own sister already viewed me as the next queen. This did much to establish confidence in my position. More, she didn't appear to resent me in the slightest. The moment she'd lost her throne to her brother, her fate as a "princess" had been sealed, never to be queen here. And princesses were married off to foreign kings. In her place, I would have hated me on sight.

"How did you find me?" she asked.

"Quite by accident, I fear. We took shelter from the rain."

She stood up quickly and glanced around. I stood as well.

Beneath her open cloak, she wore a wool gown of pale blue. The color made her blue eyes glow. This was the first time I really *looked* at her. Last night, I'd noticed she was pretty, but I now saw that even with straw in her hair, she was striking beautiful, like one of the dolls I'd played with as a child. Her silky head barely reached my shoulder. Her skin was like pure milk. Her wrists and hands were fragile.

Standing beside her, I couldn't help feeling overly tall and gangly… almost hulking.

But she didn't appear to notice this, and spoke to Captain Reynaud.

"Forgive me. But you must get us to Partheney as soon as possible. My brother will be beside himself. He'll have men searching door-to-door in the city. There's no telling what he might do."

That stuck me as doubtful. Brothers did not go to such lengths to retrieve their sisters.

"Who were those men, Princess?" Reynaud asked. "How did you come to be here?"

She winced, as if remembering. "I...I was alone in the stable yesterday, and one of them grabbed me. He put a bag over my head, and then I was pushed into the back of a wagon and felt myself being covered. I was afraid...but not overly. Our guards search any wagons passing through the castle gates, so I didn't believe the men would get me out."

Reynaud stepped closer. "But they did get you out. How?"

She shivered. "The guards at the gate did not search the wagon, and let it pass."

At this, I couldn't help a stab of pity. Though her story made little sense, women of our class relied upon our guards. I could not imagine my father's men allowing captors in tattered clothing to roll me out the gates of the keep.

"Did they say what they wanted?" Reynaud asked. "Ransom?"

"Not ransom. They said they were taking me north, to the kingdom of Samourè, to marry Prince Amandine."

That made no sense at all. Ruffians did not kidnap princesses and carry them across the border to be married...unless perhaps Prince Amandine wished to marry the girl and had failed in his own negotiations. But how did that explain why the guards allowed Ashton's captors out the gates without searching their wagon?

Reaching out, she grasped my hand again. "I am grateful to you for saving me, but please, we must hurry. The king will be distraught."

* * * *

The rest of the morning passed swiftly.

Though I'd never met a princess, Ashton behaved nothing as I would have imagined. Neither proud nor haughty—nor regal—she remained quiet much of the journey and deferred to Captain Reynaud in all things.

By mathematical accounting, she must be at least nineteen, a little older than me, but she seemed younger, almost childlike, and I couldn't help wondering why. Still, in the grand scheme, I didn't give her much thought. Though she'd stated I would be her "sister," this meant little. Again...she would soon be married off, and I would probably see her perhaps a few times over the course of the rest of our lives—if that. To me, she would be nothing.

We stopped for a simple lunch, and she thanked the captain for the apple and the biscuit he brought her. Upon seeing the protective and pitying expression on his face, I wavered in my opinion of her. He looked as if he wanted to strip off his cloak and wrap it around her like a blanket. Perhaps she was not such a fool. I'd met women who possessed the gift of making all men want to lay down their lives. Such women disgusted me. I could never simper and say "thank you" so prettily to win the heart of a man. These guards protected me because they were paid and because they were loyal to my family.

This was the only acceptable arrangement.

After lunch, we rode a few more hours, and then I saw Ashton shift uncomfortably in her saddle. She appeared nervous. "We'll see the city just over that rise," she said.

Why would she be nervous?

After glancing once at me, she urged her horse over to the captain's and began to speak softly. I wanted to hear what they were saying and followed after.

We reached the top of the rise.

Looking down, I took in a sharp breath. The city of Partheney waited below. Nothing could have prepared me for the sight.

The city stretched for leagues, but it spread out around a hill, and at the top of the hill stood an enormous eight-towered castle. Much of Partheney itself had no walls, as it had grown outward over the centuries. One section of the city—near the center—was walled, and there was a second wall around the castle itself. Not far west of the city, the ocean spread to the horizon. I had never seen the sea.

Captain Reynaud appeared to be weighing a decision.

"What's wrong?" I asked.

He looked back at me. "Since the princess was abducted, anyone seen with her might be taken for the culprits. Riding all the way through the city for the castle could be risky."

Well, we couldn't sit out here forever. "What do you suggest?"

Turning his torso to look back, he called out, "Rufus!"

A stocky young guard nudged his horse into a trot and came to join us.

"Go down into the city, and go to the guards up at the castle gate. Tell them what's happened, that we've recovered the princess and have them send us an escort."

"Yes, sir."

The guardsman was off like a shot, cantering down toward the city. Again, I was grateful for Reynaud's steady head. His precaution was wise. Or…had this been Ashton's idea?

We waited.

I expected our escort from the castle to take a while, but in a surprisingly short time, fifteen horses came galloping out of the main entrance to the city, nearly flying up the road toward us. As they grew nearer, I could see that except for one man, they all wore chain armor and tabards of light blue and yellow—the king's colors.

The leader wore a sleeveless tunic. His hair was dark. He rode like a demon, pushing his horse to its limits.

Ashton's nervousness increased to open anxiety.

"My brother," she said.

A jolt ran through me. That was the king? He'd come out himself and was riding in the lead?

Quickly, Ashton dismounted and ran a few steps ahead. When she turned back, her face shone with open fear.

"Everyone, please. Get off your horses and kneel down. Don't touch the hilts of your swords for any reason." With obvious regret, she looked to me. "You too, my lady. Get down and kneel. Please. Can't you see the state he's in?"

This plea startled Reynaud, but the group of riders was almost upon us, and the man in front had increased his lead.

"Everyone down!" Reynaud ordered. "On one knee!"

The men obeyed instantly. A moment later, Reynaud was at my side, reaching up. I was attempting to understand this chain of events. Even a woman of my status would curtsey to a king, but the thought of having to grovel on the ground was unthinkable. Still, my instincts told me to follow Ashton's plea, and I let Reynaud lift me off my horse.

Then I knelt, but I kept my head up, watching.

Ashton stood well in front of us, on her feet, waiting. The king jerked the reins of his frothing horse, and as it skidded, he jumped to the ground before it had fully stopped. I took in the sight of him. No one had warned me he was handsome, well formed and muscular. His hair was thick and dark brown and hung in waves just past his collar.

His body was in motion the instant his feet hit the ground. He ran to Ashton and scooped her up in his arms, gripping her so tightly to his chest I feared he might hurt her. His dark eyes were wild as he began striding back to his horse. There was nothing she could have done to stop him, but I saw her whispering rapidly in his ear. I assumed she was confirming our messenger's story, telling him my identity and explaining that my guards had saved her. I expected him to stop and turn and come back to both greet and thank me. He did neither.

Instead, he lifted her to the front of his saddle and jumped up behind her, gripping her again as if his life depended on it. She was still whispering quick words. Her hands were on his chest, and she appeared to be trying to get him to stop. I saw her mouth the word "please" several times.

The rest of his retinue reached us.

King Rowan glanced our way once, but at Reynaud and not at me.

He spoke to the royal guard in the lead. "Micah, manage that," he ordered.

Then, he kicked his frothing horse again and galloped back toward the city, holding the reins in one hand and Ashton with the other.

I was stunned.

I was humiliated.

Captain Reynaud's face showed fury.

I'd ridden five days, and this was the greeting from my future husband?

Quickly, I stood up, and Reynaud stood beside me

The leader of Rowan's guards appeared both mortified and dumbstruck at the same time. Dismounting swiftly, he strode toward me. He was perhaps thirty years old and one of the tallest men I'd ever seen. He wore a close-trimmed beard, and his blond hair hung down his back. There was a sheathed sword on his left hip.

I was angry and wanted to punish someone, anyone, for the initial greeting I'd received here.

But as he came before me, he dropped to one knee. "My lady, Olivia."

His tone was so filled with apology that my anger faded. He seemed to know exactly who I was and was already treating me as his queen.

"I'm Captain Micah Caron," he continued, with his eyes downcast. "Commander of the royal guard."

This surprised me. He was not overly young to have achieved the rank of captain, but he was young to be named as commander of the royal guard. Normally, such honors were awarded to seasoned soldiers in their late forties or early fifties.

I found myself unable to speak. King Rowan's nearly unhinged behavior had left me at a loss.

"The king has been overwrought with worry," Captain Caron rushed on. "But he welcomes your arrival, as do we all. The dowager queen has been preparing. A fine private room awaits you, and tonight, a banquet will be hosted in your honor. The Council of Nobles has gathered to express their joy." He looked up to Reynaud. "Bunks and hot meals have been readied for your men."

Beside me, Reynaud's taut body began to relax. He cared for his men and would appreciate Captain Caron seeing to their comfort. Now that I was safely delivered, they could begin the journey back tomorrow.

"May I escort you to the castle, my lady?" Caron asked.

Still somewhat at a loss, I nodded once—as regally as I could.

He stood up and towered over me. The effect was the opposite of when Ashton had stood beside me. His expression was still apologetic but protective at the same time. I felt small...almost delicate. Something about his physical presence unnerved me, and yet I couldn't help being grateful for how swiftly he'd altered the situation.

Motioning toward my horse with one hand, he said, "My lady?"

I let him hand me up into the saddle, and then I looked to the castle. My new home.

Chapter Three

That evening, after a few hours of rest, I woke alone in my private room, in one of the west towers of the large, drafty castle. Though not luxurious, the accommodations met my needs and expectations. It boasted its own fireplace. Tapestries depicting rose gardens graced the walls. I had a large four-poster bed with a thick down comforter. There was a wardrobe and a cherrywood dressing table with a mirror and matching chair positioned against the east wall.

All of my trunks had been delivered.

As I rose to dress, though, a problem presented itself. Most women of my class employed a lady's maid. However, my father had forbidden this practice. He'd taught us all how to listen, how to spy, and how to gather information, but he saw a danger in letting anyone get too close to a family member, and was against the idea of another woman in our rooms, seemingly invisible, listening to us talk.

As a result, my sisters and I had sometimes been forced to lace each other up. I managed to get around this as often as possible by ordering gowns that laced up the front. For formal occasions, I could call on one of our serving women.

But my finest gown, the one I wished to wear tonight, laced up the back and would require assistance. Perhaps I could choose another? No. The one I had in mind suited me too well, and I needed to look my best.

The problem resolved itself with a soft knock on the door.

"Come," I called.

A middle-aged woman stepped inside. She wore a gray wool dress with her hair pinned up rather severely. Bowing her head, she said, "My lady.

The princess informed me that you are traveling without a maid. I came to see if I could be of assistance."

I knew full well that my lack of a maid would appear odd in these early days, and I'd soon need to employ one here. It would be expected.

"Are you maid to the princess?" I asked.

She nodded. "Yes, my lady. I am Kamilla. May I assist you?"

Though I showed no emotion, her offer was welcome. "Please." I pointed to the largest of the trunks. "My gown for tonight is in there. It is the one on top."

It was emerald-green velvet with a scooped neckline and long, slender sleeves. The skirt was split, and I'd brought a white satin underskirt to wear beneath it. Kamilla got me dressed and laced me in tightly, nodding her approval at the effect of the green over the stark white.

I looked at my hair in the mirror. "Up or down?" I asked, throwing all decorum to the wind. She lived here, and she dressed Ashton. I wanted her opinion.

Kamilla studied me dispassionately. "Down, I think. You have lovely hair and should show your tresses. But sit and let me do something with the front. Do you have a clip, perhaps in silver?"

"Yes, in that box."

Without question, I sat and allowed her to brush out my hair. She took the front, pulled it back over my forehead, and pushed the top forward slightly to soften the effect. Then she pinned it. The effect was simple and elegant.

I stood up. I looked well. This was not vanity. I could see that I looked well. My burnished red hair shone, and the dress brought out the color of my slanted green eyes.

Once more, Kamilla nodded her approval. "It's good that you stand so straight. You're tall, and there's nothing for it, so you are wise to use it instead of slouching."

Her somewhat impertinent opinion was unexpected, but I couldn't help finding her words gratifying. No one had ever looked at me and approved of my height before.

Then the next problem presented itself. "I have no idea where to find the great hall."

"I'll escort you, my lady."

* * * *

Kamilla took me far enough that I could see the entry chamber before the great hall, but she did not exit the corridor. Instead, she faded back into the shadows.

I stepped alone into the vast circular entry chamber. There were entrances to other corridors along the walls, leading in all directions, but an open archway to the great hall dominated one side.

Drawing myself up, I walked through the archway to find the great hall already filled with people, milling about drinking from goblets. A large hearth stood in the center of one wall, and even in early summer it was burning, as the coastal nights could be chilly. I wondered what winters would be like here. Five long tables with chairs lined three of the walls, but it was customary for guests to drink and visit before dinner was served.

I was not alone for long.

"My dear," said a familiar voice.

Baron Augustine, an old friend of my father and a frequent visitor to my family's keep, approached me though the crowd. He was portly, with a white beard, and dressed in a burgundy tunic with gold thread. He was on the council of twelve nobles and therefore one of the most powerful men in the kingdom.

Our government was set up as a balance between the council and the reigning monarch. Council seats were for life, and an empty seat could only be filled by a majority vote from the sitting council. Most council members held one or more secondary government offices as well—for which they were paid generous stipends. Lord Sauvage served as minister of foreign affairs. Lord Cloutier, the oldest member, served as minister of finance.

Baron Augustine had studied the law in his youth. He was the keeper of our laws and bylaws. Striding directly to me, he leaned in to kiss my cheek.

"My dear," he repeated. "I cannot tell you how glad I am to see you. The dowager's announcement of your agreement, of your impending betrothal, has brought such joy to the council. She couldn't have chosen better, and you do us honor by traveling on such short notice."

Of course, he was flattering me. Any woman with an ounce of sense would have agreed to the arrangement, jumped onto a horse, and ridden five days if the crown had been offered to her, but…at the same time, his voice was warm and genuine. He'd always behaved like a loving uncle, and he was glad to see *me*. My own father would not have kissed my face or bothered with such kind words.

Even more, just like Ashton, like Captain Caron, he already viewed me as the new queen. My brother, George, had not been wrong. I would have the support of the council.

"I've not met the dowager," I said quietly. "Will you play escort and introduce me?"

"It would be my honor." He offered his arm. "She has been so eager for your arrival."

We made our way through the throngs of guests toward the hearth. I spotted the dowager queen, Genève, before Baron Augustine even pointed her out. She had the same shade of dark hair and eyes as her son. In her late forties, she was still striking, wearing a gown of gold silk and holding a goblet without drinking as she spoke to the wives of Lords Paquet and Sauvage—two other men on the council.

When she saw me coming, she went still, taking in everything about me. Perhaps she too could see who I was without being introduced.

Baron Augustine stopped and bowed to her. "My queen, allow me to present the lady Olivia Géroux."

Though she was the dowager queen, in gatherings like this, it was polite to address her by her former title. Her eyes scanned my face, my hair, my form, and gown. She smiled, but it did not reach her cold eyes. Then she handed off her goblet and grasped my hands. "My dear. You are most welcome. In his letters, your father spoke highly of you, and I can see he did not exaggerate."

Was there relief in her voice? I thought so. I could feel strength emanating from her, and perhaps she could sense it in me.

Cold eyes or not, she was my most powerful ally here.

"Olivia," said a soft voice from my right.

Turning, I saw Princess Ashton coming toward us. The sight of her took my breath away. She was almost ethereal in a gown of peach silk that made her pale skin glow. Her silky black hair was styled in a fashion similar to mine, flowing down her back with the front held by a silver clip.

She smiled openly. "Oh, how beautiful you look. You are by far the loveliest girl in the hall. I'm sorry Rowan rode off so quickly today. I wasn't even able to thank you properly."

The most unsettling thing about her was that she meant every word, and I was uncertain how to respond to someone like her. She appeared to lack any and all ability at skilled wordplay. She said what she thought, and she was a gentle creature.

Normally, I would despise such a woman, as she was clearly weak-natured. But again...she wouldn't be in my life for long. I suspected several betrothals were likely in the works, hence Prince Amandine's attempt at abduction.

"You look well," I said. "Are you recovered?"

"Yes, thank you. I rested this afternoon, and I feel safe here with my brother."

Her eyes moved partway across the hall, and I breathed in quickly to see Rowan in the crowd, speaking with Lords Paquet and Sauvage. He was every inch as handsome as he'd been that afternoon, wearing the same sleeveless tunic that showed the defined muscles in his arms. Waves of dark hair curled behind his ears. His face was clean-shaven, and his cheekbones were high.

Standing on tiptoes, Ashton kissed the side of the dowager's face. "Good evening, Mother."

"Are you certain you are recovered, my dear? This whole affair has given us such a fright."

"I feel well, Mother," Ashton answered, "and I didn't want to miss Lady Olivia's welcoming dinner. She's been so kind. She and her men saved me."

Geneve smiled at me again, but if anything, her eyes were even colder. "Yes, I was informed."

"Have you managed to learn who these captors served and how they escaped the castle gates with the princess?" I asked.

"No. But my son will learn the truth."

Again, we all looked to Rowan. He suddenly glanced around, as if missing something, and turned his head toward our small group.

Crooking his arm, he barked, "Ashton."

Ashton started slightly, as if she'd done something wrong. "Excuse me." Hurrying over, she took his arm with both hands, and he turned back to his conversation without acknowledging my existence.

Baron Augustine and the wives of Lord Paquet and Sauvage froze at this clear slight against me, but Geneve never lost her serene smile. Gazing upon her children with what appeared to be affection, she sighed. "It has been a most trying time for the king. He was overwrought at the abduction of his sister, and I fear it may take him longer to recover than her."

His pointed attempts to ignore my existence could hardly be accounted to worry over the potential loss of a sister. There was more going on here. I simply didn't know what yet.

But I nodded sympathetically. "Of course. I've not yet spoken with the king, so I have little idea of his state of mind."

Everyone waited for Geneve's next words. Again, her smile never faded. "That will be remedied soon, my dear. You are seated next to him at dinner."

This brought relief. I would finally learn more about my future husband.

* * * *

Unfortunately, dinner proved an equally humiliating affair. Baron Augustine was seated on my left, with the king to my right. Lord Moreau, another member of the council, sat to the king's right, and the two them remained engaged in steady conversation for the first three courses. Several times, Lord Moreau leaned around Rowan to speak to me, attempting to pull me into the discussion, but though Rowan never offered an impolite word to me, he also refused to acknowledge my existence. How was I to win a man so determined to pretend I was not there?

By the time dessert was served, we'd still not exchanged a word.

"Have you questioned the two guards who were on duty at the castle gate yesterday?" Lord Moreau asked him.

Rowan nodded. "Yes, and so has Micah. They both swear no one got by them with the princess...that they searched every wagon. They are loyal men, and I know them well. Perhaps the princess was mistaken about being taken past the guards. She told me a bag had been placed over her head before she was hidden in the back of the wagon, so she saw nothing."

"Then how did these captors get her off the castle grounds?"

Rowan's face darkened, and he looked down the table past Moreau. Ashton was seated several people away, on the far side of Genève. "I don't know. But I will find out."

"My king," Baron Augustine said, pulling Rowan's attention. "I hear your vineyards are producing a fine crop this year. Lady Olivia's father also grows a variety of grapes."

"Does he?" the king answered without looking at me, and then attempted to turn away again.

"I hear you do better with purple grapes here along the coast," I put in, speaking directly to the king. "We tend to grow vines of white in the south."

This was hardly a riveting topic, but I was determined to make him at least acknowledge me. He did not. He did not acknowledge I'd spoken, and went back to his conversation with Lord Moreau.

Everyone was seated and finishing the last of their strawberry tarts with cream when movement in the north archway caught my eye. Several musicians came into the hall and began setting up to play.

The dowager queen rose from the table and approached her son.

"You should lead the dance, my king," she said in her smooth voice, "and partner with our guest of honor."

A jolt ran through me at her brilliance. While a lady could never ask a man to dance, someone like the dowager queen suggesting it couldn't be ignored. Rowan would have no choice but to lead me out onto the floor.

To my astonishment, he stood up. "Forgive me, Mother. I'm not disposed to dance tonight. It's been a trying day, and I would retire to a quieter place." He leaned around her to look down the table. "Ashton, I've a mind to play chess."

She was still eating her tart, but she put down her fork instantly. "Of course." They both left the table, heading for the archway. Everyone watched them leave.

At this, even Genève froze. This was more than a slight. He'd just refused his mother's pointed invitation to dance with me and then abandoned the dinner being held for me. It was an insult. Baron Augustine appeared shocked beyond words.

I didn't let anything show on my face as my mind raced for a graceful path forward.

To my everlasting gratitude, Lord Moreau stood and held out his hand. "The king has been kind enough to give me the pleasure of dancing with our beautiful guest. Will you join me, my lady?"

I smiled back as if there was nothing in the world more pleasant than accepting his offer. "I would be honored, my lord."

I took his hand.

All eyes were upon me as we moved out onto the floor. He grasped my left hand and my waist as we began. I was skilled dancer, and so was Moreau. He was a slender man with a thin mustache. Though he was not as close a friend to our family as Baron Augustine, he'd visited our keep several times, and I knew him slightly. He had a reputation for gambling, but he was respected on the council.

Other couples soon joined us on the floor, and we were no longer the center of attention.

Relaxing slightly, he studied my face as we danced. "Don't distress yourself. You're doing well."

This was the first attempt at honesty anyone had made here, and I wanted to jump at it. But could I trust him?

"Am I?" I responded. "He's not yet even spoken to me."

"No, but neither can he send you away, and you've managed to smile through his insults. The dowager queen was wise to bring in a daughter from the house of Géroux. Your father did not raise fools."

"You wish for this wedding to take place?" I asked.

"Wish for it? I'd carry you both down the aisle myself. So would any man on the council. Rowan is a fine king, stronger in some ways than Eduard ever was, and he listens to the council. He can hold our kingdom safe, but he needs to marry and establish a line. The people expect it." He paused in his words if not his fluid movements on the dance floor. "And I can already see that you would make a fine queen."

Though I was relieved at this honest exchange, in part, it served only to frustrate me more. "Surely, he can see that as well? Why is he so opposed to marriage?"

Something flickered across Moreau's face, almost a nervous twitch. But he shook his head. "Who can know the inner workings of a king's mind? Perhaps he does not see the importance of this one element. We must protect him from himself and help him down the correct path."

To me, this seemed not only a weak answer, but also an evasion. Moreau knew more than he was saying.

"If that is the case," I asked, "how am I to seduce him if he won't acknowledge me?"

"You don't," he answered flatly, spinning me faster to an increase in the tempo.

"I beg your pardon?"

"Don't try to charm him. He's immune. Trust me on this count. Simply do what you've been doing tonight. Smile and pretend nothing is amiss. You cannot win him over. In this instance, he will only be swayed by a show of strength."

To my shame, this advice actually brought relief. I was no charming seductress, and I was only too familiar with men who responded to nothing but strength. Still...

"How does that help me succeed?"

"He'll have to be bullied," Moreau answered. "But you needn't worry about that. The dowager queen and the council can manage him. You only need make it clear that you won't respond to his insults and that you have no intention of leaving. We'll handle the rest."

This assurance should have increased my relief, but it didn't. As he'd already stated, my father did not raise fools. While I would use any support offered by the dowager or the men on the council, the only person I trusted entirely was myself.

I had to ensure my own success here, and that meant I'd need leverage over Rowan. What was his weak point?

All men had one.

* * * *

The next morning, I had a breakfast tray in my room, and then Kamilla came to see if I required help getting dressed. She didn't appear to mind serving both the princess and me.

"Which gown, my lady?" she asked, looking through my largest trunk. "I'll have a maid come in today to unpack for you."

Which gown? I wasn't certain.

"I've not been told of today's activities," I answered. "The daily rhythms of the castle are still new to me."

For some reason, I felt safe admitting such things to her. Father would have scorned me for such behavior, but I required some assistance here, and she didn't appear to judge my ignorance.

"Of course they are," she said. "You've only just arrived. I'm sure the dowager queen will invite you to tea later today to help set up your schedule, but this morning is common court day. Twice a month, the king holds court in the great hall, so the common people might bring him problems or grievances. It could be useful for you to attend."

"Yes."

It could be very useful to see Rowan interacting with his people. I might learn a great deal.

"Perhaps this one, my lady," Kamilla said, lifting a tan muslin day gown from my trunk.

In addition to green, tan was also a color that suited my red hair. I nodded to her.

* * * *

I arrived at the great hall to find it packed, so I stood quietly in the back, observing.

A dais had been set up at the front of the hall with a large chair near the front of the dais and a smaller chair set halfway behind the large one.

Rowan, wearing his crown, sat in the large chair...and Ashton sat in the small one.

This did take me aback. I had listened to some of the rumors that Rowan didn't care to share power with anyone, but if he wanted a woman's counsel in court, I would have expected the dowager queen. For one, Ashton would not be here much longer. It was already past time she should have been married off. Even more, Ashton lacked both strength and intelligence. What assistance could he possibly gain from her?

Six guards in light blue and yellow tabards stood behind them.

A well-dressed man who appeared to be a secretary of some kind stood on the floor to Rowan's right. He held an unrolled piece of paper in his hands. Two men knelt on the floor directly below the dais. They were of similar coloring and facial structure. Though still in their early twenties, their skin was rough and weathered. Rowan listened as one of them spoke.

"No matter what our father wrote down," the man said, "by right the boat is mine. I am the eldest."

"That's not what Father wanted," the other man responded angrily. "He wanted us both to have a living! He made certain before he died."

Rowan studied the brothers. "So, while your father lived, the three of you were able to peaceably run your fishing business, but now that he's gone, the two of you cannot work together?"

The elder brother spoke again. "We could if my brother would only recognize me as the captain, with greater rights of spoils, and he would follow my orders with the other men. I am the eldest. Such is my right."

The younger brother grew angrier. "Then why did Father leave a will making us equal partners?"

I absorbed this story with interest, wondering how I might solve it myself. If Rowan ordered the two men to make peace and try to work together, it appeared that only greater conflict would ensue, but…it would be unfair of him to alter the final wishes of their father.

"Could you sell the boat and divide the profits between you?" Rowan asked. "Then you might each have money to begin a new business of your own."

"Sell the boat?" asked the elder brother in amazement. "No. It has been in our family since we were boys."

Before Rowan could speak again, Ashton rose and leaned in close to his ear, whispering softly. He tilted his head and listened. After a few moments, she sat back down.

Rowan looked to the brothers. "The princess tells me that she knows your wives, and the family owns a second fishing boat, a somewhat smaller one that you hire out."

"Yes, my king," the elder brother answered.

"And this boat was also left to both of you, and you equally split the money from any profits earned from hiring it out?"

"Yes, my king."

"Would you be willing to sign the second boat over to your brother outright?" Rowan asked the elder brother. Then he looked to the younger. "If he did this, would you be willing to give up rights to the first one? This way, you would each have your boat and your own fishing business."

While this was somewhat disadvantageous to the younger brother, it did sound like the best possible compromise.

At first, neither brother appeared pleased. The elder was greedy for any profits, and the younger was indignant over being challenged for what he considered his due. But within a moment or two, they also must have seen the ultimate sense of the king's suggestion. At least they would no longer need to work together.

"Yes, my king," they both said, and rose partially to begin backing away.

But Rowan was already looking to the well-dressed secretary. "Jarvis, announce the next case."

My eyes moved to Ashton as I mulled over the realization that this compromise had come from something she'd whispered in Rowan's ear. How often did she sit up there with him when he held court?

Feeling a presence at my left shoulder, I looked up. Captain Caron towered over me.

"My lady," he whispered softly in greeting.

Though I tended to prefer clean-shaven men, his blond, close beard suited him. His eyes were so light brown they were almost transparent. Again, he made me feel small and delicate. I pushed the thought away.

"The king takes counsel from his sister?" I whispered back.

At first, he didn't answer. Then he said, "Rowan is a good king. He'd defend this nation with his life. But he has a blind spot when it comes to the daily lives of the people, and he's wise enough to know it. Princess Ashton understands the needs of the people."

I hardly believed the latter. Ashton didn't strike me as bright enough to lace up the front of her own gown. She'd most likely passed Rowan some snippet of gossip she'd heard and he had extrapolated. But I was impressed by the loyalty in this captain's voice. I hoped that someday soon, he'd be as loyal to me when I sat in the chair beside King Rowan.

As the morning passed, though, the captain stayed with me while I listened to case after case, and with each one, my confusion about the dynamics here only grew. In nearly every dispute, at some point, Ashton would rise and whisper to her brother. Only after this would Rowan make a decision or present a compromise. He was never impatient, and he clearly preferred for people to agree with his rulings rather than having to enforce them.

But Ashton was becoming more of a mystery to me. Was she actually providing him with assistance or was her presence here for show? I had to admit they did make a pretty pair of royals up on that dais, appearing to work together for the good of their subjects.

When the last case had been heard, the secretary named Jarvis announced that court was now closed.

Rowan stood. Ashton followed suit. He offered his arm, and she took it. Together, they walked through the crowd as their guards followed.

I stood near the archway.

Ashton glanced at me with a warm smile, but Rowan kept his eyes straight ahead. Perhaps it was time I learned more about Ashton.

"Where will the princess go now?" I asked the captain.

"To the old stable on the east side of the courtyard. She and some of the women do their charity work in there."

Charity work? What did that mean? But I wasn't going to ask him, lest I look even more uninformed.

I nodded. "Thank you."

* * * *

After walking outside and through the courtyard, I asked a guard for directions to the old stable. He escorted me partway and pointed to a somewhat faded building beside the barracks.

"There, my lady."

"Why is it called the old stable?"

Turning, he pointed to the other end of the barracks. "Because a new one was built several years ago."

Though I was still uncertain of the situation, I nodded and walked toward the old stable. The doors were open, and I stepped inside to see numerous tables spread all around, stacked with a wide variety of items from blankets to clothing to food stores. Several wagons were parked in open spaces between the tables.

There was a second level above, and instead of the usual ladder, a set of makeshift stairs had been arranged.

Princess Ashton stood on the main floor, near a table, and she was folding blankets. The sleeves of her gown were rolled up. She must have come directly from court.

"Reanne," she called toward the stairs. "We'll need one more sack of flour. Can you carry it, or should I call in one of the men?"

"No, I can manage," a voice called back.

Several other women moved about the main floor. Some were servants, but others looked more prosperous, not noble, but perhaps the wives or daughters of merchants.

When Ashton saw me enter, her face lit up. "Olivia, how good to see you. Have you come to help?"

Help? I wasn't even sure what was happening here.

Approaching her, I nodded. "Yes, Princess. I'm glad to help...but what is it you're doing?"

"Please call me Ashton. We're nearly sisters. I think we can use given names in private."

Again, everyone seemed so certain my marriage would take place soon—with the exception of my would-be husband.

A young woman came down the stairs carrying a sack of flour and loaded it into one of the wagons.

"We're gathering supplies for the poor," Ashton explained. "There is so much need right now. Between the drought last year and the sea storm this spring, both the farmers and the fishermen's families need whatever we can offer."

Astonished, I turned to the cart. It was laden with flour, dried beans, jerked beef, blankets, and various items of clothing.

"You're sending all that to the poor?" I asked.

She blinked. "Of course. Don't you organize drives in your father's keep?"

Drives? What did that mean?

I looked around myself at the tables. "Where did all this come from?"

"From those who are most fortunate." She still seemed puzzled by my questions. "I have a list of nobles, merchants, and city leaders who are willing to donate. I send out word of what we most need, and then twice a moon, we spend several days gathering. We organize in here, and send wagons out where they are most needed."

High windows in the barn allowed sunlight to filter inside. The light showed dust hanging in the air. I was still almost too astonished for words.

"How often do you work in here?" I asked.

"How often?" She laughed softly. "Every day. There's always something that needs to be done, even if it's just sorting and organizing. This is a large task, and winter will only bring more need."

Every day.

I could not get my head around that. The princess of our kingdom spent time every day working in an old stable to sort out food and blankets for needy commoners. How could her mother allow it?

"Do you go out gathering and delivering yourself?" I asked.

At this, her smile faded. "Not so much as I'd like. I used to go quite a bit, but I'm only allowed out the castle gate if Micah can escort me, and ever since he was promoted to commander of the guard, he has less time."

It took a few seconds for me to realize she referred to Captain Caron. She called him by his given name? Then I remembered Rowan had done the same. How odd. I didn't even know Captain Reynaud's given name.

"Captain Caron is young to hold such a command," I ventured.

She nodded. "Yes, but last year, Captain Trevar took a fall off a horse and broke his knee so badly it wouldn't mend. He had to retire, and Rowan wanted someone he could trust. He trusts Micah."

This was another interesting piece of information. King Rowan valued men he trusted over men with more experience.

"Would you like to help?" she asked.

I would not. I found all this quite beneath a person of her station—or my own. But turning around and leaving would appear impolite.

"What can I do?"

"The Compté family has a new baby," she said, "and Theresa hasn't recovered from the birth. I was able to get out and visit last week, but I've heard things haven't improved. Her husband, Cameron, is an artisan mason, but he's not found much work this summer. Go to the back of the stable and find some clean cloths for nappies. Then go upstairs. Most of the food is there. See if you can find some of last year's strawberry preserves. Theresa might need more fruit in her diet." Walking to another table, she lifted an indigo shirt with black buttons. "And I think I'll send this for Cameron."

I stared at her. She knew the given names of some mason and his wife out in the city? Thinking back to the events of the morning, I realized she had not been feeding Rowan snippets of gossip. She actually *knew* what was happening with the people outside this castle wall.

"Princess," another woman called. "Do you think there is enough flour loaded?"

"I'm coming," Ashton called back.

She headed over to check the wagon. With little choice, I started toward the back of the barn. Cloth for nappies? What exactly was I seeking? I knew that babies wore cloths. I'd simply never seen such a cloth.

But I'd only taken a few steps when a serving woman came through the open front doors and approached me.

"Lady Olivia." She bowed her head. "Captain Caron said I might find you here."

"Yes?" I asked, wondering what she wanted.

"The dowager queen requests your company for tea. It is being served as we speak."

Relief flooded through me. "Thank you. Please wait so that you might show me to her apartments."

Turning, I called, "Princess, I fear I must leave you. Your mother is asking for me."

"Of course," she called back. "I can manage here."

With another sigh of gratitude, I left the barn.

Chapter Four

Genève's apartments were exactly what I expected.

I entered her rooms in the nearest south tower to find her seated on a low velvet couch. She wore a gown of deep red today, with her hair piled up.

There were a number of couches in this main chamber, suggesting she often hosted gatherings here. She had her own large hearth, and the furnishings were opulent, from the thick carpets to the marble-tiled tables. Vases of roses graced three tables, and a porcelain tea set rested on the table directly in front of her. As she began pouring the tea, I saw a plate of small cakes with cinnamon-crumble topping. How very civilized.

"My dear," she said. "Come and sit."

Her voice held no warmth, and in spite of the opulent surroundings, I had the feeling I was walking into the dragon's lair.

"My queen," I said with deference, as I sat down on a couch across from her.

She handed me a cup of tea. "After spending an evening and morning in this castle, do you believe yourself up to the task of completing a marriage with my son?"

Accepting the cup, I tried not to react. Had her gloves finally come off? Were we about to engage in a frank conversation? I hoped so.

"I believe myself up to the task," I answered, "so long as I understand the obstacle. As of yet, I cannot see my obstacle."

"Can you not?" Her eyes narrowed. "Perhaps you're not clever as you seem." Then she sighed and sat back. "No, you are clever. You're simply too well-bred to see the truth, and that is not a shortcoming."

I was tired of mincing words, and met her gaze evenly without speaking.

She leaned forward again. "Has the prospect of another woman not occurred to you?"

I tensed. It had not. From what I'd seen and heard, Rowan had no romantic connections. If this was the truth, it could be a problem if he was hiding a mistress from the noble classes. And if she wasn't noble—and therefore not a real threat—why would Genève bring it up? Suddenly, I was afraid. I'd come here with no plan to fail, but if, somehow, I did fail, I'd be sent home to the triumph of my sisters and the retribution of my father.

"Another woman?" I asked tightly.

"Rowan has called a formal meeting of the council in three days' time. There, he will inform them of his plans to marry Princess Ashton."

At first, I felt nothing, as I could not have heard her correctly. But I had. "Princess Ashton?" I repeated in disbelief. "That...that is impossible. She's his sister."

"They share no blood. They have no blood relation to each other whatsoever. Still, the council will revolt, and they'll never approve such a reckless proposal. Rowan has sworn he will take his news to the people and announce the engagement publicly. This will have one of two results. Either the people will be shocked and view the marriage as incestuous... or worse, they will not."

For a moment, I didn't follow her meaning, and then it hit me. Rowan had been crowned king because the council had placed him on the throne as Ashton's elder brother. Though he was Eduard's adopted son, over the years, he had *become* the "king's son" in the collective consciousness of the people. Should Rowan stand up publicly and remind everyone that Ashton was not his sister by blood...would he still have a right to the throne? Would his right to rule be brought into question?

As if reading my face, Genève nodded. "You see, my dear. He cannot be allowed to do this."

"Does the council know what he's about to suggest?"

"Some suspect. I think Moreau especially. But no one knows for certain."

"Rowan has told all of this to you, though? He's told you this plan himself?"

"In great detail," she answered bitingly, showing emotion for the first time. "We've engaged in several heated arguments."

A larger question loomed, and I nearly gasped at the thought. "Does Ashton know?"

Genève shook her head. "That is what surprises me most. She's not as simple as she appears, but in this matter, she has no idea. She views him as her beloved elder brother and would be as shocked by this as anyone."

I allowed myself to breathe. "Then what is the concern? She would refuse him."

Genève tilted her head, and her expression shifted to disappointment—in me. "Really, my dear. Have you not have observed them together? He has only to snap his fingers, and she will do anything he says. She lives in his shadow, and she'll refuse him nothing."

I went cold.

Genève spoke the truth. Ashton might be horrified at the thought of marrying a man she viewed as her brother, but in the end, she'd follow any order he gave. What was to be done?

"I thought I had solved the problem before your arrival," Genève continued. "But your men blundered into that, and you brought her back with you."

The coldness settled in my stomach. "What do you mean?"

"Negotiations between myself and Prince Amandine of Samourè have concluded. His father is dead and his own coronation is imminent. It's a good match for Ashton. The council has approved. Only Rowan has refused to agree."

I still didn't follow this entirely, but an ugly suspicion formed in the back of my thoughts.

"Yes," Genève said, again as if reading my face. "I arranged for her abduction. I paid those men to take her from the stable on a morning I knew she'd be alone. Rowan was busy that day, and he wouldn't notice her absence until dinner."

"But how did her captors get her out the castle gates?"

"The guards let them out. I told you that I'd arranged this. I would leave nothing so important to chance."

"You bribed royal guards?"

Her body went rigid. "I did *not*. When you are queen, if you ever find a royal guard who can be bribed, you will have him executed on the spot. I picked two men who can be trusted, explained the situation, and appealed to both their patriotism and loyalty to Rowan. The men love him more than they loved his father. Rowan is not afraid to use military force when necessary, and they want him on the throne. I promised them Ashton would not be harmed, and she would be delivered safely to her new husband."

I was reeling. Two of Ashton's own guards had been convinced to let paid ruffians take her out the castle gates. Genève must wield more power than I'd realized.

An uncomfortable thought occurred to me—though I don't know why it should make me uncomfortable. "Did Captain Caron know?"

"Micah? No. He is as devoted to Ashton as he is to Rowan. Micah's father served in the guard before Ashton was born. He watched her grow up. He can never be taken into this confidence. Remember that."

For some reason, this made me glad. I wasn't sure why.

But...Genève was right about me. My men and I had blundered upon Ashton and brought her back.

"She'd have been married before Rowan even learned where she was," Genève continued. "And the path for you would have been secured."

I was not about to apologize. "So, what happens now?"

She leaned again. "Prince Amandine still wishes to marry her, although in order to gain approval from our council, he had to make territorial concessions that did not please his own council. I will need to arrange for Ashton's removal from this court."

"Another abduction?"

"No, I cannot play that card again. But don't think on it. I'll handle this matter so long as you can promise me one thing."

"And what is that?"

"If I clear your way, and the council puts enough pressure on Rowan that he agrees to marry you, can you tie yourself to a man who will never care for you? Rowan has had several mistresses over the years, no one of consequence, just women to sate the needs of his body. But he's never cared for any woman except Ashton. I don't believe he will ever love anyone else. Can you stomach that for the rest of your life?"

Could I stomach life with a man who cared nothing for me in order to obey my father...and to be queen?

Absolutely.

I nodded. "I can."

She smiled. "Good. Then I'll handle the rest. But be ready. Developments will be swift. We have only three days."

* * * *

Dinner that night was less strained.

For one, it was a much smaller affair with only the royal family and the families of the council. But also, Genève seated me between herself and Lord Moreau, and she did not expect me to try to establish polite conversation with the king. I understood why. We were in a holding pattern now until whatever method she'd devised to send Ashton to Samourè could be set into motion.

Rowan continued to ignore my existence, but I didn't care. I would be his queen soon enough.

Not long after dinner, he called to Ashton, and they left the great hall.

"Shall we join them?" Genève asked Lord Moreau and me.

In mild confusion, I looked to him.

"By all means," he said, "though I hope that suggests a game of cards?"

"It does," she answered. "But not for money. I know your wife isn't here on this visit, but I did so promise her."

"You crush my spirit," he said lightly.

I walked with the two of them down the north corridor and spotted an archway ahead. Through the arch, I found myself in a small room with a burning hearth, and several tables set up. Rowan and Ashton were playing chess.

He ignored our entrance.

"What about a game of Jacks and Kings?" Lord Moreau asked.

I spent half the night playing cards with him and the dowager queen while sitting not ten paces from my future husband—who never glanced our way—and everyone at my table continued to pretend nothing was amiss.

Despite my earlier promise, which I had meant, this was growing rather wearing.

The following morning, I slept until nearly noon, then I sent for Kamilla. I'd been invited to tea and an embroidery party in the queen's apartments. All the noblewomen currently residing at the castle would attend.

Today, I chose a gown of fine wool. I thought something simple might be best for a gathering of women. Although embroidery was not my passion, I understood its social importance and always had something ready inside a round wooden frame.

When I arrived at the queen's chamber, seven women were already present, but they appeared comfortable with each other. Lord Paquet's wife, Elizabeth, was a plump woman in her late thirties. As she stood by the tea table, I noted her kind face.

"Come in, my lady," she said upon seeing me. "Have you broken your fast? We have some fine cakes and sandwiches."

I was hungry. After setting down my embroidery frame, I moved to join her.

The dowager was close by, chatting with Lord Sauvage's wife, Miranda. Lord Sauvage was a hard-natured man with a reputation as a warmonger. He'd not chosen his wife for her sweet nature, and I had learned to be cautious in Miranda's company. I'd just picked up a plate when she asked, "Is the princess not joining us?"

Genève hesitated and then her face broke into a smile. "I was going to wait, but I fear I will burst if I don't share my joy. The princess will not be joining us today, as she has more important matters. She is readying herself for a journey, for a new life. Matters have been settled with Prince Amandine, and he has sent a retinue to bring her home. They arrive the day after tomorrow. My darling girl will soon be queen of Samourè."

Excited voices broke out all around as the women flocked to congratulate Genève.

For myself…I didn't know what to make of this. Why hadn't she told me yesterday? Amandine had sent a retinue, and Ashton would simply leave? Could it be so easy? What if Rowan refused to let her go?

But I had no idea what Genève had planned, and it was in my own interest to do nothing to question or hinder her. So I smiled and flocked with the other women, expressing my pleasure over Princess Ashton's betrothal.

Inwardly, I wished I understood Genève's plans better.

Somehow, I managed to eat tiny sandwiches, drink tea, and work on embroidery until it was time to dress for dinner, and then I excused myself. The dowager queen's apartments were in a south tower, and my own were in a west tower, so I made my way down the curving stone stairwell to the ground floor.

Then I slowed my pace, as my father had taught me. The corridor I entered contained several alcoves, and I must walk silently and slowly. Most assignations of note took place inside alcoves. Men and women could not meet in each other's rooms. Being discovered in a private bedchamber could be disastrous, but being stumbled upon in an alcove might be explained. My father taught me that vast amounts of useful information could be gleaned through a mix of silence and attention—and always watching the alcoves. Knowledge was power, and power meant both survival and reward. By the age of fourteen, I was so advanced in this skill that I learned my older sister, Margareta, was involved in a tryst with a handsome guard.

I was able to blackmail her for six months before she managed to have the guard dismissed and thereby remove any form of corroboration should I decide to tell Father. But it was a sweet six months, and I thought her a fool for having been caught out so easily. Father had taught her the same tricks. She should have been wise enough to avoid an alcove.

By now, the practice was second nature to me, and I didn't even think about it as I walked slowly and silently down the corridor.

Then…a voice coming from just up ahead stopped me.

"They can't. They cannot do this."

It was Rowan.

"It's already done. Mother has begun arrangements for my dowry."

Ashton.

There was an alcove to the left side of the corridor twelve paces from me. Wooden balustrades had been set two to each side of a narrow archway. Cautiously, I approached until I could peek between the corner and one balustrade and see into the alcove.

Ashton stood up against a wall with her hands clasped in front of her. By her tearstained face, she had been crying. Rowan stood in the center of the small space. He was breathing hard, and his fists were clenched.

"I won't let them take you," he said.

"You knew this day would come," she answered. The pain in her voice was clear. "I'm to be married to Prince Amandine. Mother has completed the negotiations. The council has approved. The retinue is on its way."

"Do you want to leave here? To leave me?"

"No! You know I don't, but neither do I wish you to go against the council and make enemies of your own nobles, nor do I wish you to start an international incident. I am a princess, and princesses are married to improve foreign ties. The deal is done, Rowan. There is nothing you can do to stop it."

His entire body went still, and then he nodded. "There is."

Striding three steps, he grasped her by the back of the head and pressed his mouth down hard over hers. I held in a breath, shocked as he forced her teeth apart with his tongue.

She struggled in his grip, making panicked sounds and trying to push him away.

He reached behind her back with one hand and tore loose her lacings. She let out a muffled cry and managed to pull her mouth from his.

"Stop! Rowan, please, stop."

He kissed her harder, and I realized he wasn't going to stop. He was going to force himself on her, and then openly admit what he'd done. He would not be the first nobleman to try this. She'd be ruined for Prince Amandine, and Rowan would be in a better position to insist on a marriage to her himself—after he'd violated her. I had to stop this or my own future would be lost.

A loud tearing sounded as he ripped the cloth of the back of her gown.

She was fighting and sobbing at the same time, but he didn't seem to notice. An unfamiliar feeling rushed up inside me. How could he do this? He who claimed to love her? She was so fragile, and he was hurting her.

Backstepping six silent paces, I began to walk forward normally, letting my footsteps be heard and humming a tune I'd learned as a child.

As I passed the alcove, I stopped as if surprised to see anyone inside. Thankfully, Rowan had heard someone coming and stepped away from Ashton, but he was still breathing hard.

Ashton's face was wild and lost, and she held one side of her bodice halfway up her shoulder.

"Ashton," I said with a friendly tone, using the familiarity of her given name on purpose. "There you are. I was looking for you. I wanted your opinion on my gown for this evening."

Considering the sight before me, my empty chatter was absurd, but it didn't matter.

The madness in Rowan's face faded as he looked at her. She trembled and wept and held up her gown. One side of her mouth was bleeding. He hadn't struck her, so I assumed he'd cut her with his teeth. Then he looked down at his own hands as if stunned at what he'd been about to do. For the first time, he turned his head and really looked at me.

I held my right hand out to Ashton.

"Come with me now," I said. "I cannot decide on a gown by myself."

Her eyes focused on my hand, and she ran forward, grabbing it like a lifeline. I grasped her fingers tightly and began walking back the way I'd come.

"Where are your rooms?" I whispered.

"In the tower ahead, one floor below Mother's apartments."

Even though I didn't think Rowan would come after us, I kept her moving swiftly up the stairs, and at the top, we passed a young serving girl. "Go and fetch Kamilla straight away," I ordered. "The princess has fallen and injured herself."

The girl's eyes widened. "Yes, my lady."

She ran off.

Continuing onward, I took Ashton toward her rooms. She didn't speak.

* * * *

I stayed with Ashton only until Kamilla arrived to take over. I might have saved Ashton from rape, but I was worthless as a nurse. I told Kamilla the same story about her having fallen. After one glance at Ashton, Kamilla did not appear to believe me, but I didn't care.

"I can get myself dressed tonight," I said. "Stay with her until dinner."

"Yes, my lady."

Upon leaving Ashton, I once again made my way up the corridor toward the center of the castle. When I emerged into the circular entryway, I stopped at the sight of Rowan speaking to Captain Caron.

Rowan seemed in control of himself again. "All right. We'll go over the watch rotation later," he said.

"Yes, my king."

At the sight of me, the captain nodded and left quickly.

Rowan glared at me. We both knew what I'd just witnessed, and I walked straight to him. It was time he started to learn who I was.

We were alone, and before I could say anything, he spoke first.

"Do you still wish to marry me?" he challenged.

"With all my heart," I answered coldly.

He leaned closer. "You enjoy rough wooing?"

Did he think I'd respond to threats? I had no personal fear of him. He would never grasp the back my head and kiss me like he'd kissed Ashton. Nor would he ever tear my gown. That sort of act required passion.

I whispered in his ear. "Say what you like. Do what you like. But know this. I am not leaving. I promise, no matter what you do, I am here to stay."

His eyes flashed hatred.

Good. I hated him too.

Turning, I swept off toward the west tower.

* * * *

At the conclusion of dinner that night, Rowan stood up and walked down the table to lean over Ashton. Previously, after dinner, I'd only seen him call to her to join him.

Tonight's action must have been unusual, because Genève watched. Reaching out, he touched Ashton's back, and she flinched. She wouldn't look at him, and he grew agitated, whispering into her ear with determination. After a few moments, she finally nodded once.

"We're off to play chess," he said to his mother.

Silently, Ashton rose and let him lead her from the hall.

Genève turned to me, searching my face with her eyes. I'd never seen her alarmed before...but she was alarmed.

"What was that?" she demanded quietly. "She was afraid of him just now." Her eyes shifted back and forth. "That cut on her mouth. Did he do that?"

I hesitated. She seemed to have guessed I knew something.

"Nothing happened," I said. "Nothing of consequence."

"But he...did he try...?" she trailed off.

"Nothing happened," I repeated.

The crack in her control vanished as quickly as it had appeared, and she was serene again, but I'd glimpsed a hint of desperation.

* * * *

The next morning, I slept late, as I'd tossed and turned in my bed much of the night. I had a feeling something explosive was about to happen in this castle. I just didn't know who would light the fire.

The only thing I knew was that I had to succeed.

Near noon, Kamilla came to help me dress. I'd been told yesterday that an abundance of strawberries had been picked, and all of the noblewomen were gathering in the kitchens this afternoon to help the serving women make preserves. This was an old custom, and we even practiced it at my father's keep. In the heart of winter, preserved fruit had more value than gold. The poorest of our kingdom's people lived on flatbread and salted fish, and they often grew ill from the lack of variety in their diets.

I doubted Ashton's mother knew of her penchant for giving away last year's supply to fishermen and the wives of unemployed stonemasons.

Normally, I enjoyed the practice of making preserves. Today I was filled with trepidation. Something in Geneève's face last night worried me. But what did she have to fear if Prince Amandine's retinue was scheduled to arrive? Some of the things Ashton had said in the alcove yesterday were true. Rowan could not thwart the will of the council if he wished for their future support, and he'd already risked several international incidents in refusing marriages for himself. Turning away a royal guard that had come to escort a new queen home—after negotiations were completed—would be a great insult. Wars had been fought for less.

"Pull out my oldest wool today, Kamilla. I'll be working in the kitchens."

"Yes, my lady. As will I."

Her manner was a bit subdued this morning, but thankfully, she didn't bring up Ashton's torn clothes or cut lip. Instead, she dressed me in silence.

"I'll do my own hair," I said, wanting her to leave.

"Very good, my lady."

She slipped out.

I brushed my hair and pulled it back in a sensible braid. Looking in the mirror, I saw dark circles under my eyes. Those would not do. Father wouldn't approve. I'd need to put powder under my eyes before dinner tonight.

Upon leaving my guest room, I made my way down the curving stairwell. Once on the main floor, I knew I had to head north for the kitchens. I passed a few servants along the way, and then entered an empty corridor. Without thinking, my steps slowed and my walk became silent. I passed an alcove almost without noticing it, for I was not truly focusing on the alcoves this morning, until I heard a distinctive female voice ahead.

"You'll enter the stable from the back and make certain that no one sees you, especially Rowan. Do you understand?"

It was Genève.

"I know what I'm doing," a gravelly voice answered.

An alcove awaited on the right.

Silent but swift, I rushed to one side to listen and carefully peeked between the corner and a balustrade. Inside the narrow chamber, Genève stood speaking to a middle-aged man with a shaved head. His features were sharp. He wore chain armor over a wool shirt but no tabard.

"She'll be alone this morning," Genève said. "I gave her permission to forgo making preserves today so that she might sort some donations for tomorrow's wagons. Whatever you do, don't let her scream. Just cut her throat and slip out the way you came. And remember, you cannot be seen by Rowan."

I froze.

She was speaking of Ashton.

"I told you," the man said. "I know what I'm doing, and I don't need a lecture from you."

Genève assessed him and handed him a red velvet pouch. "This isn't only about money. The good of the kingdom is at stake. Most of the nobles are sheep, but there are several wolves. If Rowan falls, it could mean civil war. Do you want that, Soren?"

Soren? She knew him by name.

The man hefted the pouch. "Doesn't make any difference to me, so long as I get paid. But you need not fear. I'll get it done."

When he turned to leave, I panicked. Whirling, I ran back up the corridor and dashed into the first alcove just in time to avoid being seen. Listening to their steps, I heard him stride past. A few moments later, Genève walked in the other direction.

I was alone in an alcove while an assassin was heading toward the old stable to kill Ashton.

I stood there, listening to my breath. What should I do?

Suddenly, the air inside the alcove began waver. Alarmed, I tried to step back, but there wasn't much room. The motion of the wavering air grew more rapid, and then…something solid began taking shape.

I drew in a harsh breath.

There, right in front me, stretching from one wall of the alcove to the next, a great three-paneled mirror now stood where there had been only empty air an instant before. The thick frames around each panel were of solid pewter, engraved in the image of climbing ivy vines. The glass of the panels was smooth and perfect, and yet I didn't see myself looking back.

Instead, I found myself looking into the eyes of a lovely, dark-haired woman in a black dress. Her face was pale and narrow, and she bore no expression at all. But there she was, *inside* the right-hand panel, gazing out at me.

Had I lost my hold on reason? Was this place and these people driving sanity from my mind?

"Do not fear," the woman said. "There is nothing to fear."

I couldn't help my rising fear, but I also could not seem to speak.

"You are at a crossroads," she continued, "with three paths." As she raised her arms, material from her long black sleeves hung down. "I am bidden to give you a gift."

Could this be real? Was it truly happening?

"You will live out three outcomes…of three different choices," she said. "Three paths await you. Three actions…or inactions you might decide upon. Then you will have the knowledge to…choose."

I shook my head, finding my voice. "Wait! What are you saying?"

Lowering both hands to her sides, she said, "The first choice."

My thoughts went blank, and the alcove around me vanished.

The First Choice
Hesitation

Chapter Five

I was in a corridor, outside an alcove, listening to the plans of a murderer and an assassin.

"Doesn't make any difference to me, so long as I get paid," said the man called Soren. "But you need not fear. I'll get it done."

I felt dizzy, disoriented, as if I'd forgotten something and needed to remember, but when Soren turned to leave, I flew into motion, dashing to the nearest alcove and hiding from sight.

He walked past me.

A few moments later, so did Genève.

My mind raced. This man…this Soren, was about to seek out Ashton in the stable and kill her. Of all the possible actions Genève might have taken, it never once occurred to me she would have Ashton removed via assassination. Genève had raised Ashton as her own daughter.

She must be more desperate than even I'd realized. But what should I do?

I must stop it. Of course I had to stop it. And yet…

I hesitated.

What if I did save Ashton and in the process Genève's guilt was discovered? What would Rowan do? If the truth came out, he could call for her execution—and he would win. Where would that leave me? My most powerful ally here would be gone. The only person capable of any control over Rowan would be gone. He'd insist on a marriage to Ashton at any cost, and I'd be sent home to my father.

I stood there for long moments, frozen in hesitation, lost in the possibilities.

With Ashton gone…the path would be cleared for me.

Shaking my head, I came back to myself. No! I could not wear a crown bought with Ashton's blood. But time had been lost, and I would have to hurry.

From where I stood now, the kitchens weren't far, and there would be a door near the kitchens leading out into the courtyard. All kitchens had an exit.

I ran.

Upon reaching the archway to the kitchens, I looked ahead to a door and hurried through it. Once out in the courtyard, I cast my eyes about for any help, but the only guards in sight were all the way down at the castle gates, too far away.

Flying into motion, I ran toward the old stable myself, not certain what I'd do when I got there. Just as I reached the door, motion from the left caught my eye, and I turned to see that Rowan had led a horse out of the new stable, and he was adjusting its bridle. Captain Caron was coming out behind him, leading a roan stallion.

Again, I hesitated.

I would rather not involve Rowan directly. He'd be the most dangerous in seeking out the truth. But I had to do something. I'd already wasted too much time, and at this point, I would need help.

Stopping near the doorway, I shouted, "Captain Caron! Come quickly!"

Upon hearing me, the captain turned his head in alarm.

Then…Ashton screamed. I could hear her terror.

The captain and Rowan both bolted, running toward me at full speed, and I hurried into the stable.

To my surprise, it was now quiet inside. I saw no one, only long tables piled with goods and dust hanging in the air.

The captain skidded through the open door first.

Then Rowan came pounding in behind, casting around for the princess. "Ashton!" He carried a thick dagger in his right hand.

I hurried forward, looking both ways. Where was she? Could the assassin have dragged her off when he'd heard me and realized he was about to interrupted? Rowan and the captain were both searching too. Rowan was in a panic and moving the fastest down the tables to my right.

Then he stopped and went pale.

A sound I'd never heard before, like something from a wounded animal, escaped his mouth. He dropped from sight, and both the captain and I hurried toward him, navigating two tables piled with dusty overcoats.

Upon reaching Rowan, I looked down at the floor and wanted to close my eyes.

He knelt beside Ashton's body. Her throat was slashed open and blood flowed in a stream across the floor. Her beautiful black hair lay around her head, and her eyes were closed. Rowan picked her up and pulled her tightly against his chest, rocking back and forth, making long keening sounds. The look on the captain's face was unbearable. I could see sorrow warring with pain...and guilt. His job was to protect the family.

I couldn't seem to move my feet, and I wanted Rowan to stop making those awful sounds. I wanted him to put Ashton's body down.

Thinking back to her scream, I realized the assassin must have been almost upon her when he'd heard me call out for help. He'd been forced to rush events, and she'd seen him coming. He'd killed her quickly and then moved out of sight.

Had I arrived here a few moments earlier, she might be alive.

My hesitation had cost Ashton her life.

* * * *

After that, events took a morbid turn.

Once more men arrived in the old stable, Captain Caron ordered two of them to lock down the castle gates. By that point, his sorrow had shifted to anger. He wanted someone to punish.

Rowan would not get up off his knees, and he refused to let go of Ashton or allow anyone else to touch her or remove her body. I didn't even try to reason with him, and instead sent a guard to bring Genève.

Before long, the dowager queen stood in the doorway with more guards at her back, and then she approached, glancing at me and looking down at the scene of the floor. Her face was unreadable.

"Has the assassin been caught?" she asked the captain.

"Not yet, my queen. But he will be."

"This must be the work of someone on Prince Amandine's council," she said with a slight break of sorrow in her voice. "There was great resistance to his impending marriage."

I had to admit she was good. She was very good.

He nodded slowly, considering her words. "I will hunt down whoever did this."

Rowan had fallen silent, but he continued rocking back and forth, still gripping Ashton tightly. Her blood ran down his left arm.

"My son," she said slowly. "Put your beloved sister down so that her body might be properly attended."

He ignored her, and she stepped closer.

"Rowan," she ordered. "Put her *down*."

Turning, I left. I couldn't bring myself to watch the outcome.

* * * *

After returning to my own room, I remained there until evening, sitting and thinking.

At one point, a serving girl arrived with a tray. I'd given no thought to food, but I hadn't eaten all day.

The tray contained bread with butter, a slice of cheese, a bowl of strawberries, and a large goblet of wine. Looking at the simple meal, I was surprised to find myself hungry.

"Did the dowager queen order this?" I asked the girl.

"No, my lady. Kamilla sent me."

That made more sense. Kamilla may be stoic, but she was thoughtful. Then I noticed tearstains on the girl's face. She'd been crying.

"You know about Princess Ashton," I said.

"Yes, my lady. The whole castle knows." Her voice broke. "The captain had his men bring a door down to the stable, and they carried her body inside and to the cellars."

Well, that was something. At least she was being treated with dignity now. It was normal to carry a body to the cellars, where it was cooler, for burial preparation.

"Where is the king?" I asked.

"In his rooms."

"And the dowager?"

"In her rooms."

"Thank you."

I sent the girl away, and then I ate slowly. My father's quiet voice sounded in my ear.

Good. Keep up your strength. Your path is clear now.

After drinking the entire goblet of wine, I felt more myself. Yes, my path was clear, but I had to go forward with my eyes open—in possession of all the facts.

Rising, I walked to the door and left the room, making my way downstairs, partway across the castle, and to the first of the south towers. There, I climbed the stairwell.

Outside Genève's door, I knocked.

"Come," she called from inside.

When I entered, she wasn't surprised to see me. But she was pale as she stood beside her hearth. Her near-constant armor appeared weaker than I had ever seen it.

"I expected you sooner," she said.

"I should hate to become predictable."

There was no reason to make this easy on her. She'd had Ashton murdered. It would be pointless for me to pretend I did not know, or for her to pretend I would not reason it out. After our last private conversation in here, when she'd promised to remove Ashton, she'd have to think me a fool to feign ignorance. But…I had no intention of letting her know how much I knew.

I knew the assassin's name.

Walking inside, I closed the door.

"How did you get Rowan to let go of Ashton's body?" I asked.

"I didn't. In the end, I ordered Micah to pull him away and pin his arms while one of the guards took her. Micah is the only one who would dare, and he could see something had to be done."

Closing my eyes briefly, I imagined the raw emotion of such a scene.

"Is the retinue from Samourè due to arrive tomorrow?" I asked.

"No. Why should it? I never sent for one."

Her machinations were becoming clearer. She was the one who'd announced to the noble ladies that Ashton's betrothal negotiations were complete and the retinue was on its way…and that some members of the Samourè council had come out strongly against their prince making a connection by marriage with a more powerful kingdom and giving up land in the process.

"Could you not have tried that path?" I asked. "Sent for the retinue and given her a chance to leave?"

"Rowan would never have let her go. He'd have gone against the council and then insulted Prince Amandine by sending the envoys away."

"But won't the nobles wonder when the retinue never arrives?"

She shrugged. "It will only deepen the mystery and foster suspicion."

"Once Rowan recovers his wits, he'll want blood. If he blames the council of Samourè for Ashton's death, he'll start a war."

She shook her head. "He'll want to, but there's no proof. He cannot invade another kingdom without a vote of support from the council. They won't give it without proof, and he'll find none."

"He won't find proof because Samourè had no part in this."

Her eyes locked onto my face. "I could not stand by and watch my son throw his crown away. Something had to be done." She dropped her gaze. "All you need do now is be ready to act when I tell you."

Yes, I would do whatever she told me. She was my most powerful ally. But right now, I wanted to be gone from these rooms, and I turned away.

"I've been mother to Ashton since she was two years old," Genève said, "and she could not have been a more devoted daughter. Whether you believe it or not, I loved her."

The problem was that I did believe her.

And that's what frightened me most.

* * * *

Rowan locked his door and would not open it for anyone, not even servants bringing trays of food.

Genève allowed this to continue for three days.

On the night of the third day, she gathered Captain Caron and me and led the way up to Rowan's rooms.

There, she knocked, loudly.

"Rowan, open the door."

We waited, but nothing happened.

Leaning in, she called through the keyhole. "Open this door right now, or I'll have Micah break it down. You know he can do it."

If anything, over the past few days, Captain Caron's countenance had grown worse. I feared he blamed himself for every tragic event playing out here. His light brown eyes were less bright, and his long blond hair was snarled. But if Genève ordered him to break down the door, he would.

A moment later, the sliding of a bolt sounded from inside. Genève hesitated only a few breaths and then opened the door.

As a stench flooded out, I put one hand to my nose, but the dowager queen pressed forward. I followed. The main sitting room was dark, and Rowan sat by the dead hearth. There was a cask of wine beside his chair and a goblet on the table beside him. He kept a cask of wine in his rooms?

I spotted a chamber pot on the far side of the chair and realized it was the source of the stench. Perhaps he'd been sitting by this dead hearth all three days. He must have unlocked the door and immediately resumed his seat.

Genève cast around until she saw two candle lanterns. "Micah, please light those."

I began to wonder why I was here, why she should include me in this. My presence would do nothing to bring Rowan back from this darkness.

As the captain lit the candle lanterns, illumination only made the scene worse. Rowan's clothes were filthy, and he'd not washed Ashton's blood from his arm. It was covered in dried, red flakes.

"Leave us," Genève ordered the captain.

After a concerned glance at Rowan, he nodded and left.

"Olivia, close the door," she ordered.

Though uncertain what she was about to do, I obeyed. Once the three of us were alone, she walked around the chair to stand in front of Rowan.

"Grieving is natural," she said, "But this is bordering on excess. Get out of that chair and I'll order you a bath."

"Go away," he whispered.

In answer, she drew her hand back and slapped him hard enough to move his face. Startled, he snarled and rose partway out of the chair.

"I'm glad to see there's something of a king left inside you," she said without flinching. "And you are not the only one who lost Ashton! All of Partheney is in mourning. The people have been waiting for you to call a common court so that the leaders and the merchants might come to mourn with you. They want to hear what is being done to find her assassin, and they want to hear it from you!"

His dark eyes finally rose to meet hers.

"If you don't act," she pressed on, "Lord Moreau will be forced to hold court tomorrow."

His eyes didn't lower. He listened.

To my amazement, I could see she had him. She *had* him.

"Lord Moreau?" he repeated.

She nodded. "Yes. Is that what you want? For the council to start ruling in your stead?"

I didn't know Rowan at all, but his mother apparently knew him well. He'd loved Ashton more than he loved his throne...but he did love his throne.

"The last blood relation to Eduard is gone," Genève went on relentlessly, "and the people want security. They want a king who will produce heirs and establish a line. They want to see him in a clean, proper marriage." Taking three steps toward me, she grabbed my arm and dragged me over. Her grip was like a talon. "Look at this girl! She is a regal, virgin daughter from the line of Géroux, one of the oldest families in the country. The people will embrace her. They will embrace you if you would get out of that chair and behave like a king."

His eyes moved to me, and I stood rigid, feeling like some prize calf on display at a village fair. Then he looked back to the empty hearth.

"The people will need something to celebrate, something to help them heal," Genève said. "And you need something to solidify your crown. Tomorrow, I'll begin plans for Ashton's burial, and after that, I will plan a wedding."

Rowan was silent for a short while longer. Then he whispered, "Do you what you will."

Genève's grip trembled on my wrist as his words hung in the air.

He had just agreed to marry me.

Chapter Six

Ashton's burial in the family crypt was a small affair, attended by only Rowan, Genève, myself, Captain Caron, the twelve council members, and any of their wives who were currently in residence. Rowan made no display of emotion as Ashton's body was moved into its place in the crypt. She'd been dressed in a white gown, with a matching ribbon around her throat. Due to her naturally pale skin, she appeared to be sleeping.

Genève had been concerned about this day, even fearing Rowan might not attend the dinner afterward, but he sat in the center of the head table in his chair as was expected of him. However, he did make one request.

"I want Micah at the dinner. I want him sitting beside me."

To me, this was gratifying. I'd worried some of the captain's actions over the past few days might have permanently damaged their relationship, but if anything, they seemed closer and spent much time in quiet discussion. I wondered of what they spoke.

Three days later, my wedding followed.

At first, it had come as a blow that Genève wanted a quick wedding, with no time to invite all the members of the noble houses—or my own family—but she explained herself.

"We need to hold it now, while he's still in agreement. Once it's done, it can't be undone. In the autumn, we'll host a grand coronation for you, and your family can attend."

After listening, I agreed.

Securing the marriage far outweighed any personal vanity on my part.

Doubts only followed when I realized the wedding party would consist of exactly the same people who'd attended Ashton's funeral. This feeling of trepidation increased when Kamilla brought in my wedding gown for a fitting. It was family heirloom from Ashton's line, and Genève wished me to wear it.

It was white.

It came with a matching ribbon to be tied around my throat.

I refused the ribbon but donned the gown and allowed Kamilla to let out the hem.

The ceremony was brief. Rowan and I each spoke our vows, most of which were lies, and then we signed the agreement. Lord Cloutier and Baron Augustine signed as our witnesses.

The noble wives tried to weep prettily and pretend it was a happy day, but everything was overshadowed by Ashton's death and the fact that my husband looked as if he would rather be anyplace else.

The echoes of my white gown didn't help.

At dinner, Rowan was not impolite, but we probably exchanged six words.

When dinner came to an end, Lord Moreau raised his goblet. "We cannot detain the happy couple a moment longer. My king, you have our blessing to retire with your lovely bride."

Though I somehow kept the smile on my face, my heart slowed, and Genève went stiff in her chair. What was Moreau thinking? How would Rowan react to that? He'd done so well with this charade, but he could still be pushed over the edge.

To my unspeakable relief, Rowan nodded and stood, offering me his arm. I took it.

Genève beamed and everyone attempted to cheer us as we walked from the hall.

A single thought echoed in my head.

I've done it. I've married King Rowan.

Out we were out through the archway and alone, Rowan drew his arm from my hand and began walking away from me, toward the east corridor, in the direction of his own rooms. I was nonplussed. A honeymoon chamber had been prepared for us at the base of a north-side tower, and we'd both been informed. Though I'd dreaded the prospect of giving my body to Rowan, it had to be done.

"My king..." I began.

He stopped. "Yes?"

"Should we not be heading...north?"

Appearing genuinely puzzled, he asked, "Whatever for?"

He walked away.

* * * *

My life changed swiftly.

Within several days of the wedding, all the members of the council departed Partheney to travel to their own estates and lands. They'd come to oversee the wedding, and the wedding was done. There were sweet good-byes—a few even sincere—and vows to return in the early autumn for my coronation and the next formal gathering of the council.

I was given Geneve's fine apartments, and she moved into Ashton's.

"This is the way of things, my dear," Geneve informed me. "Even before your coronation, you've taken on the role of queen. You will hold the embroidery circles for any visiting noblewomen, and you will oversee the household of the castle. If you have any questions, ask me."

My duties were numerous, but I'd expected this, and I'd been trained for the task of overseeing a great house. I held private counsels with both the housekeeper and the cook. I kept apprised of issues with staff, and I liked to have meals planned out a week ahead of time. I kept track of the kitchen gardens, of which vegetables were flourishing and which were failing. I kept careful accounts over what was being spent on beef and mutton and fish.

I had fittings for gowns.

Kamilla became my personal maid.

For the most part, I relished my new life.

One awkward moment came about two weeks after the wedding when I was in the great hall overseeing the proper removal of a tapestry so it could be cleaned.

A royal guard strode through the archway, looked around, and came to me. He bowed. "My lady."

"Yes?"

"There's a woman in the entryway, a merchant's wife. She's asking to see you."

"Did she say why?"

"Something about Princess Ashton's charity work."

I'd forgotten all about that. "Show her in."

A short while later, a stocky woman in a fine velvet gown bustled into the hall with an aura of energy. The same guard who'd brought the message accompanied her. She curtsied. "My lady. I'm Emilee Martine. My husband's a wine merchant in the city, but I also worked with Princess Ashton in the old stable…for the cause."

"How can I help you?" I asked.

"There's been no wagons going out with food and goods for the poor for nearly three weeks now. We've got wagons ready to go, but Princess Ashton always made a list of what goods should go to which families."

She gazed at me expectantly. I had no idea what she expected.

"We all feel the loss of the princess keenly," I answered.

Her expression shifted to confusion. "But won't you make the lists? There is so much need, and the princess always knew which families were hurting most."

Me? She expected me to know?

"Forgive me," I answered politely. "But I've not been off castle grounds since my arrival. You would have a better idea of which families to put on the lists."

"I don't know any of the fishermen. The princess did."

This made me wonder more about Ashton's life, but I couldn't help this woman, and the conversation was becoming uncomfortable.

"Again," I said, "forgive me. Helping the poor was great passion of the princess, and she is ever missed. But I know nothing of her fine work. You will have to carry on as best you can without her."

Emilee blinked. "You'll still call for goods from the nobles...send out announcements of what is needed? They won't help without you."

I held back a sigh. This grew tiresome, and she was becoming impertinent. I nodded to the guard behind her. "Do excuse me. I have many duties to attend today."

Sputtering, she found herself escorted her out.

I was sorry for her, but I had no intention of begging goods off other nobles or spending time making lists of families in need.

My days were already quite full.

* * * *

I rarely saw Rowan except at dinner. He was civil but quiet, and he'd begun drinking more wine than before, sometimes a good deal more, though I never noticed him drunk. After dinner, he often seemed at a loss. I asked Genève about his previous pastimes at night. She told me that when dancing had been scheduled, he'd stayed in the hall and danced with Ashton. On other nights, he'd often played chess with Ashton. But now, he had no wish to either dance or play chess with anyone else. Several people offered—including myself.

During his days, he'd taken to spending a good deal of his time in the barracks, often riding out into the city with Captain Caron. I didn't know what they were doing, but I suspected they were hunting for Ashton's killer. No one knew how the assassin might have escaped the castle gates. Rowan had not yet made a formal accusation that someone on the Samourè council was behind the murder. Perhaps he wanted more proof.

Captain Caron was especially sensitive to all this, as under his command, first Ashton's abductors and then her killer had somehow escaped through the castle gates. I couldn't ask Genève how she'd managed to get Soren off royal grounds, but in the end, I suppose it didn't matter. She never did anything without a plan, and she must have planned for this.

In truth, I didn't mind Rowan's absence.

Well, with one exception: every night when I went to bed. Though our marriage was signed and witnessed, I had a considerable concern about its legitimacy.

It had not been consummated.

Of course, our mutual dislike of each other would have kept us from behaving like young lovers, but the lack of consummation left me vulnerable. Should he decide to change his mind, an annulment was still possible.

I had to find a way to get him into my bed.

For now, I worked hard to make myself indispensable at the castle, and I was forming a plan to make the people see me as their future queen…to make my removal more difficult.

* * * *

Early on the morning of the next common court date, I rose and awaited Kamilla—with whom I'd made prior arrangements. She arrived shortly after the sun rose and took painstaking efforts in dressing me.

I had a new day gown of rich amber silk. The neckline was square, with tiny white pearls inset as trim. The skirt of the gown was split. The amber color suited my hair, and I'd ordered a cream silk underskirt.

Kamilla put up my hair, weaving a strand of pearls into the arrangement, and she cut a few locks in the front so they might curl around my face. When she finished with me at last, I stood before the mirror, pleased by the image.

A queen gazed back at me.

"Thank you," I said. I meant it. I had come to value her greatly. She mourned the loss of Ashton, but she was kind to me, even offering me comfort, as if I were in mourning too. When Kamilla looked at me, she saw a good person.

Of course, I wasn't. But I valued her so much for this.

"Don't let him bully you, my lady," she said. "Stand your ground today."

Though she never expressed it openly, Kamilla was not so kindly disposed toward her king.

I nodded. "I won't fail."

I had a plan.

Gathering my skirts, I left my apartments and made my way to the great hall. It was still early, before people would gather, and inside the hall, a mix of guards and servants were making ready. The dais had already been set in place and two guards carried Rowan's chair between them. They set it on the dais.

Captain Caron oversaw all of this, but his eyes widened when I entered the hall. Striding over, he took in my gown, face, and hair. I could see open admiration in his light brown eyes, but he must have noticed me noticing because he glanced away.

"My lady?" he asked.

It was too early for me to up and ornately dressed.

"Please don't mind me," I said. "I just came to check on the setup for the day, but I can see that all is well in hand."

Men were stepping off the dais.

"Have they forgotten the smaller chair?" I asked.

"My lady?" the captain asked again.

I met his gaze, and he must have realized what I was up to.

Turning, he called out, "Have the smaller chair brought out as well."

Both men stopped. "Sir?" asked one of them.

"Do it," he ordered.

I wasn't quite finished. "Have it arranged directly beside the large chair, not halfway behind."

He raised an eyebrow. "Are you certain, my lady?"

"Absolutely."

* * * *

Later that morning, I waited near the exit of the corridor that led from the east tower and emptied into the entry chamber before the great hall. When Rowan emerged, wearing his crown, I fell into step beside him. He appeared taken aback at first but allowed me to keep pace.

"Coming to watch the court?" he asked.

I will give him this. Since our marriage, he'd never been impolite.

"Not exactly," I answered.

As we moved through the vast, round entry chamber, six guards took their places behind us. Ahead waited the tall archway of the great hall, and people had gathered.

Though Rowan had spoken to leaders of the city and the heads of the merchant guilds to explain the news of Ashton's death—and allow them to ask questions—this was the first full public gathering since her death.

When I walked in, dressed in my resplendent gown, with my husband at my side and six royal guards at my back, all the people inside the hall turned to stare. News of the royal marriage had spread, but I had not yet been seen. Rowan halted when he realized what I'd just done.

Faces in the crowd before me broke into smiles and a cheer went up. More cheers followed, louder and louder until the noise was deafening. Their beloved princess may be gone, but I was here, and to them, I was young, regal, and full of promise.

They cheered.

Beside me, Rowan stiffened.

"Smile," I said quietly, channeling his mother.

He didn't smile, but nor did he stop the celebration. Then he saw the two chairs on the dais.

"Shall we?" I asked.

A flicker of surprise passed across his face as he realized he'd been outmaneuvered, but he could hardly send me away now. Together we walked through the crowd up to the dais and took our seats. The guards took up their positions behind us.

Scanning the crowd, I stopped on Captain Caron. As he met my eyes, his mouth formed the barest hint of a smile. This was the first time I'd seen him look almost happy since Ashton's death.

Rowan's secretary, Jarvis, took his place to one side of the dais, unrolled a list, and called up two men from the craftsmen's guild who were in dispute over placement of stalls in the upcoming fair. I was so nervous I barely followed the discussion, but I also realized I knew nothing of the layout of the city or the marketplace, and I'd be of no use to Rowan in this matter. Thankfully, it wasn't a complicated issue, and he managed to help the men work out an agreement. I was aware that the fair was an important event, and the crown took part of the proceeds in taxes, so I made a mental note to learn more of the inner workings.

The next case was more difficult. Apparently, a section on the seaward side of the castle had collapsed during a storm in the spring. The basic work had been completed, but now an artisan mason was needed for the fine work. This was a large job that would extend for months, and it paid well.

Jarvis had conducted the initial search, and he'd narrowed the candidates down to two men of equal skill—both vying for this important job. It was for the king to make the final choice.

The two men took turns relating their skills, and they both did indeed sound qualified. As I listened, something about one of the men caught my attention. He wore an indigo shirt with black buttons.

Then I noted that Jarvis referred to him as "Cameron Compté."

Quickly, I turned my head toward Rowan. I didn't rise and stand in deference behind him, whispering in his ear. For one thing, my height would have made this appear ridiculous. Instead, I spoke very softly.

"Cameron Compté has a wife named Theresa who is unwell. She's had difficulty recovering from the birth of a child. The family needs money, and he's not found much work this summer."

For all I knew, the other man on the floor had as great a need as Cameron, but this didn't matter.

Smoothly, Rowan leaned forward in his chair, speaking to Cameron. "I've heard your wife, Theresa, is unwell and you have a new child in the house." He gazed out over the crowd of people, and then back to the two men before him. "As you are both fine masons of equal skill, I award the position to Cameron Compté."

His words and his ruling made him sound benevolent and connected to the small lives of his people. This must have been what Ashton did over and over. Cameron's expression melted into relief, and he bowed.

"Thank you, my king."

His clear gratitude completed the picture of a just decision. Rowan shot me a startled glance. He'd not expected actual help from me.

Unfortunately, my triumph was short-lived.

I'd been in possession of this small piece of information only because of the few moments I'd spent in the old stable with Ashton. I had nothing else to offer. For the next six cases I sat in silence, feeling increasingly self-conscious and useless. None of the cases were particularly complex, and in each one, I'd have made the same decision as Rowan, but my purpose here was not to make decisions. My purpose was to offer snippets of information to assist him.

Then...a man and a woman were called before the dais. She ran a business making casks, and he was a winemaker. She had delivered a large number of casks he'd ordered, and he had not paid the bill, citing hardship and asking for an extension.

"I've already granted him an extension, my king," the woman said, "twice. He has no intention of paying what he owes, and my men worked for three months on those casks. We turned down other work because his order was so large."

The man held up both hands. "I cannot pay what I do not have. The price of burgundy wine has fallen this year, and I've not been able to cover my own costs, much less pay some of my debts."

A few faces in the crowd darkened, but no one spoke.

At this, I sat up straight as I remembered something. At one of the embroidery circles in the dowager's quarters, Lord Sauvage's wife, Miranda, had been joking about her husband's poor temper due to the increased cost of burgundy wine—which was his favorite. The sweetness of last year's crop had produced a fine vintage, and its popularity had caused a sharp rise in price.

A number of the people in the crowd must know this, but I wasn't certain about Rowan.

Again, I turned my head and spoke softly to my husband. "He's lying. The price of burgundy wine is sky-high this year."

Rowan leaned forward, addressing the winemaker. "As the price of burgundy wine has indeed not fallen, but risen, you will make good on your debt today." His voice was harsh, and he looked to Jarvis. "Take them aside and see to this. I do not care for liars or swindlers."

The winemaker blinked and then paled. He'd apparently not expected this decision. From what I'd seen, Rowan tended to prefer compromise, and the man was probably trying to buy more time so he could slither out of paying for the casks.

But people in the crowd nodded approval. With his righteous indignation, Rowan appeared both in the right, and a just leader.

My thoughts flowed. I would never be like Ashton, ready with bits of knowledge about the common people. I would never know their names or who was having children or whose husband had fallen off a roof and broken a leg. But…I could learn more about the guilds and the smaller points of commerce in this city. I could invite the wives of city leaders and merchants to teas and embroidery circles. Perhaps I would need to smooth the feathers of Emilee Martine and employ her assistance.

I couldn't help with the next few cases, but I *had* helped with the two most difficult decisions, and when court came to a close, Rowan looked at me with cautious assessment.

Then he stood, and I followed suit. Our guards fell in behind. We swept from the great hall together, passing a sea of smiling faces.

As I passed Captain Caron, he silently mouthed, "Well done."

To my shame, I was grateful. For some reason, I cared what he thought.

Once through the archway, I wondered if Rowan would turn and censure me for my bold actions today.

He didn't.

Instead, he headed off for the courtyard, but he called back. "I will see you at dinner." He paused. "My lady."

Chapter Seven

Early autumn arrived and the Council of Nobles returned for my coronation.

The castle was bursting with activity, and it seemed I was constantly being shown a variety of lists for approvals. There were endless meals to plan and nobles to house. Everyone was coming to see me crowned. In addition to the entire families of every man on the council, my own family was en route.

They would all need rooms.

And their guards…preparing housing for the guards alone took up a good deal of Captain Caron's time.

Thankfully, Genève took a good deal off my hands, as I also had gown fittings and rehearsal sessions with Lord Cloutier, who was the eldest member of the council, for the ceremony. It would not be complicated, and he himself would place the crown on my head,

I rarely saw Rowan during the weeks leading up to the grand event, and I had no idea how he spent his days. He was certainly not assisting his mother or me, but neither of us expected his help.

On the day of my family's arrival, though, he did stand with me in the courtyard as they rode in. I could barely breathe for joy. This would be a sweet moment I would savor.

My father rode in the lead and dismounted with his usual grace. I walked out to greet him and Rowan followed.

"Father," I said.

He nodded. "Daughter."

It was then I realized this would be the extent of his approval. I don't know why I expected more.

He bowed to the king.

My brother, George, dismounted his horse next—and then both my sisters. He bowed and they curtsied, and I must admit enjoying a thrill of pleasure at the jealous hatred in both Margareta's and Eleanor's eyes. Neither of them had made my childhood easy, and I planned to make their next few days as miserable as possible. Of course, they would be given the best rooms, but I wanted them suffering at my triumph.

"I trust you had a good journey," Rowan said politely.

"Yes," my father answered. "The roads were very dry." Then Father turned to me. "I've brought you a surprise."

The words alone were startling. Father had never thought to arrange a surprise for me in all my life. He turned and looked back at an unusually tall guard on a roan horse. The man had a hood over his head, but I noticed he was not wearing the green tabard of Géroux under his cloak, but the light blue and yellow of the royal military. He dismounted.

When he tossed his hood back, exposing a head of thick, burnished red hair and slanted green eyes, I gasped. "Henri!"

My other brother, the only member of my family to ever show me kindness. Father had brought him down from the northern border and allowed him to come to my coronation. Throwing decorum aside, I ran to him, and he swept me up his arms, holding me tightly.

"Olivia."

He was nearly as tall as Captain Caron, and, like the captain, had always made me feel diminutive by comparison. I felt small and safe in his arms.

Grasping my shoulders, he held me back to look at me. "By the gods. You're about to be queen. Will I have to kneel and kiss your skirt?"

"Absolutely." I smiled. We did not exactly share love, but we *liked* each other, and I was so glad for his presence.

What surprised me most was that he seemed at ease and happy. His lightly freckled skin was tan, and he appeared in excellent health. I'd thought to find him subdued when we next met, as Father had thwarted his life's plan.

"You are well?" I asked quietly, "even after being sent north?"

He held both my hands and matched my low voice. "I am quite well. Though I'd never admit it to our father, he was right. I am suited to the military and enjoying more freedom than I thought possible. Plus…I'm needed on the border. I am necessary."

Rowan came up behind us with a queer expression on his face, almost wistful.

Henri bowed. "My king."

"This is my favorite brother," I said, still feeling playful and not caring if George heard.

Then I wondered why Rowan was watching us so strangely, a brother and sister who were fond of each other and did not fear to express it. Some of my happiness faded. I'd bought this crown at a high price.

But Rowan also assessed Henri quickly. "Lieutenant Henri Géroux? You've been up on the northern border?"

"Yes, my king."

Rowan nodded. "I would speak with you later if you have the time."

"I am at your disposal."

More of my happiness faded. The northern border separated our kingdom from Samourè.

* * * *

On the day of my coronation, I rode a horse from the outer edge of the city all the way to the castle gates. Rowan rode behind me. Twenty royal guards and forty members of the royal military followed him.

Thousands of people lined the streets.

It was the finest day of my life.

My gown was gold with a red underskirt, and I wore a white cape with fur trim. People cheered and tossed roses in our path. We were loved, and I felt loved. I let my horse, Meesha, walk slowly, so I might embrace every moment.

When we finally passed through the castle gate, Captain Caron lifted me down, and Baron Augustine awaited me.

Rowan went inside ahead of us, and we waited.

All the other nobles were already inside.

After enough time had passed, the baron offered me his arm. "My lady."

Together, we walked through the doors of the castle, down the main corridor. The royal guards followed.

I walked in to find a sea of finely dressed nobles. Forty serving woman had spent three days lining the walls with long strings of flowers. A red carpet had been spread from the archway to the dais.

Baron Augustine led me up the red carpet. Rowan sat in his chair on the dais. He wore his crown. My empty chair waited beside him. Lord Cloutier stood in his formal robes, and a second crown rested on a pedestal.

Unbidden, the dark thought filled my head that Genève had worn that same crown for years. She stood at the front of the nobles, beside my father. They were an appropriate pair.

Baron Augustine led me to the dais, and I took my chair beside Rowan.

After that, everything became a blur.

Lord Cloutier anointed my forehead with oil, and I remember swearing to a number of vows to put the kingdom before all else.

He placed the crown upon my head. Then he stepped to the side and motioned to me with one hand. "Queen Olivia."

Rowan and I remained seated.

The crown was heavier than it looked, but I held my head high.

I was queen.

* * * *

The celebration that night was quite merry. Typically, if a royal family decided to choose a queen from among the daughters of their kingdom's own noble families, the infighting could be savage. But my family was of old blood and my father was not on the council—not in a position of political power—and everyone was so glad to see Rowan married and the young queen crowned, that most of the congratulations were sincere.

Geneève had suggested earlier that we forgo any dancing after dinner and just allow people to mingle and talk. I agreed. There would much for people to say.

As the night wore on, I felt more and more happy. I was the queen and the lady of this great hall.

To make things even sweeter, neither of my sisters could stop casting astonished glances at Rowan. In a purely physical sense, even I had to admit he was striking, with his defined arms, high cheekbones, and dark wavy hair. I'd married a handsome king. Margareta and Eleanor must be positively writhing with jealousy.

How delicious.

Thankfully, they didn't know him on a more personal level. They didn't know he was in love with a ghost and had not a single care for me.

But even Rowan appeared to enjoy the evening. He drank only two small goblets of wine and spent much of his time in close conversation with my brother, Henri. Those two seemed good friends already.

Near midnight, the lively chatter had still not begun to abate, and I found myself growing weary. It had been a long day. I wondered if I might take my leave for a moment or two. When no one was looking, I extracted myself and walked out the main archway, wanting a short span of time to myself.

To my mild consternation, Geneève followed me. I was well aware how much I owed her for the events of today—but her presence always reminded me how much I owed.

Somehow, I smiled. "My lady. It was a successful day."

She didn't smile back and moved closer. We were alone out here in the round entrance chamber.

"Yes, the council is pleased, but a few have expressed concerns." Her voice was so low I strained to hear it.

"Concerns?" I repeated. Had I not done well so far?

"You are still at some risk. Why have you not managed to take Rowan into your bed?"

I felt the blood drain from my face. Months had gone by, and she'd not said a word in this regard. Another thought struck me.

"How would the council members know?"

"Don't be a fool. They have spies among the staff. They all have spies. It's to be expected."

I wanted to fade into the wall. The council knew. They *all* knew that the new queen held no attraction for the king.

"Your task is to provide heirs," she went on. "I've not spoken because you're clever, and I assumed you'd manage him." Her voice hardened. "Get him into bed, Olivia. He must plant his seed inside you."

All my confidence fled. I was no temptress. Even knowing how weak I sounded, I whispered, "I don't know how. I don't know of any way to make him want me."

Her voice grew harder. "Find one."

* * * *

Over the next few days, I smiled and feigned enjoyment as we continued to host our guests. But much of my joy was tarnished, and I wasn't sleeping well at night.

Finally, most of the guests began heading for home.

Only the council remained, and would soon convene for autumn business.

My father bid me a polite good-bye, but he glanced at my flat stomach, as if he wondered when he would be the grandfather of a king. Henri hugged me, picking my feet up off the ground. I reveled in his affection and wished he were not leaving.

"Thank you for being so kind to the king," I said, and I meant it. "He is well liked, but he finds conversation in large groups to be difficult."

I'm not sure how I'd reasoned that, but I had. Rowan wasn't comfortable in large groups of other nobles where he was expected to mingle and make conversation.

Henri waved one hand. "He's splendid. My time here has passed too quickly." Then he kissed the side of my face. "You are a fortunate girl, and you've done well. You deserve this happiness."

Had we been alone, I'd have broken down and begged him to tell me how to seduce a man.

But we were not alone.

My family rode away. By that evening, the castle achieved a more normal state of existence, but I was now alone in this place with Genève and the men of the council…and they all expected the same thing from me.

* * * *

A few nights later, an idea came to me. At first, the very prospect was so revolting that I pushed it away, but it kept creeping back, and by this point, I was willing to try anything.

I was already in bed, in my nightgown.

The idea would not leave me alone. More details began to form.

Rising, I donned my silk robe over the top of my nightgown, and I slipped from the room. At this time of night, the castle would be empty but for a few guards. I hurried downstairs and up the corridor, stopping at the entry chamber before the great hall. Then I dashed across, into a corridor leading east, and I made my way to the first tower. Climbing the curving stone steps, I made my way to Rowan's room.

Outside his door, I hesitated, wondering if I could go through with this. Then I knocked.

It took a few moments, but the door opened from the other side, and he looked out. His hair was tousled as if he'd just woken up, but he still wore the same tunic and black pants he'd worn at dinner. Had he fallen asleep dressed?

At the sight of me, his eyes filled with alarm. "Olivia? What's wrong? Is my mother ill?"

How tragic that a wife should knock on her husband's door in the middle of the night, and his only assumption could be that some emergency was taking place.

"No…I…I only wanted to speak to you. May I come in?"

Discomfort crossed his features, but he stood back and held the door to let me in. Once inside, I slowly pulled the door from his hand and closed it.

He frowned upon noticing I wore nothing but my robe and white nightgown. "Did you cross the castle dressed like that?"

"No one saw me."

"What is this about?" he asked carefully.

We were in his main sitting chambers, but the door to his bedroom was open, and I could see his rumpled bedclothes.

Desperately, I hoped I would not need to employ the plan in the back of my mind. Perhaps if I approached him on a platform of honesty and reason, he might agree and take advantage of the fact that we were alone in his chambers.

"Your mother has been to see me," I began. "She and the council know you and I have not consummated the marriage."

He didn't react.

"Your mother applied pressure on me," I continued, "to resolve the matter and find a way to get you into my bed."

"And what did you say to her?" His voice was tight.

"That I didn't know how." I looked into his eyes. "I don't know how. That's why I've come to you."

His tension vanished, and he ran a hand over his face. "Olivia, I am sorry you've been trapped by all this. I've not known what to say, but I have been sorry for you."

He'd been sorry for me? I wish he'd spoken sooner. It might have made some days more bearable.

"And you don't find me repellent?" I asked.

"No man would find you repellent."

I couldn't believe he was saying these things to me, and felt a weight come off my shoulders. I would not need to employ my dark and degrading plan.

"Then can we not at least…consummate our union? Can we not make an heir?" As these words left my mouth, his tension returned, and I rushed on. "Please forgive this indelicacy, but your mother told me that you've kept mistresses…for the needs of your body. Can you not try to see me as one of them?"

This suggestion was beyond indelicate, but the two of us were beyond polite sparring.

He sighed and moved toward a couch. "Come and sit with me."

Seeing this as a good sign, I obeyed, sitting beside him.

"Yes," he said. "I've kept mistresses, but not since…not since…"

He didn't finish, but he didn't need to.

"Not since Ashton's death," I finished for him.

His eyes flew to my face.

I nodded. "I know you loved her as much more than a sister."

"She was *not* my sister." As opposed to offended, though, he sounded relieved to be speaking of this. "You don't understand. When I first came to this castle, I was twelve years old, and I didn't want to be here. My father was dead, and I was expected to be overjoyed at the prospect of a new father. But when I first entered the great hall with some of our retinue, I saw a little girl with black hair. She was so tiny and so pretty. She'd barely learned to walk. One of our dogs barked, and it frightened her. She ran to me, and I picked her up." He paused. "Whenever she was startled or frightened, she ran to me. She always ran to me for protection."

Yes, but who could possibly protect her from you?

I remained silent.

"Ashton is the only person I've ever loved," he said. "And now that she's gone, I can't...I can't...I'm sorry, Olivia. I know what is expected of us, but I can't."

As the truth washed over me, I began to feel ill.

Honesty and reason would not work here. I needed to employ other methods.

"Close your eyes," I said. "Let me try something. Just close your eyes and keep them closed."

"Olivia—"

"Please. For me."

He closed his eyes. Leaning in, I let my mouth almost touch the side of his ear, the way she used to whisper to him. "It's not Olivia sitting here. It's Ashton. I've come back to you. My hair is long and silken and black. My skin is pale, and my eyes are blue. I play chess with you after dinner, and I would do anything to make you happy. You are my protector."

Though I'd not known what result this would bring, I couldn't help being startled by his rapid intake of breath.

I kept on whispering, describing every detail of Ashton in her peach gown. "You are all that I love. You protect me, and you are my world." I let my voice soften even more. "I am Ashton, and you are my world."

Suddenly Rowan's hand was around the back of my head, and his mouth was pressing hard against mine. He pushed his tongue between my teeth and pulled me off the couch onto the rug below.

He was on top of me, using his weight to pin me down.

His hand was on my leg, pulling up my nightgown.

The strength in his body was unsettling. Besides a friendly kiss on the cheek from Baron Augustine, the only other man who'd ever touched me was Henri—for an occasional hug. I knew men were stronger than women, but I hadn't known how much. Although I had no intention of stopping Rowan, I was alarmed to realize I could not have stopped him had I wanted to.

He pushed my nightgown up around my waist, and then he was thrusting inside me.

It hurt, but I bit the inside of my mouth.

"Ashton," he breathed, thrusting again.

Thankfully, this didn't last long, and he let out a gasping breath as his body convulsed. His weight came down on top of me, and we lay like that for a long moment. Then he rolled off. I sat up and began arranging my clothing for modesty. We did not look at each other.

I couldn't help remembering Genève's words that first day we spoke alone in her chambers.

He's never cared for any woman except Ashton. I don't believe he will ever love anyone else. Can you stomach that for the rest of your life?

How easily I'd promised her.

Neither Rowan or I spoke as I slipped from his room. There was nothing to say. I felt soiled and ashamed at what I'd just done. My body was sore, and I was bleeding.

But I had the king's seed inside me.

Chapter Eight

I didn't know a great deal about the science of procreation, but I did know that a single such act with Rowan might not be enough. Four more times, I made the trip to his rooms in the night. He always let me in. He'd close his eyes, and I'd whisper a spell in his ear to conjure the image of Ashton, and only then would his body respond. During the act of our encounters, he never once opened his eyes until it was over.

After the fifth time, I couldn't bring myself to go through it again and stopped the visits, hoping fervently that my efforts had been fruitful. The dowager queen said nothing, but I suspected she knew I'd been visiting his room. She seemed to know everything that went on.

Several weeks later, when my courses were due, they did not arrive. As I had always been regular, I dared to hope…but not too much.

The following month, they did not come again.

One night at dinner, as a slice of ham was set before me, I turned away, fearing I was about to be sick at the table. Genève was on her feet and at my side.

Her face filled with hope. "My dear. Are you…do you think you are…?"

"I think so."

By then, I was certain I was pregnant. Rowan turned in his chair. "You think what?"

Genève leaned close. "Your queen is with child."

"With child?"

Had that possibility not occurred to him? What did he think that sordid business between us was all about?

But in the days that followed, I pushed the memory of those nights to the back of my mind as the council, and indeed the entire city, celebrated our news. A young, pregnant queen was the cause of much joy and much fuss, and I allowed myself to enjoy it all.

Pregnancy agreed with me, and once I'd gotten past the feeling of being ill when I looked at food, I began to blossom. I loved the swelling in my stomach and the proof of my child growing. Autumn passed into winter. I turned nineteen over the solstice holidays. Winter passed into spring.

Then one night at dinner, Rowan turned to me. "Did you know I've been in contact with your brother?"

"With George?"

"No, Henri. There've been some troubling events taking place along the border up north. Lord Sauvage has tried to bring this to my attention before, but I didn't realize the extent of the issue until now. Raiding parties from Samourè have crossed over to steal crops and livestock. Several homes have been burned."

"Burned?" This surprised me. Normally, a careful peace was maintained between our kingdoms.

"I need to ride up and look into this myself," he said.

"How long will you be gone?"

"About a month."

"A month?" My voice sounded strained. I might not love Rowan, but I was heavy with his child and didn't like the idea of him leaving me at this time.

"Don't worry," he said. "The captain will be here, and he'll look after the castle's protection. I've counted the months in my head, and I'll be back in time for the birth."

At least now he sounded like a husband, and his words calmed me. Of course Captain Caron could protect the castle, and Rowan had promised he'd be back for the birth.

"Can you manage the common courts by yourself?" Rowan asked.

"Yes."

And I could. Following through on my instincts, I'd cultivated relationships with wives of the city leaders, wives of merchants, and female members of the artisan's guild. I knew little of the daily lives of our people, but I knew a good deal about local trade and commerce, and to my mind, this mattered more.

No, I didn't fear attempting to rule without Rowan. My thoughts in regards to his journey turned to worry that he was looking for a reason to invade Samourè. I knew Lord Sauvage often counseled for the invasion of neighboring kingdoms. He saw threats everywhere, and his idea of diplomacy was always at the point of a sword. Rowan tended to politely listen, but he'd never acted before. Now...he was looking for a reason to find fault with Samourè. I knew he still blamed their council for Ashton's death, and though he may not speak of this, he'd never let it go.

Rowan left two days later.

I was interim ruler of the kingdom and handled many of Rowan's duties, conferring with Captain Caron, Jarvis, and Lord Cloutier in his role as minister of finance. I was surprised to learn that Rowan intended to raise taxes.

"Why?" I asked.

"To increase our stock of weapons, my queen."

I didn't like the sound of that.

Rowan was gone nearly two months, and the day following his return, my pains began. This was a first child, and first children often take longer. I was in labor nearly fifteen hours. But in the end, my beautiful son came into the world, and I nearly wept at the sight of him.

He had a head full of burnished red hair.

Genève rocked him with adoration in her eyes. "He is perfect. I think he looks like your brother, Henri. Perhaps he will be tall."

She had what she wanted. Her son had established a line, cemented his throne, and she was now the mother and grandmother of powerful kings. But as much as I appreciated her grandmotherly sentiments, I didn't like the sight of her holding my son, and I vowed never to leave her alone with the baby.

Over the next two days, some of the noblewomen staying at the castle came to visit and coo over the young prince. He was fine and strong, and my pride swelled every time I held him. Of all the tasks required of a queen, this one by far took precedence: the creation of an heir.

Only one aspect of his birth troubled me.

Rowan had not come to visit. For a royal couple, even with a marriage as strained and distant as ours, the one thing in which we might triumph and share intimate personal joy was the birth of a healthy child. I wanted to celebrate with my husband, the father of my son.

On the third day, I was still recovering and had not left my rooms. When Genève came to visit, I asked, "Where is Rowan?"

She glanced away. "He is busy, my dear."

Busy? Too busy to see his wife and rejoice in the birth of his son?

That evening he arrived, and I sent the women away so that we might be alone with our baby. Rowan's normally pale skin was tan, and I could see he'd been spending much of his time outdoors. He'd not cut his hair since winter, and it reached his shoulder blades. A hint of a dark beard covered his jawline, as if he'd forgotten to shave.

Our son was asleep in his cradle.

"Are you well?" Rowan asked me politely. "You are recovering?"

He sounded like a near stranger inquiring after my health.

"Yes," I answered. "Thank you."

With a curt nod, he took in a breath and walked to the cradle, but once there, he shifted his weight back and forth between his feet as if he would rather be gone.

"A fine child," he said. He did not smile or rejoice or even attempt to lift our son and hold him.

My heart began to sink, and I ventured, "I thought to name him after my father, Hugh, or perhaps my brother, Henri?"

I believed Rowan would turn to me and insist we name the child Eduard, after his adopted father.

But instead, he nodded once. "As you wish."

For the first time since the day of our marriage, I knew the feeling of true regret. His lack of love for me extended to a lack of love for his son. He didn't see the child in the cradle as remotely connected to himself. The baby was not Ashton's.

Genève's words echoed in my ears.

Can you stomach that for the rest of your life?

Yes, I could stomach it, but reality was proving much, much harder than the image I'd held back then in my mind.

Rowan turned back toward me. "And you are well? You are recovering?"

"Yes, my lord."

"Good." He started for the door. "I have a meeting with Lord Sauvage. I will inquire after you tomorrow."

He was gone.

Rising, I walked to the cradle and looked down at my beautiful son. I loved him more than I could express.

"Henri," I whispered.

That was his name.

* * * *

By a week later, I'd recovered from the birth enough to hold a scheduled gathering in my apartments. Three or four times a month, I hosted the wives of city council members, the wives of merchants, and wives of members of the artisan's guild for tea, cards, embroidery, and other pastimes. At first Genève had protested, as she would never have entertained women who lacked noble birth in her private apartments.

But then she saw what I doing and fell silent.

Though these women were "only" wives, most of them ran the family businesses. They were glad to share knowledge with me and to keep me informed—as I often now sat alone as the head of common court. I was becoming concerned that Rowan had raised taxes again, and his measures were becoming a burden for many of the people.

Emilee Martine was my strongest ally in this faction. I'd earned her friendship by assisting her with Ashton's charity work as best I could. I handed off the mantle of creating the lists of needy recipients to her, but I worked actively to help keep the donations flowing.

Today, about fifteen women had gathered in my sitting room, and I'd kept baby Henri with us. We spent several hours drinking tea, eating cakes, and sharing information. Henri received no end of attention. Five women had set up a game of cards at a table, and Emilee's adult daughter, Merry, was working an embroidery pattern I'd given her.

I'd just sat down to offer thoughts on a choice of thread when Kamilla entered and came to me.

"My queen. Captain Caron is here, and he's asking permission to see the child."

Something about this caused me to draw a quick breath. Micah was just outside asking to see Henri?

"Oh, please let him come in, my queen," Merry begged. "The captain is ever so handsome, and we could use a man's company about now."

The other women laughed.

"Merry!" Emilee admonished. "Don't be coarse. Remember where you are." But her eyes were lively, and I could see she agreed with her daughter.

Nodding to Kamilla, I said, "Show him in."

A moment later, the tall captain walked into the sitting room. These chambers were a world for women, from the low couches to the porcelain teacups to the tiny sugar cakes to the embroidery frames. Any man would have seemed out of place, but Micah was the soul of masculinity with his close beard and his height and his chain armor. Thankfully, he'd forgone his sword.

Upon entering, he bowed to me, but before he could speak, the chattering women surrounded him, leading him to the cradle where Henri lay. I remained seated on the couch.

Micah's face broke into a broad smile, and to my amazement, he reached down and picked up my son, cradling the infant with some skill. I wondered where he'd learned to do that. I knew for a fact he wasn't married.

Rocking Henri back and forth, he spoke to the child a loving voice. "Well, young prince. You must grow swiftly. I'll soon teach you how to use a sword and ride a horse."

The women laughed happily, and the happiness spread to me.

"Not too soon, I hope," Emilee joked.

"You can never start soon enough," Micah answered. He cooed over the baby like a woman, and in between coos, he looked over at me with more smiles. He was so comfortable with Henri.

As I sat there, watching him, unwanted images filled my mind.

I thought of a life with a man like him…a decent man. I might live in a small home perhaps, but I'd have a pure marriage with a man devoted to me, devoted to his family. I wondered how the soft hair around his mouth would feel if he kissed me. His kiss would be gentle, of that I was sure.

Walking over, Micah leaned down to hand the baby to me. "Come and see your beautiful mother," he said to Henri.

The words were like daggers in my heart as I fought to push all the unwanted fantasies away. This was what I'd wanted from Rowan.

Micah's eyes flashed with concern. "My lady? Are you well? Would you like me to leave?"

I forced my face into a serene expression. "I am well, and don't wish you to leave. We are all glad for your company. Sit down and tell us more of your plans to teach Henri to ride. How soon should we find him a pony?"

The concern didn't fade from his eyes, and the last thing I wanted was his pity.

"Merry," I called. "Please bring the captain some of those cakes."

The chatter continued, and we went on with our afternoon.

Chapter Nine

A month later, Rowan called a formal meeting of the council, and he asked for a vote to invade Samourè. He never once mentioned Ashton's name. From what I understood—via snippets I was told later—he recounted brutal tales of raiding parties crossing our borders to burn homes, kill men, rape young girls, and steal crops and livestock.

I don't know how much of it was true.

I only know that it worked, and with Lord Sauvage's added urging, the council voted to give the king a free hand. Only Baron Augustine argued for another strategy, as apparently Amandine—who was now King Amandine—had offered financial reparation, and his offer was ignored.

Genève told me she'd gone to Rowan and argued fiercely that he abandon this path, but he ordered her from his rooms. This came as quite a blow to her. She'd intended to rule through him, at least in part, and she'd now lost any semblance of control.

And I'd been right on the night Ashton died, that Rowan would want blood. It took him a year, but he was on the verge of wetting his sword. He wanted to make Samourè's council suffer, and he wanted them to know what horror they'd brought down upon their own lands. Our army was larger and stronger. Yes, some of our own people would die, but I had no doubt that Rowan would kill a good deal more of theirs. He wanted revenge. He wanted retribution on a grand scale.

However, in order to avoid resorting to conscription to fill the ranks, he had to sell his war to our people.

At the next session of common court, he sat in his chair and passed out decisions, and at the end he stood and held up both his hands to signal that he would speak. The great hall was especially crowded. I think perhaps word had spread that news was imminent.

"My people," Rowan began. "Our kingdom faces a threat. You all know I have been to the north and back myself. I do not rely on the eyes of others in this matter. It is too important. Raiding parties from Samourè have been attacking our citizens with no regard to life or honor. I've seen girls no old older than twelve who were raped and murdered, lying on the ground with blood between their legs. I've seen the bodies of their fathers and brothers. I've seen homes burned and livestock killed for sport and left in the fields to rot."

Everyone in the hall listened in silence. Again, I knew some raids had taken place, but I didn't know how much of Rowan's account was true.

"They are pressing inward," Rowan called. "And they must be stopped! We will gather an army and invade them first. I only ask this of you to protect your own families." He raised a fist. "We will stop them before they press further!"

A roar in the hall went up. Word of this speech would spread quickly. He had the people at his back. They would sacrifice money and lives.

We were going to war.

* * * *

It took Rowan another month to raise a full army. Men like my brother, Henri, and others in the royal military were his helping hands in this effort.

All the nobles sent men from their own lands, including my father. Many of them even sent personal guards. Samourè would surrender in a matter of days...if Rowan would accept surrender.

Strangely, all of this seemed distant from myself, almost unreal.

My days rotated around the running of the castle and the raising of my son. He was the light of my life, and every day he grew stronger and more aware. I could not seem to spend enough time holding him and gazing into his eyes.

Finally, though, he was old enough that Genève insisted he sleep in the nursery, at least at night, with maids to tend him. "Your affection for him is admirable, but it grows unseemly," she said. "You have responsibilities."

I knew she was right.

Then she added, "And of course you will be breeding again soon. He must have a brother. The nobles will expect it. The people will expect it."

She must know Rowan and I had not shared a bed since Henri's conception. I didn't think myself capable of ever going through that act again.

By early fall, Rowan was ready to lead his army. Again…our world at the castle would not change much, as we would not lose all our men. Captain Caron and the royal guard would remain here, exactly as before.

But I ached for the women of our kingdom, and the wives of Partheney. Their men were leaving, and some would not return.

The night before Rowan's departure, I sat up late in my apartments, gazing into the fire.

Near midnight, a knock sounded. Puzzled, I stood up and answered the door. Rowan stood on the other side.

"What's wrong?" I asked. "What has happened?"

As with him, so many months ago, his presence outside my door in the middle of the night suggested an emergency or a tragedy.

But then I saw his face. It shone with a mix of shame and desperation.

"I'm leaving tomorrow," he said quietly. "I don't know when I'll be back. One more time, would you…would you do what you do."

I couldn't mistake his meaning. He wanted to come in and close his eyes and have me whisper in his ear and conjure the image of Ashton. He wanted to spend himself inside me while imagining I was her.

The thought made me ill, and my first instinct was to tell him to go away.

But his mother was probably having him watched, and so was the council. I couldn't send him away.

Wordlessly, I stepped back and let him in.

* * * *

A week following Rowan's departure at the head of his army, I held a gathering of noblewomen in my apartments. In Rowan's absence, Baron and Lady Augustine had taken up temporary residence at the castle, as had Lords Paquet, du Guay, Moreau, Cloutier, and their wives. Lord Sauvage and several other members of the council had accompanied their king.

All the ladies, including Genève, met in my apartments for embroidery and companionship. Henri was with us in his cradle, and today, I'd arranged for a special surprise. An hour into our gathering, I'd invited the men to join us, including Micah. Though he held no title, he was one of the few in a position to walk in both social worlds.

When Genève was queen, she would never have included the men, but I was not she.

Though the ladies feigned shock at the men's arrival in my feminine apartments, I could see everyone was pleased, and we were a merry party.

The servants brought fresh tea and pastries. Within moments, Micah hefted Henri from his cradle and carried him around.

"He's gaining weight, my lady."

What a good man he was.

I tried not to think on that last night before Rowan's departure, of the depraved acts I'd committed on the floor of this same room. Instead, I counted my blessings.

I had friends here in Partheney.

I had the loyalty of a fine captain.

I had my beautiful son, who was the light of my world.

And most of all...I was queen.

* * * *

The lavish sitting room around me disappeared. I found myself standing once again in the alcove of the castle, staring into the right-hand panel of the three-paneled mirror.

Pressing my back against the wall, I fought to take in air, thinking on all that I had just lived through.

But the dark-haired woman was now looking out from the center panel.

"What was that?" I gasped.

"That would be the outcome of the first choice," she answered. "But now those memories will vanish, and you'll go back to the beginning, to the moment of the crisis, to live out the second choice."

"Wait!" I cried. "I won't remember anything of what I just saw?"

"Back to the beginning once more," she answered. "To live out the second choice."

My mind went blank, and the alcove vanished.

The Second Choice
Instant Resolution

Chapter Ten

I was in a corridor, outside an alcove, listening to the plans of a murderer and an assassin.

"Doesn't make any difference to me, so long as I get paid," said the man called Soren. "But you need not fear. I'll get it done."

I felt disoriented and touched one side of my head, but when Soren turned to leave, I flew into motion, dashing to the nearest alcove to hide from sight.

He walked past me.

A few moments later, so did Genève.

An assassin was about to seek out Ashton in the stable and kill her. I was desperate for the crown. But not at this price, not for Ashton's life, and I had to save her. From where I stood now, the kitchens weren't far.

Without hesitation, I ran.

Upon reaching the archway to the kitchens, I looked ahead to a door and hurried through it. Once out in the courtyard, I cast about for any help, but the only guards in sight were all the way down at the castle gates, too far way.

Running toward the old stable myself, I resolved to do anything necessary to save Ashton. Just as I reached the door, I turned my head in time to see Rowan leading a horse out of the new stable.

He would have been my last choice. He was too unpredictable and too rash when it came to Ashton, but I needed help to save her…and I was determined to save her.

"Rowan! Hurry! Ashton needs help!"

Upon hearing me, he turned his head in alarm. Captain Caron came running out of the new stable. He must have been inside, right behind Rowan.

I dashed inside the open door.

Ashton stood about twenty paces from me, next to a table piled with coats. "Olivia, was that you shouting? Whatever is wrong?"

My gaze continued moving and then stopped. Soren was only about four tables behind her. Sunlight coming in an upper window glinted off his shaved head. He carried a long knife, and his eyes narrowed at the sight of me.

"Ashton," I cried. "Run to me!"

On what must have been instinct, she followed my gaze and saw Soren. With a gasp, she ran toward me as he flew into motion after her, but then Rowan came skidding into the stable with a thick dagger in his right hand.

At the sight of Soren, his features shifted to shock. "You?"

Shock was replaced by a snarl that curved his mouth, and he charged. Ashton reached me. Grabbing hold, I pulled her up against the wall.

The captain skidded through the doorway with his sword drawn.

"My king!"

Rowan reached Soren, and the assassin slashed with his blade. Slashing back, Rowan tried to sweep the man's leg with his foot. He succeeded, but Soren grabbed him and both men went down. The next thing I knew, Soren was partially up, and as he thrust hard, his blade pierced Rowan's rib cage, sinking up to the hilt.

Ashton screamed, fighting to break away from me, but I was stronger and held her back.

Three more guards came flying through the open door. The captain reached Soren and kicked him off Rowan.

Rowan's eyes were open and unblinking. He didn't appear to be breathing. The repercussions of this hit me with a jolt.

As Soren fell backward, the captain raised his sword, but I cried, "Don't kill him yet."

Though his face was a mask of murderous rage, somehow Captain Caron stopped. His men rushed, and they pinned Soren to the floor. While this distracted me, Ashton broke away and ran to her brother. A cry of pain escaped her, echoing off the walls of the barn.

"No!"

Her fingers were on his throat and then his chest, but as I walked up behind her, I knew she'd find no signs of life. The blade must have gone right into his heart.

King Rowan was dead.

Ashton began keening and leaned over to press her face against his body. I didn't know what to do. I'd never loved anyone enough to experience such loss.

In alarm, I looked to the captain for help.

But he jerked Soren to his feet. "I'll make your death last for days," he rasped.

With stony eyes, the assassin remained silent, and my thoughts churned. Rowan was dead. My entire world shifted in less than a minute. Genève had been my most powerful ally to force a marriage with her son, but now he was gone, and I was unwanted baggage…and she'd told me in detail how she'd arranged to have Ashton kidnapped. I knew too much.

No longer an ally, Genève had just become a threat.

"Captain," I said, moving toward the doors. "Please."

He loved Rowan, and he was not himself at the moment, but after one more glare at Soren, he strode to me.

"What?" he asked rudely.

Ashton stopped keening, but her face was pressed against Rowan's chest.

"I overheard the dowager queen hire that man to kill the princess. That's why I ran down here."

Captain Caron went still. He didn't even breathe.

"You'll find a red velvet pouch on his person," I continued. "They were in an alcove and I saw her give it to him."

"Why would the queen assassinate the princess?" he whispered.

He was certainly astute and aware enough to reason this out for himself.

"Question that man," I said," and make sure Lords Moreau and Sauvage are present, but do not mention the dowager's name. Torture him at first. Promise him a swift death, a single stroke, if he'll name who hired him, and then swear to lock him in the depths of the cellar and leave him there in some hole to slowly starve to death, alone and forgotten in the darkness, if he won't. He will name the dowager."

More guards were arriving.

The captain looked to Ashton. Her body was racked by grief, and her face was still hidden against Rowan's chest. The sight was beyond unsettling.

Turning to a guard beside him, the captain said, "Lock the prisoner in a barracks cell. I'll take the princess to her rooms and join you directly." After walking to Ashton, he crouched down. "Princess, come away." He reached out for her.

"No! Micah, no! I can't leave him here."

"I'll take care of him. I promise."

As he grasped her shoulders to draw her away, she struggled. "Micah, stop!"

He shook her once, gently, but his voice hardened. "Ashton. Put your arms around my neck. *Right now.*"

With a final sob, she looked into his face and obeyed him. Still sitting in a crouch, he swept one arm under her legs and lifted her. She clung to him, and he stood up.

"Lieutenant Arye," he barked to a man near the door. "Take three men and confine the dowager queen to her apartments. No one is to see her but me. Do you understand?"

The man paled. "The dowager?"

"Those are my orders. If you fail, I'll have you demoted, dismissed, and sent back to the border guard."

"Yes, sir."

Carrying Ashton, the captain strode out.

Walking over slowly, I looked down at Rowan. There was a pool of dark blood spreading out beside him. This was what my swift action had wrought: the death of my future husband and the end of my chance to be queen.

I felt nothing for him, no sorrow over his loss.

But I feared greatly for myself. What would this mean for me?

* * * *

With little control over the outcome of my actions, I went to my room and hid there.

Events moved swiftly.

Though I never learned what methods the captain used to get a confession so quickly, I later heard rumors that Lord Sauvage was involved, and he had a reputation for brutality.

Soren named Genève before the sun even set.

He was beheaded an hour later. Genève was arrested and taken from her apartments. But instead of locking her in a barracks cell, the Council of Nobles had her housed in the far south tower, which was seldom used.

Lords Sauvage and Moreau came to question me, and I told them everything I'd heard in the alcove and of how I had run for the stable. Only when I reached the part about Rowan's death did I feel the need to express false emotion, calling up a single tear.

"I should not have called on the king for help. I only wanted to save the princess."

"His death is not of your doing," Lord Moreau said.

"But why would the dowager wish for Ashton's death?" I asked, allowing confusion and misery into my voice.

They glanced at each other. They knew why. They both knew. Genève would now have to fight for her life.

She would lose.

"Where is the king?" I asked. "When I last saw him…his body was… it was…" I allowed my voice to break.

Sauvage grew alarmed. There was probably nothing he feared more than a weeping woman. I knew him mainly by reputation, but he was a striking figure, of medium height with a solid, muscular build. His hair was thick and prematurely silver in an unlined face. His jaw was square, and his nose boasted a bump at the bridge. Like Genève, he exuded an aura of strength and determination.

"The king's body is in the cellars," he said quickly, "to be prepared for burial. You must rest. Should I have dinner brought on a tray?"

"That would be kind."

To my relief, they left.

* * * *

Sitting alone in my room, I'd never been so afraid. Rowan was dead, and Ashton would be crowned as queen, and I would be sent home to my father. He'd see me as an utter failure and act accordingly.

I'd be suffering at Lord Arullian's hands inside of a month. The fear brought an acrid taste into my mouth as I tried not to panic. But I could see no way to save myself.

A soft knock sounded on my door, and it opened without invitation.

Kamilla looked in. Her normally tidy hair was in disarray. At the sight of me, sitting in a chair by the hearth, she breathed in softly.

"My lady, you're still awake."

I stood. "What is it?"

"The princess is in a bad way."

Ashton? Of course she was in a bad way. She'd watched as an assassin thrust a knife into Rowan's heart, and the woman she viewed as a mother had been arrested.

"That's to be expected," I answered. "It has been a trying day."

At the moment, my pity for myself was so great it could not be extended to Ashton—who would be queen.

"No, my lady," Kamilla answered. "She is in a *bad* way, and she does not need a maid to care for her. She needs family, and you are the closest thing she has."

"Me? Would not Lady Elizabeth or Lady Miranda know her better?" The wife of a council member seemed a far better choice than myself.

"I fear not, my lady," Kamilla answered. "King Rowan…discouraged her from fostering friendships with anyone but himself." She paused. "But you were to be her sister. She needs you."

You were to be her sister.

Something in this broke through my fear-laden haze. Kamilla viewed me as the closest thing the princess had to family? That meant something, but as of yet, I didn't quite understand what. I only knew a lifeline had been thrown, and I had to grasp it.

"Yes, of course. I'm coming."

As I was still dressed, I left my room immediately and followed Kamilla to Ashton's apartments.

There, I saw what Kamilla meant.

Ashton sat on a couch before her own hearth, but she stared into the flames without blinking and whispered unintelligible words to herself in an endless stream. The skirt of her sky-blue gown was stained with Rowan's blood.

"She won't let me remove the gown," Kamilla whispered.

Walking over, I leaned down to touch Ashton's shoulder. "Princess?"

She didn't respond or acknowledge I'd spoken. Her whispering continued. No wonder Kamilla had gone for help. But with Rowan dead and Genève arrested, was I really the only option? I might have a use here yet.

A small voice at the back of my mind whispered, "Don't fail."

The problem was that I had no idea how to offer comfort. Worse, I didn't understand Ashton's feelings for Rowan. Yes, she'd loved him, but she had also feared him, not only physically, but she'd feared displeasing him for his own sake. I didn't understand her, and I couldn't fathom loving someone I feared.

And yet…she now suffered over his loss. How could I help? What could I do?

My thoughts flowed backward to night when I was twelve years old. From the time I could walk, our family's spaniel, named Emma, had been my sweet friend, nearly always at my side. She had soulful eyes and long soft ears. Though my father forbade it, I often snuck her into my bed so she might sleep with me. He never checked, so he never found out.

When I was twelve, she went to sleep one day and did not awake.

I was beside myself with a sense of loss and sorrow.

My father and my brother, George, barely noticed. My sisters didn't care. I sat on one of our couches before a fire that night and felt as if I were bleeding inside. Henri came to me. Like everyone else in the family, he'd never witnessed one member offering another comfort, and he would have had no more idea what to do than I would in his situation. But he got a blanket, and he sat down beside me and covered me with it. Then he called a servant and ordered hot tea with milk and honey.

We never spoke of Emma, but when the tea arrived, he made me drink some of it, and he sat with me on that couch all night.

"Get me a blanket," I ordered Kamilla.

"What about her gown, my lady?"

"Leave it. It's not important. Just fetch the blanket."

Kamilla struck me as the type of person who believed all would be well so long as everything was neat and clean. She viewed the real problem right now as the blood on Ashton's gown. But after a brief hesitation, she did as I asked.

Sitting down close to Ashton, I covered us both with the blanket.

"Stoke up the fire," I told Kamilla, "and then go to the kitchens and bring back a pot of hot tea with honey and milk."

As if glad for a real task, she nodded. "Yes, my lady."

After building up the fire, she hurried away.

Henri had not touched me on the night he tried to offer comfort, but I took his idea and extended it. Wrapping my arms around Ashton, I pulled her close to me and held her. She let me.

She stopped her unintelligible whispering.

Neither of us spoke. I just held her and kept her covered with the blanket.

When Kamilla returned, I poured Ashton a half a cup of tea, blew on it until it was cool enough, and brought it near her lips. An image of Captain Caron appeared in my mind, and I remembered how he had managed her.

"Ashton," I said firmly. "Drink this. Right now."

When I held the cup to her mouth, she drank from it. I helped her to finish it and then set down the cup.

Settling back, I again covered both of us with the blanket.

"Kamilla, there's nothing more you can do. You may as well go and get some sleep."

"Are you sure, my lady?"

"Yes. I'll stay with her. Get some rest. She'll have need of you tomorrow."

"Thank you, my lady."

Once Kamilla was gone, I took Ashton back into my arms and held her. Hours passed, and she rested against me, but she never closed her eyes.

Finally, when my arms began to ache and my shoulder grew sore, I whispered, "It's late, and you've not slept. Do you think you might lay down in the bed?"

"Will you stay with me?" she whispered back.

These words were a good sign. She was still lost in grief, but at least speaking coherently now.

"Yes. I'll stay." I helped her up, and when we'd walked into her bedroom, I said, "Let me unlace your gown so you will be comfortable."

Like a child, she did my bidding and stopped. Quickly, I unlaced the back of her soiled gown and slipped it off her shoulders, leaving it in a heap on the floor. The skirt of the white shift she wore beneath was a little spotted, but that didn't matter now.

After helping her into bed, I crawled in beside her. I was still fully dressed, but that didn't matter either.

"Sleep now," I whispered.

"You won't leave?"

"No. I won't leave. I promise."

Chapter Eleven

The following day, Kamilla brought gowns and stockings from my room, and I moved into Ashton's apartments. Ashton didn't speak much, and she ate little, but I remained with her.

As the days passed, several of the noblewomen residing at the castle came to check on the princess, but I wouldn't allow them inside—I didn't want Ashton to be seen in her current state. As opposed to resenting this, they all seemed relieved, gratefully remaining outside the door and expressing sympathies while thanking me for my kindness. I was not kind. I was self-serving. But I had the feeling that none of them wished to step inside and be faced with Ashton's grief. Perhaps they'd heard about the scene in the stable after Rowan's death. Women of our class did not show open emotions for others to witness.

Lord Sauvage's wife, Miranda, appeared especially uncomfortable as she stood in the doorway. By this point, I'd been cloistered with Ashton for four days.

"Is she improving?" Miranda asked.

"She's sleeping now."

"I've heard she is…unhinged."

Who could have told her that? It was certainly not Kamilla, so it must have been one of the serving girls bringing in meals. I'd need to check the list of who was coming in.

"She is recovering, my lady," I answered. "But slowly."

I could see that Miranda didn't believe me, but she nodded. "Thank you, Olivia. For all you are doing."

She gave me the oddest feeling she was after something, but I had no idea what.

* * * *

The next day, I left Ashton long enough to go to the kitchens to fetch her a meal by myself. I wanted to limit the number of servants coming into her rooms.

As I reached the large, round center chamber near the entrance to the great hall, I came upon Captain Caron speaking to several guards. I'd not seen him since he'd left the stable that day carrying Ashton.

As I came into sight, he stopped in mid-sentence and broke off, walking to me. "My lady. How is the princess?"

He looked as if he hadn't been sleeping, and his long hair hung in snarls.

With him, I didn't need to protect Ashton, and I didn't need to pretend. "I don't know," I answered honestly. "I'm getting her to eat a little, but not much, and she rarely speaks. I sometimes fear she is shattered."

He closed his eyes and opened them again. "I've heard reports of all that you're doing for her. I cannot tell you how grateful I am that you're here."

His voice was anguished and sincere at the same time. While caring for Ashton, I'd been cut off from castle news.

"When is the burial?" I asked.

"It's done. Lord Sauvage ordered it, and no one gainsaid him."

Rowan had already been buried at Lord Sauvage's order? Something about this unsettled me, but then again, with the lack of an acting monarch, the council would need to make such decisions.

"What of the dowager?" I asked.

"Her trial begins tomorrow, but it will be a closed-door affair in the private council chambers. You can expect to be called to testify."

Yes. I had expected this.

The poor captain looked weary to his core, and I knew it was more than a lack of sleep. He probably held himself responsible for Rowan's death, and for the fact that he'd not seen the extent of the threat Genève posed.

For some reason I couldn't explain, I looked up into Micah's light brown eyes. "And how are you? How are you really?"

The honesty of my question appeared to unman him. He blinked several times. "Lost."

Then he turned and walked away, and I watched his broad back. In many ways, Rowan had been a fortunate man. He'd struck me as one of the most selfish people I'd ever met—and I'd met a few. He always put his own needs first...and yet two decent people had loved him so much. Two people mourned his loss with open wounds.

I couldn't say this of myself.

No one loved me like that.

* * * *

By a week following Rowan's death, I was able to leave Ashton for longer periods of time, such as to dine in the great hall.

I explained to her that it was time she allowed herself some interaction with at least the noble wives. But she refused. She wouldn't leave her rooms or accept guests. She did not ask after Genève.

The trial began, and as expected, I was called to testify.

In my time here at the castle, I'd never been to the council chambers. The room was large and rectangular, with a polished wooden table long enough to accommodate twenty people. When I arrived, all twelve council members were present.

Genève was not.

I later wondered how much of her own trial she even witnessed. It struck me more as a matter of these men questioning witnesses for the sake of decorum before they made a formal vote.

Lord Cloutier sat at one end of the table. An ornate, but empty, chair sat at the other. I knew this must have been Rowan's.

While testifying, I was expected to stand.

Lord Moreau asked most of the questions, and I believed he was most informed of all that had taken place. Answering his questions was an easy matter, as I spoke nothing but the truth. I told them everything I'd overheard in the alcove.

The red velvet purse had been found on Soren.

"And you've been residing with the princess since the king's death?" Lord Sauvage asked, even though this was common knowledge. "Do you believe it likely she will recover her wits?"

The question was so sudden it left me momentarily speechless. Several council members looked to him in alarm.

"That is hardly relevant to our business here," Baron Augustine sputtered.

"Forgive me," Lord Sauvage said. "I asked simply out of concern."

As I didn't think him capable of concern, I wondered what he was up to.

"Is there anything else, my lords?" I asked.

"No," Lord Cloutier answered. "You may go."

* * * *

The following day, Genève was pronounced guilty of treason and sentenced to death.

I would be expected to attend the execution—as would every noble at the castle. It was considered our duty to watch a traitor die.

However, I made a formal request to the council that Ashton not be required to attend.

My request was granted.

The execution was held in the courtyard, and the morning dawned warm and clear. A platform had been set up, with a simple wooden block positioned on one side. The axman wore a black hood.

About two hundred people gathered around the platform. The crowd was a mix of nobles, guards, city leaders, and merchants. Everyone spoke in hushed tones. I'd heard sometimes these events could take on an almost carnival atmosphere, but not this one. The king was dead, and his mother was about to die for the crime.

As I stood near Baron Augustine, I scanned faces around me until I spotted Captain Caron. Slowly, I moved in his direction until I stood beside him. He looked down at me with bleak eyes.

Then Geneve was led out the castle doors by four royal guards. I'd not seen her since that day outside the alcove.

Walking with her head high, she appeared defiant, wearing a gown of golden silk.

Once up on the platform, she cast her gaze around at the crowd, stopping briefly on me before moving on. I wondered if she knew the part I'd played in her conviction.

"I am innocent of treason," she called clearly. "I loved my son. What I did, I did for him and for this kingdom."

Even in the end, she couldn't accept the smallest responsibility in Rowan's death. I found this lack of self-knowledge somehow tragic.

The executioner motioned to the block, and without fear, she knelt and laid her head down. She had courage.

But I tensed for what was to come. I'd never seen a beheading, and had no wish to be here. Something lightly touched my left hand. The captain's fingers wove through mine, and he gripped my hand. I gripped back.

"Close your eyes," he said quietly.

I did as he asked, and a moment later came the sound of the chop. Even without sight, I couldn't help wincing. After a few breaths, I opened my eyes to see Geneve's headless body on the platform. Blood flowed from the stump of her neck.

Quickly, I pulled my hand from the captain's before anyone saw, but I was grateful to him.

Chapter Twelve

Two more days passed.

What struck me as most strange about my situation with Ashton, was that it did not feel strange. Her apartments were less lavish than Genève's, but they were more comfortable, with softer couches, piles of pillows, and thick carpets.

I remained with her during the days, and then I would go down to dinner. Once there, the council members and their wives often questioned me about her state, and I tried to answer ambiguously.

But I was necessary, and this mattered.

No one even mentioned sending me home.

At night, I returned to our rooms and slept with Ashton in her bed. We spoke of little things, and I protected her from everyone else. She needed time to heal.

On that second day following Genève's execution, I was setting out a light lunch of fruit, bread, and cheese for us when Ashton looked at me directly.

"Kamilla said my mother hired that man in the stable to kill me. Is it true?"

This caught me off guard. Had Kamilla been so blunt? As of yet, Ashton and I had not spoken of realities, but I nodded. "Yes."

"Why?" she asked.

"I don't know," I lied.

"Is my mother dead now?"

"Yes."

"How?"

"She was executed."

"Where you there?"

"Yes."

"Did she suffer?"

"No," I assured her. "It was quick."

To me, this seemed a breakthrough on her part, and I would have answered anything she asked. As Genève had died as a traitor, her body had not been buried in the family crypt, but I didn't know what became of it. I wondered if Ashton might ask, but instead, she glanced away.

"I have no memories before Rowan and Mother," she said. "My first clear memory is the day they arrived. The hall was so crowded, and there were guards everywhere, and a great dog standing beside me began to bark. I saw someone with dark hair, and I ran to him. Somehow...I knew he would keep me safe. He would always keep me safe. He picked up me and held me. That was Rowan."

It was then that I understood why Ashton and Rowan viewed each other so differently. He'd been twelve years old upon arriving at this castle, with memories of a prior life and a prior father. He'd never viewed Ashton as his sister.

Ashton could only see him as a beloved brother, her protector. She'd never known a life without him. In our time here together, in these apartments, she'd never mentioned that day in the alcove when he tore her gown while she wept and begged him to stop, and he'd cut the side of her mouth with his teeth. She seemed to have pushed this from her mind.

I knew he would keep me safe. He would always keep me safe.

This was how she chose to remember him, and now that he was dead, I saw no reason to remind her of his darker side.

However, well before the dinner hour that evening, I grew restless and dressed early to go down.

"Won't you come with me?" I asked Ashton.

She was sitting by the fire again, staring into the flames. She'd been wearing her nightgown and robe all day. "Not tonight. Soon."

She'd said this for the past three nights.

Knowing that pressing the matter was hopeless, I slipped from the room and descended the tower to the main floor. As always, I slowed and moved silently down the corridor. For my part, this was more instinct and deeply ingrained training from my father than from any wish to overhear a conversation. No voices drifted from the alcoves.

When I reached the entry chamber before the great hall, I resumed my normal walk, heading toward the archway, but a voice came from just inside and to the right of the arch.

"How soon do you think he will move?" Baron Augustine asked.

The hushed, furtive tone of his voice caused me to stop. Father had also taught me that numerous conversations of value took place in public. He taught me to listen for the tone, for the sound of someone who did not wish to be overheard.

"As early as tomorrow, I fear," Lord du Guay answered. "Sauvage has never been known for subtlety."

Quickly, I moved to the wall outside the archway and crept to the corner to peer inside. Though I couldn't see either man, the hall was alive with the activity of servants setting up dinner.

"How much support does Moreau have?" asked Baron Augustine.

"Not enough," du Guay answered. "Sauvage is determine to head the provisional government, and I think he has the votes. Moreau may try to roust him, but too many on the council don't trust a man with his gambling debts. They'll back Sauvage."

"The gods save us," Augustine said. "The people won't like it. Ashton is too well loved. But with the king dead and the princess lost to us, Sauvage has precedent. I don't know if he can be stopped."

I drew away from the wall and hurried back to the corridor. Every word of their conversation echoed in my ears. It all made sense. Lord Sauvage had been suggesting that Ashton had "lost her wits," and she had done nothing to alter this perception.

Forcing away my father's careful training, I ran down the corridor and up the curving stairs to Ashton's apartments, slipping through the door.

"You must get up!"

Still sitting by the fire, she turned to me. "What's wrong?"

I walked straight toward the back of the couch. "Lord Sauvage intends to set up a provisional government and name himself as the head."

"What?" she asked in disbelief. "Why would he do that?"

"Because with you shut away in here, the kingdom has no ruler." Stepping around the couch to face her, I pressed on. "Can you imagine Lord Sauvage in control of our military? With absolute power over the lives of our men? Can you see him up on the dais of the common court dispensing rulings to the people? Is that what you want, Ashton? Is it?"

She stood. Her eyes moved back and forth. A light seemed to come on inside her. "Sauvage in common court...no. I do not want that." Though she wasn't power-seeking like Rowan, she cared deeply about the people. "Olivia...what do I do?"

"Let me call Kamilla. Don your finest gown and have her pile up your hair. Walk into the great hall tonight and take Rowan's chair in the center of the first table. Let everyone see you there. Be the queen."

A long moment of silence followed. Then she nodded.

* * * *

I savored the look of utter shock on Lord Sauvage's face when we walked through the archway into the great hall.

It was gratifying beyond description.

Ashton wore a rose-colored gown with a split skirt and burgundy underskirt. Her hair was elaborately coiffured, and she wore a diamond tiara. Though diminutive, she was every inch a queen.

There were about forty people in the hall, and Lord Moreau reached us first. "My princess," he said, bowing. "Are you well? It is a joy to see you."

She smiled. I don't know how she managed a smile, but she did. "I am well, as you can see. Would you act as escort and show me to my chair? I should like you on one side of me and Olivia on the other."

He bowed again. "It would be my honor."

A sea of inquiries and well wishes followed us to the table.

Moreau was quick-witted, and he pulled out Rowan's chair for Ashton. She sat gracefully, as if this place was her due—which it was.

Sauvage's face went pale. Standing before her on the other side of the table, he actually had the nerve to say, "You take the king's chair, my lady?"

She gazed up at him innocently. "Of course. I will soon be queen."

A muscle in his jaw twitched. "The council holds a meeting at noon tomorrow. Perhaps you might be good enough to join us?"

"It would be my pleasure," she answered.

With a curt nod, he walked down the table to find a seat. Ashton's countenance remained serene, but I could see her hands under the table. They were shaking.

* * * *

The next day, Ashton dressed with equal care, choosing a gown with a flowing blue skirt and a cream bodice. She chose to wear her hair down, and I wondered if that might be a mistake, as she already looked younger than her age, and leaving her hair down made her appear as a girl.

I gave little thought to my own appearance and wore my tan muslin.

"Come downstairs with me," Ashton said. "I need your strength."

I was glad to walk with her to this meeting. She was about to go alone into the lion's den with her kingdom at stake. Her success was my success at this point, and I had to make myself indispensable to her. Yes, playing nursemaid to Ashton was quite a step down from my recent ambitions, but I would have done almost anything to avoid being sent home.

And...I didn't mind helping Ashton.

Together we descended from the tower and made our way to the council chambers. Some of the men were already inside and some were milling about out front. Baron Augustine smiled at me warmly. As of yet, everyone appeared to be laboring under the impression that my care of Ashton was entirely selfless.

"Shall we begin?" du Guay asked, starting for the chambers.

"Lady Olivia will be present for this meeting," Ashton said, taking my hand and leading me past him.

Taken aback, I followed, but I was on uncertain ground. She wanted me *in* the gathering? Several men inside the room must have heard her and watched us enter.

"Princess..." Lord Moreau began. "It would be best if Lady Olivia waited outside."

"Why should she not be present?" Ashton returned. "She would have married the king and been my sister. She would have been queen in my place."

While this was true, Rowan's death had rendered me less than useless here at court. I was now nothing more than an extra daughter of Hugh Géroux.

"She has a right to be here," Ashton continued as she turned to an attendant. "Please get Lady Olivia a chair."

The young attendant scurried to obey, pushing a chair up beside the ornate chair at the table's head. Ashton sat in the ornate chair and motioned me beside her. Still uncertain of this, I obeyed. Until now, I'd been nearly invisible to the council—caretaker of the princess in her grief. This would bring me to their full attention.

Though nonplussed, the twelve council members began to sit. This entire situation was so unprecedented that my presence here may not have seemed worth a battle. The king had been murdered, the dowager queen beheaded, and now the path forward was unclear.

Only Lord Sauvage glared at me. The others appeared to forget my existence.

I had no idea how this would begin, but the moment all the men were seated and the door was closed, Ashton stood up.

"My lords," she said. "In the privacy of this chamber, let us not mince words. I understand your concerns and your recent decision to consider setting up a provisional government. But the people of our land are loyal to my family, and they will expect me to be crowned as queen, and *you* need the goodwill of our people." She paused. "In turn, I need your goodwill and your support to rule. So, I believe we are saddled with each other."

The room was dead quiet while every man listened.

Her expression softened. "Though no one has spoken the words, I know as well that you are reticent to crown a girl not yet twenty years of age. Who could blame you? But I am aware of my age and my gender, and I do promise to be counseled by you in all things and to depend upon your experience."

She had their attention. She was right in one thing. The people of this kingdom would expect to see her crowned as queen. She was the heir. All the men here knew this.

But now, many of the expressions shifted to various states of interest, and my hopes rose. I looked at her through their eyes and saw the image she was painting. She had promised to be counseled by them. They saw a pretty figurehead whom the people loved. They saw a biddable girl who would stand on the dais of common court and keep the people happy while they governed behind the scenes.

"My lady," Lord Moreau said carefully. "It is common for a reigning monarch to appoint a chancellor. Would you consider this?"

What was he after?

"My brother did not," Ashton answered.

"No, but he was ten years your senior, and your father made certain he had experience in the workings of the council and the military. We suggested he choose one, but in his case, we did not press the matter."

This was a threat. Compromises were being considered here, but Lord Moreau was insisting she take on a chancellor if she wanted his support.

"Who would act as chancellor?" Lord Sauvage challenged.

"She would choose for herself," Moreau answered.

"And you assume she would choose you?"

"I assume nothing," Moreau answered.

"My lords," Ashton said. "I am not opposed to choosing a chancellor, but I've not yet read the bylaws. Must I choose a member of this council? I would not wish to be seen as showing favoritism. Could I choose someone like Baron Cornett or perhaps Viscount Bretagne?"

Another moment of silence followed, but I could see them mulling over her suggestion, and no one appeared displeased. It seemed they might even approve her idea of choosing a man who was not on the council—therefore not disturbing the balance of power. Viscount Bretagne was getting on in years, and Baron Cornett was known to enjoy his pleasures a bit too much, but both men were of noble blood, loyal to the kingdom, and friends with every man on this council. Neither was objectionable, and either one could keep her in check.

Baron August spoke up, "Yes, princess. According to the bylaws, you may choose someone not on the council. He need only be from among the noble families and a landowner." He paused. "And there is no rush. You need not choose until after your coronation." He looked about the room. "Are we all agreed in this?"

I held my breath.

Coronation.

The men of the council nodded one by one, even Lord Sauvage, and I exhaled. She had them.

Ashton would be queen.

* * * *

The next morning, Ashton and I were having breakfast in our sitting room while Kamilla reorganized our gowns in the bedroom.

"You'll want to give extra thought to your gown today," Ashton said. "We're due at common court in an hour."

I knew today was a bimonthly common court day.

"You wish me to attend?" I asked, taking a sip of tea.

"No. I've made arrangements with Micah for the chair placement. I want you up on the dais beside me."

I set down my cup. Last night at dinner, I'd noticed several members of the council glancing at me askance, perhaps wondering about my growing influence. My presence in the council chambers yesterday was one thing, but this could create powerful enemies.

"Ashton, I can't. I have no royal title."

"Well, I can't do this alone, and I need you up there with me. I need your strength."

Me? Sitting beside the future queen on the dais? Though a part of me feared the repercussions, another part slowly began to revel in the image. In addition, my survival here depended on Ashton continuing to need me. I was the one who'd started down this murky path, and I couldn't stop now.

So we helped each other choose a gown for the day.

She held up one of her own dresses to my shoulder, a beautiful amber silk. "It's a pity we cannot share gowns," she said. "This color suits you better than me."

The difference in our sizes was so great that we'd never be able to share clothing, but her words touched me. My own sisters would not think to be so generous.

Once we were dressed, Kamilla piled up our hair, and we each wore a simple gold chain.

As we left our apartments and descended the curving stairs, I could see Ashton was nervous. The people might love her, but Rowan had always done the public speaking in common court, and he passed down decisions.

This would be her first time standing in his place.

I began to see why she wanted me beside her.

When we emerged from the corridor into the vast entry chamber, six guards fell into step behind us. Ahead waited the tall archway of the great hall.

When the princess walked in with me beside her, all the people inside the hall turned to stare at us. As of yet, no one had spoken to the public of the tumultuous events of last week. Linking her arm in mine, Ashton walked through the crowd. Ahead, on the dais, the large chair and the smaller chair had been placed side by side.

After we'd ascended, Ashton turned to the face the crowd.

"My people," she said, and her voice carried. "I beg your forgiveness for not having come to you sooner. I have been in a place of darkness, bleeding over the loss of my brother, of our king."

The emotion in her words had impact, and I saw tears running down a number of faces in the crowd. These people had not been given a chance to publicly mourn their king. My gaze paused on Captain Caron, who stood rigid, near the back, hanging on her every word.

"His loss leaves a hole in the world that can never be filled," she continued. "But you have my love, and you have my ear, and I will do my best to serve you, as you have always served me."

Even I found myself caught up in her speech. It was so genuine, so real.

Turning, she motioned to me. "This is the lady Olivia Géroux. She would have married my brother and been your next queen. She would have been my sister. From now on, she will sit beside me here in court and lend you her ear as well."

From now on...

I fought to keep my expression still. We did not live in a world of "would have beens." We lived in a world of what *was*. I had not married Rowan. I would not be queen. I was not Ashton's sister.

And yet...not a single face in the crowd frowned in confusion or disapproval. Ashton spoke, and they listened.

Her words were all these people required.

She seated herself, and I followed suit.

"Bring forth the first case," she said.

Jarvis took his place to one side of the dais, unrolled a list, and called up two men from the craftsmen's guild who were in dispute over placement of stalls in the upcoming fair. I was still so rattled I barely followed the discussion, but I also realized I knew nothing of the layout of the city or the marketplace, and I'd be of no use to Ashton in this matter. Thankfully, it wasn't a complicated issue, and she managed to help the men work out an agreement. I was aware that the fair was an important event, and the crown took part of the proceeds in taxes, so I made a mental note to learn more of the inner workings.

The next case was more difficult. Apparently, a section on the seaward side of the castle had collapsed during a storm in the spring. The basic work had been completed, but now an artisan mason was needed for the fine work. This was a large job, requiring months of work, and it paid well.

Jarvis had conducted the initial search, and he'd narrowed the candidates down to two men of equal skill. He wished for Ashton to make the final choice.

The two men took turns relating their skills, and they both sounded more than qualified. As I listened, something about one of the men caught my attention. He wore an indigo shirt with black buttons.

Then I noted that Jarvis had referred to him as "Cameron Compté."

Ashton leaned forward. "You are both fine masons of equal skill, and we are fortunate to have such artisans here in the city. This decision is most difficult, but Master Compté's family is in the greatest need at present, and I award the position to him."

While this seemed an unusual reason to award the post to one man over the other, the people in the crowd nodded at her choice. Perhaps it made her seem more connected to their daily lives.

Unfortunately, it caused me to begin to feel self-conscious and useless sitting up there. When Rowan had sat in the large chair, Ashton whispered snippets of information and advice to him in almost every case. I knew nothing of the workings of this city or the people who lived here.

None of the cases were particularly complex, and in each one, I'd have made the same decision as Ashton, but my purpose here was not to make decisions. My purpose was to listen and offer her assistance.

Then...a man and a woman were called before the dais. She ran a business making casks, and he was a winemaker. She had delivered a large number of casks he'd ordered, and he had not paid the bill, citing hardship and asking for an extension.

"I've already granted him an extension, my princess," the woman said, "twice. He has no intention of paying what he owes, and my men worked for three months on those casks. We turned down other work because his order was so large."

The man held up both hands. "I cannot pay what I do not have. The price of burgundy wine has fallen this year, and I've not been able to cover my own costs, much less pay some of my debts."

A few faces in the crowd darkened, but no one spoke.

At this, I sat up straight as I remembered something. At one of the embroidery circles in the dowager's quarters, Lord Sauvage's wife, Miranda, had been joking about her husband's poor temper due to the increased cost of burgundy wine—which was his favorite. The sweetness of last year's crop had produced a fine vintage, and its popularity had caused a sharp rise in price.

A number of the people in the crowd must know this, but I wasn't certain about Ashton.

Turning my head, I spoke softly. "He's lying. The price of burgundy wine is sky-high this year."

Ashton leaned forward, addressing the winemaker. "As the price of burgundy wine has indeed not fallen, but risen, you will make good on your debt today." Her voice was firm, and she looked to Jarvis. "You will see to this."

The winemaker paled. He'd apparently not expected this decision.

But people in the crowd nodded approval. Ashton appeared both in the right and a just leader.

I would never be like Ashton, connected on a personal level to the common people. I would never know their names or who was having children or who was out of work or who was ill. But…I could learn more about the guilds and the smaller points of commerce in this city. In this way, I could make myself useful to her.

Several more cases were presented, and then common court ended for the day.

Ashton stood, and I followed suit. Our guards fell in behind as we swept from the great hall together.

Once through the archway, Ashton exhaled. "Thank you," she whispered.

"I wasn't much help," I whispered back.

"You were. I could not have done that without you."

At the mouth of the corridor leading to the south towers, she stopped. "I have a gown fitting, then I'm going down to the old stable to check the progress of the sorting of donations. I've not been there since…since…" She trailed off, and then added. "Would you like to stay with me, or do you have other plans?"

Though I had no plans, my mind was full, and I was too restless to sit through a gown fitting.

"I think I've been indoors too much," I answered. "A walk in the courtyard might do me good."

She smiled. "Yes, of course. If you can, come find me in the stable later. We can always use the help."

Though I hardly relished sorting through hand-me-down blankets and fetching sacks of flour, such acts might be part of my life now—and they were certainly preferable to being sent home.

"I will."

Turning, I made my way back through the entry chamber to the corridor leading out the front of the castle. Upon stepping outside in the fresh air, I closed my eyes and breathed in, smelling salt from the sea on the air. There would be repercussions from what Ashton had done today…seating me beside her on the dais.

Of this, I was sure.

When I opened my eyes again, Captain Caron stood not ten paces away, watching me.

Chapter Thirteen

"Captain," I said.

He came closer, studying me. "I think in private, it's time you started calling me Micah."

Yes. Ashton always called him by his given name. So had Rowan and Genève.

"That was risky in the hall today," he went on.

As always with him, I seemed to have no defenses. "I don't have a choice."

"What is it you want, Olivia? What are you striving for, here?"

"It's not so much what I want, as what I don't want...and I don't want to be sent home."

His eyes continued to scan my face. "Are you afraid?"

I wasn't about to answer that. "I need to be useful to Ashton. I was not useful enough on the dais today."

"You were. She knows nothing of the price of wine."

An idea struck me. He was a man who walked in a mix of social circles, and therefore rare. "I should like to learn more of the city's commerce, of the workings of the merchants and the artisans, so I might be of help to Ashton. Do you know such people? Could you bring a few here and introduce me?"

He considered this for a long moment. "I'll do you one better. Come with me."

As he started for the castle gates, I felt awkward hurrying after him. "Where are we going?"

"Into the city. You said you wanted to learn more. The best way to do that is firsthand."

* * * *

At first, the thought of passing through the gates and exploring the city with Micah seemed terribly wrong. I had no permission. I'd asked no permission. This somehow seemed a breach of all propriety and rules.

Then I realized there *was* no one to ask. My father wasn't here. I certainly didn't need Ashton's permission to leave the courtyard. In many ways, at this moment, I was…free. So, I walked out the castle gates beside Micah and out into the streets of Partheney, alone in the company of a man to whom I was neither married nor related. Yes, he was the commander of the castle guard, but today he was not playing that role.

It all felt rather scandalous.

I liked it.

"Have you eaten lunch?" he asked.

"No." I'd barely eaten breakfast.

"Come this way," he said.

I followed, and we walked down a street of fine houses. After about five city blocks, he turned west, and I found myself amidst several streets of fine shops with colorful signs and awnings.

"There," he said, pointing to a shop with a bright yellow awning and numerous tables with chairs set up out front.

As we approached, my mouth began to water at the smell of freshly baked bread.

About thirty people already sat at the tables, drinking mugs of tea or eating rolls and sausages.

Micah pulled a chair out at an empty table. "Sit, my lady."

No matter how polite he was, it sounded like an order. Perhaps he was simply accustomed to spending his days giving orders?

Nevertheless, I sat. I was hungry, and this experience was new. Eating with common people at a table outdoors? Several people called greetings to Micah and looked at me with open curiosity. With a slight thrill, I realized they'd have no idea who I was. Young noblewomen did not sit in public with soldiers wearing chain armor.

A large man with a thick mustache strode up to our table. He wore an apron. "Captain. Good to see you? How are you this morning?" Then he glanced at me.

Micah didn't introduce me. "I'm well, Bertram. Could you bring us rolls, sausages, and spiced tea?"

With a nod, Bertram left, but he returned almost immediately with a tray, and my mouth watered again. The rolls were light brown and still steaming. I could smell the spice in the tea. With some alarm, I realized I carried no money, but Micah paid for our meal, and I was in no position to object.

Once we alone at the table again, he gestured to the food. "Eat, my lady. You won't find finer bread anywhere in the city."

The sausages were warm, but not hot, and I enjoyed the food more than anything I'd eaten at the castle. The day was fine, and I was comfortable without a cloak even with the sea air blowing softly through the streets. The life of the city pulsed around me, and white clouds floated overhead in a blue sky. Again, I felt...free. Micah stretched out his long legs and ate three of the rolls. For a moment, I allowed myself to become lost in an illusion that this was real, that I belonged with him, and I belonged at this table among these people.

"Your home is in the southeast?" he asked.

"Yes."

"Did you grow up in a manor?"

"No. A drafty stone keep. I was never fond of it."

Why did I always tell him what I was thinking? Father would warn me to hold my tongue.

"What about you?" I asked.

"I grew up in the castle barracks. My mother died not long after I was born, and my father served in the royal guard."

"So you have no siblings?"

"No, and I was raised in a world of men, so I often wished for sisters."

"Well, you can have both of mine," I said lightly. "They're awful."

Looking up from his tea, he laughed. It was the first time he'd even smiled since Rowan's death. His light brown eyes glowed. A fresh gust of sea air blew across my face, and I felt happiness rising inside me. I wished I could stop this moment and remain here forever.

A stocky woman in a fine velvet gown came striding from the street with an aura of energy.

At the sight of her, Micah sat straight. "Emilee."

Turning her head, she brightened at the sight of him and came over. "Captain. Did you finally get an afternoon to yourself?" Then she glanced at me. "And you've brought fair company."

I found her blunt manner a little off-putting, but Micah surprised me by saying, "May I present the lady Olivia Géroux."

At first, she offered a short laugh, as if he were joking, but then she took in the cut of my gown and the blood began draining from her face.

"Olivia Gér..." She cast her eyes about and then spoke to Micah. "You're serious? The lady who was to marry the king? Are you mad? You can't bring her down here. Are you *alone*?"

Suddenly, I was self-conscious. The pretty illusion around me vanished. Micah had been mad to bring me here and have us sit in public with no other escort. What if word of this got out?

"Sit down," he told her. "Then we won't be alone."

With a startled huff, she sat.

He looked to me. "My lady, this is Emilee Martine. Her husband owns one of the most profitable wine trades in all of Partheney, but Emilee runs the business. If you want to talk to someone connected to commerce here, she's the one."

This rendered Emilee silent, and she stared at me.

I wasn't sure what to say, as I had no idea what to ask her.

Finally, she said, "I heard you were in court this morning, sitting beside the princess, and you helped her put Milton le Grange in his place."

Milton le Grange? Was he the winemaker trying to wriggle out of his debt? Word had certainly traveled quickly. But this gave me an opening.

"Yes," I said.

"How did you know about the price of burgundy?" she asked.

This was not an impertinent question. I wasn't managing a household, and women of my station often had no idea of the price of common goods.

"Sheer dumb luck," I answered. "I'd heard that Lord Sauvage was complaining."

She was taken aback at first, and then she smiled broadly. "But you want to talk to me about commerce?"

"Yes." I nodded. "The princess intends to have me on the dais, and I wish to be of help to her and to the merchants. But I need to know more, much more. I promise if you will teach me, you'll always have my ear in the common court."

Her smile faded as she listened, as if she wasn't hearing me correctly. Then she glanced at Micah. "She means this?"

He nodded. "I think so."

"All right, then," she said to me. "I'll tell you anything you want to know." Turning her head, she called to a woman at another table. "Adela! Come over here and sit." Lowering her voice, she spoke to me again. "Adela and her husband trade in wool."

Wool was an important industry here on the coast, where the winters were long and cold.

Coming over to join us, Adela sat down. "What?"

Emilee jutted her chin toward me. "Meet the lady Olivia Géroux."

Adela's mouth fell open.

Micah leaned back and stretched out his legs again.

* * * *

After a most enlightening afternoon, Micah got me back to the castle in time to dress for dinner.

Though I didn't yet feel safe, I felt safer than I had since Rowan's death. At least I was forearmed with useful information. The merchant women of Partheney had been generous with their time and knowledge. Emilee introduced me to a number of women, and in a matter of hours, I'd learned a great deal about the guilds and taxes and tariffs and current prices of goods for this year.

Also, though Micah certainly must have had duties at the barracks, he remained with me for as long as I wanted to stay. I could not express my gratitude to him enough as we passed through the gates and reentered the courtyard. Royal guards milled all around us.

"Thank you, Captain" I said to him, wishing I could say more. For the span of the afternoon, he'd played the part of a…friend. Now that we were back in my world, he'd again become the captain of the guard.

"It was my honor," he answered, but his voice was low, and I saw a flash of longing pass through his eyes.

Quickly, I turned and walked toward the castle doors, trying to put Micah from my mind. The sun was setting, and I'd be late for dinner if I didn't hurry. Upon slipping inside the castle, I followed the corridor to the round entry-chamber near the great hall and then entered the corridor leading toward the south towers. Ashton would be wondering where I'd been all afternoon.

Though my father's training caused me to slow, I was not paying my usual attention and was caught entirely off guard when someone stepped from an alcove.

I stopped.

It was Lord Sauvage. His expression was tight, and his eyes narrowed. He'd have heard about my inclusion in common court this morning. Had he been waiting for me?

"A word, my lady," he said coldly.

I knew something of his reputation, and we were alone in this corridor. A hint of fear passed through me, and I tried to step around him. "Forgive me, my lord. Perhaps we could speak at dinner? I am late to dress."

His right hand snaked out and grabbed my wrist, jerking me back. I fought not to wince at the sudden pain in my arm. He was as strong and solid as he looked, and his grip felt like a manacle.

"I don't know what you're playing at," he whispered. "But it won't fly here. You're a fool if you think the council will stand by and watch some slip of a girl advise the princess…who will be queen."

The pain of his grip grew worse, but I knew better than to show fear. "That is up to the princess, and it is her pleasure to have me by her side."

"Not for long. I wrote your father today and told him of your shameful acts here. If I know him, and I do, he'll bring you home and have you whipped."

My stomach tightened at the hatred in his voice. I could only imagine what he'd written to my father, exaggerating tales of my behavior here. My father would be outraged. He'd sent me to marry a king and play the part of queen, not to insult the members of the noble council by pushing my way into private meetings and then standing on a dais and appearing to think so highly of myself that I might rule beside Ashton. He'd view me as having embarrassed him, and I could only image what punishment he might devise.

Lord Sauvage leaned closer. "Maybe he'll have me whip you here at the castle myself, so you won't forget the ride home."

When I tried to jerk my arm away, he let go.

Turning, I fled down the corridor. The afternoon I'd spent evaporated like mist.

* * * *

By the time I reached Ashton's apartments, I was in a panic.

After rushing through the door, I closed it behind me. I could hear Kamilla in the bedroom as she walked with quick steps, accompanied by the sound of rustling silk, as she was probably laying out my gown. But across the main room, Ashton was already dressed for dinner and appeared on the verge of being ready to go down.

"Oh, Olivia," she said. "There you are. Where have you been? I was growing worried. If you don't hurry, you'll miss the first course." Then she saw my face. "What's wrong?"

It went against all my instincts to turn to her—to turn to anyone—for help, but I was desperate.

"Lord Sauvage has written to my father, and I fear the letter was vile. He's told of my presence at a closed-door council meeting and of my sitting beside you in common court. He's most likely painted me as some power-seeking girl pushing myself upon you. He will shame my father as a man unable to control the behavior of his daughter." I put hand to my stomach.

"The moment my father reads this letter, he'll send Captain Reynaud and a contingent of guards to bring me home."

The words came from my mouth in a rush, and I expected her to be shocked and upset. She was the one who'd put me in the public eye with little thought of how the men of the council might react.

But she offered me a measured gaze. "Your father will not send guards. He will not bring you home."

"He will."

"No. I wrote to him myself yesterday, using the royal seal. I explained that it is my express wish for you to remain here with me, even after my coronation."

"The royal seal?"

She nodded. "My letter will reach him first, and I made myself quite clear. He will disregard Lord Sauvage's letter. He will not call you home."

We stared at each other.

Everyone thought her so naïve—including me—but she'd foreseen this.

"You have protected me," she said. "Now I will protect you."

* * * *

We celebrated her coronation just over a month later.

Ashton followed the tradition for a new monarch to ride from the outer edge of the city all the way to the castle gates. It was still summer, and the sun shone brightly. However, once again, she angered the council by insisting I ride through the streets directly behind her as she presented herself to the people of Partheney.

Micah rode directly behind me.

Twenty royal guards and forty members of the royal military followed him. Thousands of people lined the streets.

Ashton's gown was gold with a purple underskirt. People cheered and tossed roses in her path, but many of them now recognized me from having attended common court, and I was cheered as well. Some of the roses were thrown in my path.

A part of me reveled in this. Another part shuddered at how the council would react when they heard.

After we finally passed through the castle gate, Captain Caron dismounted and lifted Ashton down first, then me. Baron Augustine awaited us there in the courtyard. He'd not been unkind, but I could see that even he was growing increasingly concerned by Ashton's favor of me.

"You'd best go in, my lady," he told me.

"Yes," I answered.

He would escort Ashton in a few moments.

Turning, I headed through the main doors of the castle and made my way to the great hall. All the other nobles were already inside. My father and brother, George, both stood in a place of honor at the front. Forty serving woman had spent three days lining the walls with long strings of flowers. A red carpet had been spread from the archway to a dais that contained a single ornate chair. Lord Cloutier stood by the chair in his formal robes.

A crown rested on a pedestal.

Avoiding stepping on the carpet, I walked to join my family. Every eye in the room followed me, and I knew I'd been much discussed in the past month. No one knew what to make of Ashton's insistence that I be treated as her sister—with all the rights and privileges of a royal.

My father nodded once as I stood beside him. He was as puzzled as everyone else, but by now, he understood that Ashton's favor for me was more than a passing fancy. His mind had already turned to how our family might benefit.

Heads began turning toward the archway.

Ashton and Baron Augustine entered the hall, and he escorted her up the red carpet. I marveled at her beauty. The top of her head barely reached the baron's shoulder, and yet she was a queen in her golden gown with silken black hair streaming down her back.

Baron Augustine led her to the chair and she took her place.

Lord Cloutier anointed her head with oil, and he recited the vows for her to protect this kingdom and place the welfare of its people above all else.

When she swore her promises, I believed her.

Finally, he placed the crown upon her head. Then he stepped to the side and motioned to her with one hand. "Queen Ashton."

* * * *

That night, my father and George were given places at the head table. This was not lost on the council, especially not Lord Sauvage. I'd managed to avoid him this past month, but he was now powerless to insist my father bring me home and punish me.

Clearly, my father had no intention of doing either.

The Géroux star was on the rise.

I sat on Ashton's right, and as the second course was served, she turned to me and spoke quietly. "There will be some changes for us beginning tomorrow."

"Such as?"

"I'll need to move into my mother's apartments. It's expected of the queen. You're welcome to come with me or you can keep our current apartments for your own."

I thought on that. I had a few plans for the future in which having my own sitting room could be useful. "I would stay in our current apartments, if that's agreeable."

"Of course. I also wish to give you something to show my gratitude. I've arranged to sign over a fief about twenty leagues south of the city."

My hand stopped with my goblet halfway to my mouth. "What?"

"It was left to me by my grandmother, and it's mine to give. I've signed it over to you. There is a vassal in place, but you'll receive most of the rents and a portion of the taxes."

I was speechless.

"You must have an income," she went on as if we were discussing the weather, "and I'd rather you weren't forced to ask your father for an allowance."

In truth, I'd been worrying about this myself. My basic needs of meals and housing were supplied here at the castle, but I had no money of my own.

I could hardly believe what I hearing. A fief? With income from taxes and rents?

"Ashton…"

"Don't thank me. It's nothing."

It wasn't nothing. She'd just made me an independent woman.

Chapter Fourteen

A week later, I hosted my first gathering of the merchant wives. I'd made a few changes to Ashton's apartments—which were now my apartments—adding more small tables and chairs, and the sitting room was better set up for multiple guests.

I'd told the women to bring their sewing or embroidery. I'd arranged tables for cards. I'd ordered tea, cakes, and small apple tarts. I considered asking Ashton to join us, but then I remembered she'd be cloistered with the council today. Lord Sauvage had called a meeting. After that first time, Ashton had not pressed her luck by insisting I attend.

I looked forward to my afternoon.

At first, the arriving women appeared nervous, even Emilee, but less than an hour in, the sitting room was alive with activity and conversation. We spent a good deal of time discussing the upcoming autumn fair, and as I knew this would be a frequent topic in common court, I made many mental notes.

By late afternoon, when we said our good-byes, I felt much better informed…and oddly, as if I were making new friends. Emilee grasped my hand before she left.

"You are an unusual noblewoman, my lady."

I took it as a compliment.

A few serving girls arrived to clean up, and not long after, Kamilla arrived to help me dress for dinner. The sight of her caused me to wonder about our current arrangement.

"Do you mind serving both myself and the queen?" I asked. "Now that we're in separate apartments, this does make more work for you."

"I don't mind," she answered. "You are both kind-natured and easy to please. I'm glad to attend you both."

I was not kind-natured, but that was hardly worth arguing because her answer brought me relief. I trusted her loyalty. She was as devoted to Ashton as Micah, and no matter what my father had warned about ladies' maids, I knew she'd never spill secrets.

"Which gown tonight, my lady?" she asked.

"The cream silk, I think."

Kamilla went into my bedroom to lay out my gown, and I was just moving to join her when the door to the sitting room opened and Ashton rushed inside without knocking. Her normally pale face was white.

"What is it?" I asked, hurrying to reach her.

She trembled and seemed barely able to speak. Then she said, "Lord Sauvage wants to go to war."

"War?"

"Yes, he wishes me to propose an invasion of Samourè, so the council might vote and uphold my decision."

"On what grounds?"

"There have been a few raiders crossing the border and attacking farms. He sees this as a violation of the treaty between our kingdoms."

"What does King Amandine say?"

"He's offered reparations and promised to stop the raids himself, but several men on the council won't accept his offer. They say we'll appear weak if we allow ourselves to be bought off, and we don't strike back hard."

"And what do you think?"

"I am against war in this instance. A war would mean raising taxes, and many people can barely afford what they're paying now. It would mean the deaths or suffering of innocent families in Samourè. It would mean the deaths of some of our own men." She paused. "Am I wrong?"

"No," I answered, agreeing with every word. "You are exactly right."

Kamilla stood in the bedroom doorway, listening. I didn't mind. Again, she could be trusted.

But Ashton's voice was anguished. "Lord Sauvage belittled me in the council chambers as if I were a child. He said a prince or a king would not hesitate to show strength, and he suggested I would be a weak woman if I did not propose war."

Suddenly, I understood Sauvage's position. No man on the council could propose an invasion. This was our law. The reigning monarch proposed war, and the council voted. He needed for Ashton to make the proposal.

Her blue eyes shifted back and forth.

"Perhaps Rowan would agree," she said. "He would never flinch from using strength."

Reaching out, I took her shoulders in my hands. "*You* are not Rowan. What do you think is best?"

"I would not hesitate to propose war were it necessary...but this is not necessary. We can solve the issue by other means."

I agreed. "Then tell that to the council."

* * * *

Two days later, Ashton called a meeting of the council, and she insisted I attend. Though I argued against this, she was firm.

"There is a reason," she said. "Trust me. You must be there."

I still thought it a mistake. I had no legal right to be present in a closed-door meeting of the queen and the council, but in my heart, I did trust Ashton.

I loved her.

Once the great doors to the council chambers were closed and everyone was seated, as if in echo of the first meeting I'd attended, Ashton rose to her feet at the head of the table, signaling that she would speak.

"My lords," she said, "I have called this meeting because I've come to an important decision."

Everyone present, including me, waited to hear what she would say about the situation in Samourè.

"I have made my choice of chancellor," she said.

Flickers of open surprise crossed a number of faces. This was not what the men had expected. She'd chosen a chancellor? She'd not said a word of this to me.

Motioning with one hand, she said, "I have chosen the lady Olivia Géroux."

Without a semblance of decorum, the room broke out in shocked protests. I sat frozen. Lord Sauvage's hands curled into tight fists.

Only Ashton remained calm, waiting for the initial protests to pass.

Finally, Baron Augustine spoke directly to her in a strained voice. "My queen...you cannot choose Lady Olivia."

"Oh, but I can," Ashton answered. "Do you remember me asking to borrow the bylaws last week? I read them carefully. There is no stipulation that the chancellor be male. The laws state only that the chancellor be from among the noble families and a landowner."

Some relief followed in the faces around us.

"Well, then. You see?" Baron Augustine said. "Lady Olivia does not own land."

"She does," Ashton returned. "She owns the Papè fief twenty leagues south of the city, and she collects an income from the rents and taxes."

Silence fell.

"So," Ashton said, resuming her seat. "I have chosen and appointed my chancellor, as the council requested." She turned to me. "My chancellor, what your thoughts on the invasion of Samourè in retaliation for these border raids?"

Lord Cloutier went pale, but Lord Sauvage's face turned red, and a vein in his left temple throbbed.

I met Ashton's eyes and began to truly understand her. She trusted her own judgment, but she needed me. She needed my strength.

And she'd just handed me a position of joint rulership.

I answered, "My queen. I would not hesitate to counsel war to protect our kingdom. But from what I understand, King Amandine has offered to pay reparations for any past raids and to work with our northern border's military to stop future raids. An invasion would accomplish little more than to cause suffering to the people of Samourè. In this case, I see no reason to spend treasure and the lives of our own men in what amounts to little more than misplaced revenge."

She nodded. "I am in agreement with my chancellor. For now, we will work with King Amandine to secure our northern border and revisit the issue should it not be resolved."

The table was still silent.

But I met the gaze of every man around me. Lord Sauvage emanated hatred, but Baron Augustine and Lord Cloutier showed a mix of startled confusion and relief.

"This was all my business for today, my lords," Ashton said. "Does anyone wish to discuss other business?"

The men were still speechless, and she rose. Quickly, they rose as well, as was expected in the presence of their queen.

"Good day, my lords," she said. "I will see you all at dinner."

I stood as well and followed her out of the council chambers. Only when we reached the corridor to the south towers did she stop and lean against one wall, breathing deeply.

"Have you been planning for this since you gave me that fief?" I asked.

She took her hand off the wall. "Rowan taught me to play chess when I was thirteen years old. Since then, he and I played countless games. Success in chess depends upon the player best capable of examining the board and visualizing outcomes up to four moves ahead." She looked at me. "In my many games with Rowan, who do you think most often won?"

I'd never given this any thought, but I did now.

* * * *

To describe the weeks that followed as "strained" would have an understatement. In all fairness, even I understood the reticence of the council in regards to my chancellorship. For the kingdom's twelve most powerful noblemen, the prospect of being ruled by two women they viewed as girls would have been nearly unbearable.

Reactions among them ranged from concern to bitter rage—with most expressing the latter. Baron Augustine and Lord Cloutier were only slightly more amenable because they agreed with Ashton's decision regarding Samourè. But given the fact that Cloutier was sixty-five years old, and Baron Augustine was not far behind him, I think they worried more about our age than our gender. However, Lords Moreau and Paquet made it clear that her decision in my appointment had cast her in the role of a novice girl playing at being queen. Normally, Lords du Guay and Sauvage were at each other's throats, but in this matter, they joined forces in their anger.

To make matters worse, Ashton had promised to be guided and counseled by them in all things, and as a result, they'd helped walk her up the red carpet, and Lord Cloutier placed a crown upon her head. Now, all the council felt betrayed.

And yet...she did not back down.

Together, she and I sat at the front of common court, and we saw to the management of the city while the council worked with her regarding the management of the kingdom. She wrote to King Amandine herself to open discussions regarding the border raids. Jarvis now served as her personal secretary.

I did note one oddity in relation to the council. Now that the coronation was over, I expected most of the men to pack up and ride home to their own estates for a few months—to gather again in the autumn. But they didn't. No one left. The entire council remained at court as if they feared leaving Ashton and me at the helm.

Rumors were floated that a few of them even hoped the people would revolt at my appointment.

They did not.

The people of Partheney were accustomed to seeing me on the dais beside Ashton. They knew I listened to the merchants and artisans. No one objected to my appointment.

There was also one man in the castle from whom we held full support: Micah.

He treated me as chancellor from day one, and I noticed small things, such as guards in the entry carefully leaning around corners to watch me walk down corridors, as if assuring my safety from one end to the other. This was Micah's way of protecting me. As opposed to feeling resentment, I was grateful. I had no wish for Lord Sauvage to step from an alcove and catch me alone.

However…for me, Micah was becoming a distraction in other ways. It was nothing he did, but rather that when he stood close to me for any reason, I had trouble concentrating on matters at hand. I found myself caught up in his light brown eyes or the soft blond hair around his mouth. I'd forget what we were discussing and notice the sinews in his forearms.

It was all quite foolish, and I vowed stronger self-discipline.

So, although it was not exactly smooth sailing, Ashton and I slowly began settling into our roles as joint leaders.

The first awkward encounter we faced came from an unexpected corner.

In writing, she handled the tenuous Samourè situation with grace and diplomacy, exchanging letters with King Amandine and assuring him of her support in any fashion he felt best in stopping the border raids. He paid reparations, and Ashton had the money sent to families who'd been affected so they might rebuild and buy livestock. She then sent Colonel Marlowe, who commanded our northern border guard, into Samourè to coordinate with their own guard.

Within a month, the issue was under control.

Unfortunately, Ashton's grace and diplomacy produced an unexpected side effect: King Amandine asked to reopen marriage negotiations, and rather than submitting the proposal to Ashton herself, he sent an envoy to speak to the council.

To complicate matters, the Council of Nobles was torn. Half the men were so uncomfortable being ruled by a young woman that they were ready to entertain the thought of a foreign king. The other half—led by Sauvage—were more opposed to the prospect of a foreign king than being led by Ashton.

And that was saying something.

I learned all of this later. Apparently, tempers flared the day the proposal was delivered, and a shouting match ensued.

Ashton wasn't told until that evening before dinner, when she and I arrived in the great hall to sip a goblet of wine and visit with the other nobles. Lords Moreau and Cloutier were the messengers, and I very much wish I'd been warned ahead of time. Both men were on the side of Amandine.

Upon hearing of the proposal, Ashton's expression went blank. "No," she said immediately. "You will politely decline and send the envoy back."

"But, my queen," Lord Cloutier sputtered, shocked at her instant refusal. "You should consider the possible advantages of such an arrangement. And you must marry, to found a line of heirs."

"No," she repeated. "Not Amandine." Then she walked away.

Of course, I agreed with her. Amandine was already a king in his own right, and he would expect to rule here should they marry. Ashton could not hand her power over to him, but the speed and finality of her decision weren't wise.

She should have nodded and tilted her head and thanked Lords Cloutier and Moreau and assured them she would give the proposal all proper consideration. Then she should have pretended to labor over the decision for at least a week, and finally refused on the grounds of concern over Amandine's possible ambitions to rule our kingdom. At least half the council would have supported her fully and the other half would have been forced to at least respect the carefully made decision.

But she'd simply said, "No," and walked away. Even Lord Sauvage—who opposed the idea of this marriage with every fiber in his being—watched this response with interest. It was the first time she'd not behaved as a queen.

I sometimes wondered if her prior life under Rowan's thumb had affected her in ways she couldn't openly acknowledge. Her deep love for him negated any criticism of him on her part, and yet he'd bullied and manipulated her into shunning relationships with anyone other than with himself.

Now that he was gone, she appeared to react out of instinct when threatened with losing her independence.

In the end, the envoy was sent back with a polite refusal on the grounds that Ashton had only recently been crowned and was not yet entertaining marriage proposals. This would leave Amandine with enough hope to ensure his good behavior.

But…the council had been forced to smooth over this unfortunate affair, and Ashton had handled it badly. It faded from court discussion within a few weeks, but I feared it might come back later to haunt her.

* * * *

By autumn, the entire council was still in residence, as were many of their wives, and at dinner one evening, Lord Sauvage casually delivered a piece of news.

His son, Guy, a lieutenant in the royal military, would be coming to court over the winter solstice holidays.

"He's serving on the northern border under Colonel Marlowe," said Lord Sauvage, "but he has a month's leave coming up. It will be good to see him."

Ashton nodded politely, but I wanted to wince. That was all we needed, another arrogant Sauvage at court throwing his weight around.

Still, Guy held no real power, and I put the thought of him from my head.

I was dealing with a situation of more personal impact. My father had written to me in regards to a land dispute with a neighbor on the western border of our estate. He asked me to intervene in his favor and suggested that if I could not succeed from Partheney, he'd need to call me home to be of assistance.

Was this a threat?

Even though I functioned as the kingdom's chancellor, I was still technically under my father's authority. I decided to speak to Ashton and have the matter handled for him. But I worried about the precedent this set. What might he ask for next?

I was troubled as I left the hall that night and made my way up to my rooms. Faithful Kamilla waited for me, and she helped me undress and let down my hair.

"Good night, my lady," she said. "I must go and see to the queen, now."

"Good night," I answered, "and thank you."

She left, and I went to turn down my bed.

A knock sounded on my door.

Upon opening it, I found a serving girl on the other side. "Forgive me, my lady. Captain Caron sends word that your mare is ill. He asks that you come to the stable to approve treatment."

"Meesha is ill?" I asked. "What's wrong?"

"I don't know, my lady. A guard downstairs came with the message."

Meesha had remained here when Captain Reynaud departed with the rest of my family's guards. Back home, I rode her several times a week, but there was plenty of room on our estate. Here, there was little opportunity for riding, but Micah had assured me that she was well cared for and the men were taking her out for exercise.

I felt remiss in not having visited her sooner.

"I'll be down to the stable directly," I told the girl.

She nodded and left.

Though I was in my nightgown, I didn't bother getting fully re-dressed. Instead, I tied on a cloak to cover myself and donned a pair of boots.

Leaving my room, I made my way downstairs and then outside into the courtyard. The hour must have been near midnight, and I worried that Meesha must be very ill if Micah had sent a messenger all the way to the south tower for me.

Crossing the courtyard, I passed a few guards on night duty, but they simply nodded a bow as I walked by. I was chancellor here.

Upon reaching the new stable, I lifted a candle lantern off one wall and walked toward the back. With the exception of the horses hanging their heads over the tops of stalls to greet me, there was no one here.

"Micah?" I called.

Where was he?

I found Meesha located near the back, and she whickered at the sight of me. I felt even more remiss and opened the door to her stall, stroking her nose. Though eager for my attention, she seemed well, and my puzzlement grew.

A footstep sounded behind me, and I looked back.

There stood a tall guard I did not know, but I'd often seen him in the company of Lord Sauvage. His expression was intense, and he held a dagger in his right hand. Everything suddenly made sense. Meesha was not ill, and Micah had not sent for me. I'd been lured down to the solitude of the stable.

There was a bucket of water on the floor of Meesha's stall. In a flash, I reached down and grabbed hold of the handle as my assassin charged. When he reached me, I swung hard, catching him with the bucket, knocking the dagger from his hand and splashing cold water on him. As he stumbled to one side in surprise, I threw shame to the wind and screamed as long and loudly as I could.

Twisting back around, he saw the dagger on the floor about ten paces to his left, and then his eyes moved back to me. He was a trained soldier and would not need a blade to end my life. Whirling, I dashed for the front doors as fast as my long legs could run, praying to reach them before he caught me.

Just before I reached them, a strong hand caught my hair and jerked me backward. A breath later, I was on the floor and his hands were around my neck. My airflow was cut off. Grasping his wrists, I tried to pull his hands away, but his fingers only tightened and his thumbs pressed down at the base of my throat. The pain was intense, and the walls around me began to fade as I choked and struggled.

A loud crashing sound echoed around me, followed by a roar.

"Faucher!"

The guard flew backward off me, and I gasped for air, still choking. I looked over to see Micah slam my attacker into a wall and then thrust forward with a sword, driving the blade into the man's chest.

Other guards ran in the doors.

Micah jerked his sword from my attacker's chest, and the man fell dead to the floor. The incoming guards stared at this with wide eyes.

"Sir?" one of them asked.

"He attacked Lady Olivia," Micah spat, striding back to me.

I was still on the floor, fighting for air, and he dropped by my side, drawing my torso up into his arms.

"Olivia," he said. "Try to breathe slower. Take slower breaths."

I tried to do as he asked, and soon, more air passed into my lungs. Reaching out with his left arm, he moved to scoop me up, but I stopped him with one hand to his chest.

"No," I whispered. "I can walk."

I didn't care to be seen being carried though the castle.

"Are you sure?" he asked.

"Yes, just get me up to my rooms."

* * * *

With no thought to propriety, Micah took me inside my apartments and closed the door.

"Sit down," he ordered.

I sat, and he untied my cloak, letting it fall back so he could examine my throat. Somehow, it didn't feel strange to be sitting here in my nightgown, alone with him.

"Can you breathe without difficulty?" he asked, lightly touching the hollow above my collarbone. "Do your bones hurt here?"

His voice was taut, and I could hear underlying fear. Was he so concerned for me?

"I can breathe," I answered. Thanks to him. "You heard my scream?"

"Yes…but I could not believe what I saw. Faucher was bribed…How could a royal guard be bribed?" He closed his eyes. "And I stupidly killed him. Now he cannot be questioned."

He sounded as if he was speaking to himself, but I answered.

"He was most likely not bribed. The dowager assured me royal guards could not be bribed, but she managed to convince two of them to let Ashton be taken out the castle gates on the day she was abducted."

Micah opened his eyes, stood, and stepped away from me. "What?"

I stood as well. "Genève told me that she appealed to their sense of patriotism. They believed they were doing the right thing for the kingdom. I'm sure Lord Sauvage tried the same tactic tonight. You should not even attempt to pursue Sauvage with no proof, but I suspect this was how he convinced Faucher to act. Remove me, and Ashton would be left to face the council alone…and under the control of the council more *patriotic* decisions might be made."

"No," Micah whispered.

I knew this was hurting him, but an attempt on my life had been made, and he needed all the facts.

Putting his hands on his head, Micah turned all the way around once. His world had shifted, and I couldn't help but pity him. Rowan was dead. The dowager queen was dead. The council did not support Ashton's rule. One of his own trusted men had just attempted to strangle me, and he could not risk accusing Lord Sauvage without proof.

"You never should have come here," he said quietly, "into this nest of vipers. You should have married some young viscount in the south, with a vineyard, and grown grapes and raised children, and lived your life in peace away from all of this."

"And had I done that, what would have become of Ashton?"

A mix of pain and longing flashed across his eyes.

He closed the distance between us, grasping my face in his hands and pressing his mouth against mine. Though his kiss was gentle, a jolt ran through my body, and I kissed him back with hunger. No man had ever put his mouth against mine, and the sensation washed through me in waves.

Wanting more, I reached up to touch him.

Without warning, he wrenched away, and his voice filled with anguish. "I can't do this, not to you. We'll never get permission to marry, and if I stay here tonight and we're found out, you'll be ruined."

Wrapping my hands around the back of his neck, I whispered. "I don't care. Do you hear me? I don't care."

Then I touched my mouth to his again, and he was lost.

* * * *

An hour before dawn, I lay naked in his arms, in my bed. My body was spent and sated, and I marveled that no one had ever told me the joy two people could experience together.

I ran my hands up his bare chest and heard his sharp intake of breath.

"Don't start that again," he said softly. "I have to leave before the servants wake."

Though he sounded pained to admit this, he was right. I was the lady Olivia Géroux, chancellor to the queen, and he was commander of the castle guard. Even a hint of connection between us would cause a scandal deafening enough to ruin us both.

And yet, I kissed him again.

He kissed me back.

But time was our enemy, and we went no further than this final kiss. Not long after, he dressed himself and slipped from my room.

Chapter Fifteen

I was in love…madly, recklessly in love.

Micah and I couldn't get enough of each other, and could not stop ourselves from taking risks. We weren't entirely foolish, and never again met alone in my apartments, nor did we often meet at night when I might be watched. But he had a private room at the back of the barracks.

I'd go into the stable in the afternoon to visit Meesha and slip out the back, making sure no one saw me. He'd meet me there, and we'd secretly slip into his quarters. I'd taken to wearing dresses that laced up the front and often had my gown halfway off before he'd finished locking the door. I couldn't stop longing for the feel of his mouth on mine, for his hands on my body, for the words of love he breathed into my ear.

This was a new world, and I longed for every moment I might spend alone with him.

Autumn passed into early winter. No matter how careful we were not to be seen, it was a miracle we'd not been found out. I tried not to think on the future. I tried to lose myself in our stolen moments.

My life with Ashton was separate, though, and I made sure she had my full focus when facing the men on the council. Lord Sauvage was not satisfied with the reparations King Amandine had paid, and he showed the council reports of a few raiders still crossing the border. I suspected the reports were falsified, and counseled Ashton to write to Colonel Marlowe directly to get an accurate report. In the meantime, Sauvage continued pushing for war and pressing Ashton to raise taxes in preparation for war. With me at her side, she was able to stand up to him in her renewed refusals.

Micah began assigning himself to duties inside the hall at the dinner hour. He only wanted to see me, to be close to me, but we couldn't look at each other too often or dare to speak.

The winter solstice holidays offered a welcome distraction, and Ashton and I oversaw the decoration of the great hall. I ordered a new gown in dark red velvet with green trim. She and I pored over menus and planned dances and games. We hired musicians and actors for three nights of entertainment.

On the night of the first winter banquet, we walked into the great hall, arm in arm. The hall was already crowded, and I stopped at the sight of a man I'd never before seen, but who struck me as familiar. He was solidly built with a muscular chest and arms. His brown hair was thick. His jaw was square, and he boasted a bump at the bridge of his nose. Even from a distance, his posture and expression exuded a mix of arrogance and strength.

He looked like a younger version of Lord Sauvage.

Lady Miranda smiled at us and drew him over. She curtsied. "My queen, may I present my son, Guy."

Then I remembered Lord Sauvage had mentioned his son's arrival for the holidays.

To my amazement, Guy took the queen's hand and kissed it. "I am honored to meet you."

He had more charm than his father. I gave him that, but his eyes were hard, and I wasn't surprised by how quickly Ashton drew her hand back.

She nodded politely. "Welcome to court. Forgive me. I would speak with Lord Moreau on a matter. He promised to help organize the dance tonight."

She swept off, and I followed, but I could see she was unsettled. She was not comfortable in the company of confident, arrogant men, especially when they insisted on touching her.

Soon, she seemed herself again, and dinner was a merry affair. We'd ordered pheasants roasted with apples, which was one of her favorite dishes. A team of four jugglers entertained us with all variety of feats.

There was laughter and applause.

I tried to enjoy myself, but Micah had assigned himself to stand duty at the archway, and it was hard not to keep glancing at him. I wanted to share my plate with him. I wanted to dance with him after dinner was over.

However, when the music began, I turned to Baron Augustine. Of late, he'd begun to see that Ashton and I were better suited to making decisions for the kingdom than a number of men on the council, and his uncle-like affection had returned.

"Will you ask me to dance, sir?" I teased him.

He smiled. "I can think of nothing I would rather do."

"My queen," said a strong voice.

Guy Sauvage stood directly before the table, bowing to Ashton.

"Would you do me the honor of the first dance?" he asked.

I could see she wanted to refuse, but unlike Rowan, she knew better than to give open insult to the other noble families. Rising, she walked around the table and let him lead her out.

The music began, and on a purely physical level, they made a striking couple. But he held her too tightly, and her discomfort was clear.

I glanced over at Micah, who had been watching this, and I caught his eye. He appeared tense, but there was nothing he could do.

"Shall we?" the baron asked me.

Yes, at least I could move closer to her on the dance floor. For his age and girth, the baron was a spritely dancer, and I let him lead me out. By the time the first song ended, eight other couples had joined us on the floor.

Guy turned to the musicians, and ordered, "Play 'Evalada'."

Ashton blanched and began drawing away. "My lord, I do not think…"

"Stay with me," he said.

At this, even Baron Augustine appeared uncomfortable at Guy's manner, but he said to me, "I fear I must step off the floor, my dear. I'm not the man I once was."

Knowing exactly what he meant, I stepped off the floor with him, but I asked quietly, "Does she know 'Evalada'?"

"Yes." He nodded. "Rowan taught her. He would only dance it with her."

The music began and four couples remained. This was a challenging dance with fast turns, and after every ten steps, the man grasped the woman by the waist and lifted her above his head.

Guy was a skilled dancer and could lift Ashton with no effort. I watched tensely, willing her to get through it, and she did, but at the end, when the men all lifted their partners for a final time, Guy held Ashton in the air longer than necessary. She gripped his wrists in clear distress.

It was all I could do not to order him to put her down. Lord Moreau walked over. He was frowning.

Looking across the hall, I saw Lord Sauvage watching this like a hawk.

Finally, Guy set Ashton on her feet, and she moved away from him, hurrying to me.

"Olivia," she said, and her voice shook. "I fear something at dinner has not agreed with me. I should like to retire early."

"Yes, I'll take you up."

"What?" Guy stood directly behind us. "The evening has just begun."

"The queen is unwell," I said, putting an arm around her and ushering her away. As we passed through the archway, I stole a glance at Micah.

* * * *

There were two more nights of celebration, but they were ruined for Ashton. Guy continued to pay her unwanted attention, and I had no idea what he was after. If he wished to win her affection or goodwill, he could not have gone about it in a worse fashion.

Baron Augustine and Lord Moreau did their best to run interference, but both nights, I took her up early.

On the final night, once she was sleeping, I felt restless and wandered out to the courtyard to seek fresh air.

I'd learned to love the smell of the sea.

Standing with eyes closed, I breathed in the salty scent.

"Olivia."

My eyes opened to a welcome sight: Micah.

There was no one else about but a few guards on duty down near the gate.

"How is Ashton?" he asked.

"Sleeping," I answered, "while the court celebrates."

"Do they all believe you are with the queen?" His voice was soft, and inviting at the same time.

"I believe they do."

"Perhaps you might go to the stable and check on your horse in a short while."

I smiled. "Perhaps I might."

* * * *

We hid away for two hours in his room in the barracks. We'd never have risked this at night, but with the raucous festivities going on in the castle, and the fact that I'd left the hall to take Ashton to her apartments, everyone would assume I was with her.

Micah's lovemaking was intense tonight, as if he wanted to hold on to me.

Something about this made me vain, perhaps needy, and in his bed, with my arms around him, I asked, "When did you first know you loved me?"

He pulled away, propped himself up on one elbow, and looked down into my face. His answer was quick, not requiring a moment's thought.

"The first time I saw you," he said, "standing on that hill. You were so beautiful and so angry, your eyes blazing. Rowan had just insulted you, and all I wanted was to drop to my knees and beg your forgiveness."

I remembered this moment as if it were yesterday. "But why did that make you love me?"

"Because I've never begged forgiveness from anyone in my life." He paused. "When did you know you loved me?"

My answer came just as swiftly. "When you reached down and grasped my hand at Genève's execution."

Above me, his body went still, and for an instant, I thought his eyes were wet. Then he buried his face in my neck.

* * * *

Just when I thought the men of the council might never return to their own estates, six of them announced they were packing to leave. I took this as a very good sign. They may not be happy with the arrangement of Ashton as queen and me as chancellor, but at least they were beginning to accept it.

Lord Sauvage caught us unawares by calling a formal meeting of the council before anyone left. He requested that Ashton and I attend. All winter business had been concluded, and I hoped he was not going to make another push to raise taxes and invade Samourè. Every time he did this, he implied that the only reason we'd not yet retaliated on a grand scale was because the kingdom was saddled with a weakling girl.

As Ashton and I walked to the meeting that day, I could see she was weary. Guy Sauvage had not let up with his unwanted attentions, and I hoped he would be traveling back to his duties on the border soon.

Once all twelve men of the council had gathered, an attendant closed the door to the chambers and everyone waited for Ashton to sit. As she took her seat, all the men followed...except Lord Sauvage.

He was the one who'd called the meeting and, apparently, he planned to waste no time.

"My lords," he began, addressing only the council, "I called you here today to offer a proposal that will bring you joy and strengthen our kingdom. I offer to open marriage negotiations between my son, Guy, and the queen."

"What?" Lord Moreau asked.

I sat straight, casting my eyes about the long table. Moreau, Baron Augustine, and Lord Cloutier all appeared stunned. But...the other men did not. Even Lord du Guay, who was often at odds with Lord Sauvage was calm, as if he'd known.

"Guy is a fine choice," Lord Sauvage went on. "He is of old noble blood and will father strong sons. He's shown bravery in defending our kingdom from all foreign influence and will prove a steady right hand for our queen."

To my horror, I could see that most of the council agreed. Ashton must marry and provide heirs, and they preferred one of our own nobles to a foreign king.

"And you would see him crowned king?" Lord Moreau spat, not bothering to hide his anger.

This was a tenuous point for Sauvage. When a sitting king married, his wife was crowned queen even if she'd not been a princess, but when a sitting queen married a man who was not of royal blood—which did not often happen—the man was crowned as prince. This kept most of the power in her hands.

"No," Sauvage answered. "I would stand in joy to see him as prince."

He's lying, I thought. I could see it. He'd find a way to have Guy crowned king inside of a year. Ashton would be rolled flat, taxes would be raised, men would be conscripted, and we'd be invading Samourè.

However, the entire argument was rendered moot as Ashton shot to her feet.

"No," she said flatly.

I looked back to her in alarm. She'd done it again…refused instantly.

"My queen?" Sauvage said. "You will not even consider the proposal?" For once, his tone sounded calm and reasonable.

"No," she repeated, and then she swept from the room, opening the doors herself.

Silence followed in her wake.

Then Lord Sauvage shook his head. "It seems our queen is adamantly opposed to marriage."

His eyes glinted with triumph. He'd known exactly how she would react. I'd always viewed him as a blunt instrument, but perhaps Ashton was not the only one who could play chess.

* * * *

I found Ashton alone in her apartments, sitting on a couch by the hearth and staring into the fire. I'd not seen her do this in many months.

Picking up a blanket, I sat down and covered us both, pulling her against my shoulder.

"I should not have refused so quickly, should I?" she whispered.

"No. You should not."

"They'll try to force me."

"They cannot make you agree to a marriage you oppose, and you know I'll fight them for you."

She pressed her cheek against my shoulder and nodded.

But Lord Sauvage's final words affected me more than I wished.

"Ashton?" I asked. "Are you against the idea of marriage?"

She sat up, as if the question had not occurred to her. "No. I must provide heirs. I am not against marriage. But as queen here, I won't marry a man like Amandine, who is already a king in his own right. He would take my throne. And I won't marry a bully like Guy. I've already been…"

She stopped, but I finished the thought for her.

I've already been bullied enough.

Well, that was certainly true.

So, we needed to find a nobleman willing to respect her rule and to share power.

Rather a tall order.

* * * *

Within hours of the council meeting, gossip flooded through the castle that Queen Ashton was a woman who would not marry, that she valued her crown above her duty to provide heirs. Sauvage also managed to start rumors that I was the cause of her reticence, that I was the one whispering poison in her ear so that I might not be forced to share power.

I'd taken on some of the castle household duties, and as I walked to the kitchens to see about dinner menus, many suspicious glances were cast my way.

Was this to be the rest of my life? Would I be forever locked in battle with men who both resented and hated me for my position?

After conferring with the cook, I felt weary and walked outside in the courtyard, hoping Micah might see me.

He did.

Slowly I strolled over to the nearest north tower, and he came to join me. We were well apart from any activity in the courtyard and could speak freely.

He looked as weary as I felt.

"You've heard," I said.

"Yes, and you know Sauvage won't give up easily."

"I won't let him force her."

"Sometimes…" he said, "I dream of taking you and leaving this place, of leaving this all behind and going to live where no one knows who we are."

The picture he painted both soothed and pained me at the same time.

"I dream of that too," I answered. "But we're the only ones Ashton can trust. The people need her, and she needs us."

"I know."

* * * *

That evening after dressing me for dinner, Kamilla left to go up and help Ashton. I had time before I needed to go down to the hall, so I sat on the couch in my apartments in front of my own hearth, thinking. I needed to find a way to squelch the doubts Sauvage had planted in regards to Ashton. Somehow, I needed a graceful way to show that she was not opposed to marriage—only opposed to marriage with Guy.

If she just hadn't refused King Amandine so instantly and thus set a precedent.

A knock sounded on my door, startling me.

If Kamilla had forgotten something, she would not have bothered knocking.

Rising, I crossed my sitting room and opened the door. To my astonishment, Baron Augustine stood on the other side.

"My dear," he said. "May I come in?"

For a man, even one as old as him, to ask permission to enter my private chambers alone…well, it simply wasn't done. But I could see he needed to speak to me, and I stood aside.

"Of course."

His expression was drawn, and he entered slowly, looking about. "I've never been in these apartments."

Were we making small talk?

"They are most comfortable," I answered.

He sighed. "Come and sit, my dear."

A feeling of anxiety began to rise as I wondered what he was about to say, but I sank down on a couch across from him.

"I've no wish to beat about the bush," he said. "I know you are engaged in a tryst with Captain Caron."

My body went rigid, not only at his blunt confession, but at his words.

Whatever connected Micah and me, it wasn't a tryst.

The baron raised one hand. "I neither judge nor blame you. You are young, and in your current position, marriage with a man of your own station would be nearly impossible. I'm only here to tell you that if you wish to survive as chancellor, that you must give up the captain."

I stood and clenched my hands into fists.

But the baron was relentless. "Lord Sauvage has learned of your affair and has been seeking proof."

All my anger evaporated.

"Does he have any?" I asked.

"If he did, you can be assured he'd have used it by now. I don't know how you've managed to avoid discovery, but you must never again seek out the captain in a fashion where you might be seen in a compromising position. If Sauvage gets proof, you will fall."

"Half the men on the council keep a mistress!" I shot back, even knowing it was a pointless thing to say.

"You are not a man," he answered calmly. "If you are discovered with the captain, you'll be called out for a whore. No one, not even the queen, could save your chancellorship."

"And what if I get permission from the queen to marry him?"

"Marry him? Good gods, girl. If you marry him, your father would disown you. You'd no longer be the lady Olivia Géroux, daughter of Hugh Géroux. You would be Mistress Caron, wife of the commander of the royal guard…and you would lose your chancellorship." He paused. "You must give him up, Olivia."

"No."

"Then you must give up the queen and leave her to the mercy of the council."

"I can't." My voice caught, and in the moment, I hated him for coming here tonight. "In all this world, only two people love me, and I won't give up one for the other."

He stood. "I fear you must."

Turning away, he walked to the door and left my apartments.

Whirling back to the fire, I crossed my arms.

I won't give up one for the other.

* * * *

But that night, when I entered the hall, I passed Micah on the way in. He stood guard near the archway.

Ashton was already there, and Guy Sauvage was attempting to engage her in conversation, standing at her side, as if that was his place.

At the sight of me, her face filled with relief.

"Will you excuse me?" she said to him, coming to join me and taking my arm.

He appeared momentarily nonplussed, and then shot me a look of anger. His father watched from halfway across the hall. But Lord Sauvage actually smiled at me. Then he glanced at Micah and back to me.

For all my protests, my heart was breaking.

Everything the baron said was true. I could never again risk being found in bed with Micah. If so, I would fall, and Ashton would be alone. I could not marry him, or I would fall, and Ashton would be alone.

Turning my head, I locked eyes with Micah, and his expression turned quietly alarmed. Perhaps he could see the pain in my face. He did not know it yet, but I had just given him up.

I was forced to choose between Ashton and him.

And I chose Ashton.

* * * *

The great hall around me vanished, and I found myself standing once again in the alcove, standing in front of the three-paneled mirror.

As before, I fought to breathe, thinking on all that I had just seen and all that I still felt.

My aching love for both Micah and Ashton was like a dagger in my chest.

But the dark-haired woman now looked out at me from the left-hand panel.

"That would be the outcome of the second choice," she said. "Now you'll go back to the beginning again, to live out the third choice."

"Wait!" I begged. "Give me a moment."

I needed to think.

"To the beginning once more," she said. "To live out the third choice."

My mind went blank, and the alcove vanished.

The Third Choice
Independent Action

Chapter Sixteen

I was in a corridor, outside an alcove, listening to the plans of a murderer and an assassin.

"Doesn't make any difference to me, so long as I get paid," said the man called Soren. "But you need not fear. I'll get it done."

I was dizzy, disoriented, but when Soren turned to leave, I flew into motion, dashing to the nearest alcove to hide from sight.

He walked past me.

A few moments later, so did Genève.

This man…this Soren, was about to seek out Ashton in the stable and kill her. Of all the possible actions Genève might have taken, it never once occurred to me she would have Ashton assassinated. Genève had raised Ashton as her own daughter.

She must be more desperate than even I'd realized. But what should I do?

I must stop it. Of course I had to stop it.

From where I stood now, the kitchens weren't far.

I ran.

But as my legs carried me swiftly, I couldn't stop my mind from turning. What if in the process of me saving Ashton, Genève's guilt was discovered? She was my most powerful ally. Without her, the only person capable of any control over Rowan would be gone. He'd insist on a marriage to Ashton, no matter what it cost him, and I'd be sent home to my father.

I had to save Ashton. I would not take the crown at the expense of her life…but I must be cautious in my actions.

I had to do this alone.

Upon reaching the archway to the kitchens, I looked ahead to a door and hurried through it. Once out in the courtyard, I cast my eyes about, but thankfully, the only guards in sight were all the way out at the castle gates.

Hurrying toward the old stable, I formed a quick plan. My path here had been swift and via a short route. I was certain that I'd arrived before Soren. All I need do was get into the stable and get Ashton out.

Soren would never attack her in the courtyard. I would come up with some reason for her to accompany me into the castle. Once I got her to safety, I could seek out Geneve and confront her—threaten her if I must.

She and I would succeed, and I would marry Rowan, but by other methods than this, not with Ashton's blood on our hands. I would make that clear.

Just as I reached the door to the old stable, motion from the left caught my eye, and I turned to see Rowan on the other end of the barracks, leading a horse out of the new stable.

I didn't want him to see me, and slipped inside.

Ashton stood alone at table about twenty paces away from me.

Looking up, she smiled. "Olivia, will you not make preserves with the other women? Have you come to help me?"

My eyes continued scanning and stopped.

Soren stood in a half-crouch six tables behind her, dagger in hand, and he'd frozen at the sight of me. I'd failed to reach the stable first.

"Ashton, run!" I cried.

On instinct, she followed my gaze and her eyes widened at the sight of a man with a dagger.

"Run!" I shouted again.

She flew into motion, running for the doors, but Soren bolted after. I held my ground, with my hands gripping the table directly in front of me. Just as he reached me, trying to catch her, I hefted as hard as I could and turned the table over so that it fell against him, knocking him off his feet.

Just outside the doorway, Ashton skidded to a stop, looking back wildly for me. "Olivia?" Then she began screaming. "Rowan! Rowan!"

Soren gained his feet quickly, and his eyes narrowed on me. But I heard the sound of pounding feet. What would happen if he were caught?

"Run, you fool," I said.

He looked at me in alarm.

But it was too late.

Rowan came flying in the door, a dagger in his hand. At the sight of Soren, his expression went blank. "You?"

Soren whirled to flee, but Rowan was faster, darting between the tables and cutting him off. Captain Caron ran in the door, and three guards followed close on his heels.

With four men behind him, Soren tried to rush Rowan, but Rowan was ready, and instead of attacking, he swept with his leg and watched the man fall. The captain reached them in seconds, falling on Soren and pinning him as Rowan kicked the man's dagger away.

Ashton came back to me, but her eyes were on Rowan's face.

"Rowan?" she asked.

My gaze followed hers. As opposed to being startled or righteously angry or even triumphant, the king's expression was dark with a kind of rage I'd never seen. First, he looked over at Ashton, and an instant of fear crossed his features, as if he were imagining what might have happened. Then he reached down, grabbed Soren by the front of his shirt, and jerked him to his feet.

"Were you sent to this stable to kill the princess?" he demanded, his voice rasping. "Soren, did my mother hire you?"

I went cold. Rowan knew his name.

"My king!" the captain said in alarm, perhaps shocked at Rowan's accusation of the dowager.

Soren stared stoically ahead.

Rowan turned to one of the guards. "Go and fetch the dowager queen. Tell her nothing of this. Just bring her. Do it now!"

The guard glanced at Captain Caron and then ran out of the stable.

Rowan leaned close to Soren's face. "You know me. You know my word is good. You're a dead man, but you can choose how you die. If you tell me the truth, I swear I'll make it quick, a single stroke. If you don't, I'll have you roasting over a fire for three days, and I'll feed you water while your skin sizzles, to keep you alive as long as I can. Near the end, I'll cut you down and gut you myself, and I'll take my time." He paused. "Do you believe me?"

Soren breathed rapidly, and his stoic expression wavered.

"Did my mother hire you to kill Ashton?" Rowan asked.

With a single, short nod, Soren answered, "Yes."

Despair flooded through me. I'd managed to save Ashton, but otherwise I had failed. Geneve's guilt was known. There would be a trial, most likely followed by an execution.

I'd lost my strongest ally.

The rage in Rowan's face grew darker, and Ashton took a step toward him. "It's a lie," she said. "Mother would never do this."

Footsteps sounded outside, and the guard who'd been sent off returned with Genève at his side. At the sight of Ashton…and Rowan…and Soren held captive, startled guilt crossed her features. Then it was gone. But it was enough, and Rowan saw it.

He strode toward her with his dagger still in his hand.

"Rowan, no!" Ashton cried, stepping into his path. He pushed her to one side and kept going.

"Stop!" Ashton shouted. "Micah, stop him!"

The captain didn't move.

Perhaps Ashton knew her brother better than Genève knew her son, because Genève did not flinch or even take a step back, as if she had no reason to fear.

Upon reaching his mother, Rowan grabbed the back of her head and drove his dagger into the hollow at the base of her throat. Blood spurted, and her face contorted in pain and disbelief, but he held on to her and kept pushing with the dagger until she stopped moving.

She was dead.

He dropped her body.

Ashton screamed and rushed at him, hitting him with her fists. The blood and death and raw emotions around me were like nothing I'd ever seen. Reaching down, Rowan swept Ashton up into his arms, holding her tightly against his chest as she continued trying to hit him.

The captain and guards all stood frozen.

Jutting his chin at Genève's body, Rowan said, "*That* was royal justice." Then he looked to Soren. "Micah, take his head off in one stroke."

Turning, he strode from the stable carrying Ashton, heading for the castle.

For a long moment, no one spoke. Genève's body lay on the floor with a red pool gathering around her head.

The captain said to me, "My lady, please leave this place."

I was only too glad to obey his request.

* * * *

Hiding alone in my room, I tried to ponder the magnitude of my failure. By attempting to act alone to save Ashton, I'd not only exposed Genève but had brought about her death.

And yet…I had not abandoned hope for my own situation. I might still find a way to force Rowan's hand into marriage. For one, this afternoon, a wedge had been driven between him and Ashton. She'd watched him murder the woman she viewed as her mother.

And also, the council would still back me.

All was not lost.

A knock sounded on my door. Opening it, I found Lords Moreau and Sauvage on the other side. Both men appeared rattled. I'd never seen Sauvage rattled before. They bowed as a show of respect.

"Forgive the interruption at this time, my lady," said Lord Moreau, "but we've heard the captain's account of what happened. The princess is unable to speak to anyone, and we must have some support for Captain Caron's story."

He spoke with deference, and I felt on solid ground, as they still treated me as their future queen.

"Please come in," I said.

"Our purpose is only to protect the king," Sauvage said.

This was certainly true. These two men were often at odds, as they had different views on national issues, but they were unified in their mutual support of Rowan. Thinking on that, I realized I could give them what they needed: proof that Rowan was justified.

"Why were you at the old stable this afternoon, my lady?" Moreau asked.

This was a perfect opening.

"Because I had just overheard the dowager queen hiring an assassin to kill the princess."

"What?" Sauvage asked.

I told them everything I'd heard and seen. "She gave him a red velvet pouch filled with money. If you have his body searched, you will find it."

Both men stared at me. When the pouch was found, they'd have proof of my account.

"And that's why you went to the stable?" Sauvage asked. "To try and stop it?"

"I ran, but I was not fast enough. The man...Soren was already there. I called out to Ashton, and she called for Rowan. He came running in... and he seemed to know the assassin."

"Yes," Moreau answered. "We've spoken to the king. He said this man was someone his mother has used over the years for unsavory tasks, and that she brought him from Tircelan when she married Eduard."

Lord Sauvage shook his head. "It's hard to believe how sly she was. I had no idea." He paused. "You'd be willing to repeat everything you've just told us, and swear to its truth?"

"Yes."

"Well, then. The king may have acted rashly, but once the truth is known, he'll be seen as justified."

Moreau shifted uncomfortably and assessed me. "My lady, do you understand why the dowager might have been desperate enough to assassinate the princess?"

Sauvage shot him a quick look, but I was glad to finally be speaking openly. "Yes," I answered.

"For the good of the kingdom," Moreau continued, "it would be best to see you wed to the king soon."

"Perhaps it's time someone explained that to him," I answered levelly.

Sauvage nodded. "We'll speak to him."

They both made to leave, and Moreau glanced back. "Thank you, my lady. You have been most helpful."

"Have the body searched," I repeated. "You'll find the pouch."

* * * *

Dinner in the hall that night was canceled, and a serving girl brought me a tray in my room.

She appeared shaken and nearly dropped it before setting it on a table.

"Does the castle know about the dowager?" I asked, already knowing the answer.

"Yes, my lady," she whispered. "Guardsman Baudine told me the king cut her throat."

The guards were gossiping? Captain Caron should put a stop to that.

"Is there anyone in the great hall?" I asked.

She hesitated and then nodded. "A few…but the king and Lord Cloutier are shouting at each other because the king doesn't want the dowager buried in the family crypt." Her voice caught. "He's calling her a traitor, but Lord Cloutier says that since there was no trial, she must be placed in the crypt."

Oh, for the sake of the gods. Did Rowan have no sense? He was shouting at Lord Cloutier over the burial? Did he not mourn his mother at all?

"Where is the princess?" I asked.

"No one has seen her, my lady. I think she is in her apartments."

"Thank you."

Alone, I picked at some of the food, a rabbit stew with a side of raspberries, but I wasn't hungry. I did drink the entire goblet of wine. Regardless of my unforgivable mistakes this afternoon, I still viewed myself as in a solid position. Lords Moreau and Sauvage were indebted to me, and they'd promised to try to make Rowan see reason. He would get away with his reckless act of killing his own mother, but it would place him in a more tenuous position, and marrying me would go a long way toward restoring public confidence in his rule.

I sat there, thinking, into the early hours of the night.

A low knock sounded on my door, and it opened without invitation.

Kamilla looked in. Her normally tidy hair was in disarray.

"My lady, you're still awake."

I stood. "What is it?"

"The princess is in a bad way."

Ashton? Of course she was in a bad way. She'd watched her brother murder the woman she viewed as a mother—after learning that her mother had tried to have her assassinated.

"That is to be expected," I returned. "It has been a trying day."

"No, my lady," Kamilla answered. "She is in a *bad* way, and she does not need a maid to care for her. She needs family, and you are the closest thing she has."

"Me? Would not Lady Elizabeth or Lady Miranda know her better?" The wife of a council member seemed a far better choice than myself.

"I fear not, my lady," Kamilla answered. "King Rowan...has discouraged her from fostering friendships with anyone but himself. But you are to be her sister. She needs you."

You are to be her sister.

I had a role to play here, and I'd better play it.

"Yes, of course. I'm coming."

As I was still dressed, I left my room immediately and followed Kamilla to Ashton's apartments.

There, I saw what Kamilla meant.

Ashton sat on a couch before her own hearth, but she stared into the flames without blinking and whispered unintelligible words to herself in an endless stream.

"She won't speak to the king," Kamilla whispered. "She won't even look at him. When he left here, he was in quite a state, and he ordered me to care for her."

How very like Rowan.

Ashton was in shock, and she was grieving.

Walking over, I leaned down to touch her shoulder. "Princess?"

She didn't respond or acknowledge I'd spoken. Her whispering continued. No wonder Kamilla had gone for help.

The problem was that I had no idea how to offer comfort.

Then I remembered a night when I was twelve years old, and my brother Henri had tried to offer comfort to me.

"Get me a blanket," I ordered Kamilla.

Once I had the blanket in hand, I sat down close to Ashton and covered us both.

"Stoke up the fire," I told Kamilla, "and then go to the kitchens and bring back a pot of hot tea with honey and milk."

"Yes, my lady."

After building up the fire, she hurried away.

Wrapping my arms around Ashton, I pulled her close to me and held her. She let me.

She stopped her unintelligible whispering.

Neither of us spoke. I just held her and kept her covered with the blanket.

When Kamilla returned, I poured Ashton a half a cup of tea, blew on it until it was cool enough, and brought it near her lips. I had feeling she might respond to an order.

"Ashton," I said firmly. "Drink this."

When I held the cup to her mouth, she drank from it. I helped her finish it and then set down the cup.

Settling back, I again covered both of us with the blanket.

"Kamilla, there's nothing more you can do. You may as well go and get some sleep."

"Are you sure, my lady?"

"Yes. I'll stay with her. Get some rest. She'll have need of you tomorrow."

"Thank you, my lady."

Once Kamilla was gone, I took Ashton back into my arms and held her. Hours passed, and she rested against me, but she never closed her eyes.

Finally, when my arms began to ache and my shoulder grew sore, I whispered, "It's late, and you've not slept. Do you think you might lay down in the bed?"

"Will you stay with me?" she whispered back.

These words were a good sign. She was still lost in grief, but at least speaking coherently now.

"Yes. I'll stay." I helped her up and when once we'd walked into her bedroom, I said, "Let me unlace your gown so you will be comfortable."

Like a child, she did my bidding and stopped. Quickly, I unlaced the back of her gown and slipped it off her shoulders, leaving it in a heap on the floor. After helping her into bed, I crawled in beside her. I was still fully dressed, but that didn't matter either.

"Sleep now," I whispered.

"You won't leave?"

"No. I won't leave. I promise."

Chapter Seventeen

I stayed with Ashton all the next day and night. Kamilla brought us trays of food, but Ashton did not eat much. I sat with her and spoke of small things. I had Kamilla bring me a book of stories of knights and maidens, and I read to her.

When visitors knocked on the door, I stood as both messenger and guardian, and no one resented me. They all viewed me as Ashton's sister and the future queen.

I was exactly where I was supposed to be, caring for my sister in a time of need.

Late morning of the second day, she asked for more tea with milk and honey. We were alone, and by that point, I needed a short break, so I told her I'd go down and fetch it myself.

It felt good to walk down the curving stairwell through the long corridor. Upon reaching the round entry chamber, I stopped at the sight of Captain Caron speaking to a few of his guards. As I entered, he saw me and broke off, coming right to me.

"My lady," he said. "Are you well?"

His face was so genuinely concerned that it touched me. Was he worried I might be too delicate to recover from that awful scene in the stable?

"I am well," I answered, "but I'm caring for the princess. The king committed a brutal and reckless deed. He should have had the dowager arrested and put on trial."

The captain glanced away. He might agree with me, but it was clear he didn't care to hear Rowan criticized.

"Well, it's done now," he said.

"Yes. It is." Having been cut off from all news, I asked, "Will there be...repercussions?"

"I think not. It seems you supplied proof that the dowager had arranged for the assassination. I searched the man's body and found a red velvet pouch."

"So, the council ruled Rowan's actions as justified?"

He nodded.

"What else has happened?" I asked. When his face began closing up, I added, "Please. This affects me."

He sighed. "He was in a closed-door meeting with Lords Moreau and Sauvage this morning, and when he came out, he had a face like thunder. I don't know of what they spoke."

Fortunately, I did. Those two had wasted no time in pressing Rowan to complete the marriage with me. Good. He must be made aware of his current position. A wedding with a young noblewoman from an old family—with the promise of heirs—would go far to establish the goodwill of the people.

"Thank you, Captain," I said, and headed off to the kitchens.

Once there, I put together a tray of tea with milk and honey, and I carried it back upstairs.

But when I reached Ashton's apartments, the door to the sitting room was open, and I knew I had closed it.

Rowan's voice carried out into the corridor.

Stepping up to the open doorway, I looked inside. Ashton sat on a couch, and Rowan was on his knees before her. His position would have seemed conciliatory, except for the fact that he had his hands placed on the couch, one to each side of her, so she couldn't rise.

His expression held the same mix of intensity and determination as that night after dinner on the day he'd attacked her in the alcove—only this time it contained a hint of anxiety. I had a feeling he'd been here for a while.

"I had to do it," he said. "I had to protect you."

Her head was tilted down, and she wouldn't look at him.

"You understand?" he went on. "She paid an assassin to have you murdered, and she would have done it again. You know that everything I do, I do to protect you."

When she didn't speak, one side of his jaw twitched.

"Do you love me?" he asked.

"Yes," she whispered.

"Then you forgive me?"

She nodded once.

"Say it," he told her. "Say the words."

"I forgive you," she whispered.

Then he was up on the couch beside her, pulling her close. She leaned into him and for the first time since Genève's death, she began to cry, weeping against him while he held her.

"It's all right," he said, "I'm here."

Somehow, he'd gotten her to turn to him in her sorrow. I did not understand them.

With a light step, I entered the room, carrying the tray, and stopped at the sight of him, as if I'd just arrived.

"My king," I said, "the princess wished for some tea."

At my intrusion, hostility shone from his eyes. "Set it down and leave."

Ashton pulled away from his arms. "No, Rowan. Olivia has been staying with me. I want her here."

His glance moved between the bedroom door and me. "Staying here?" he asked Ashton. "Why?"

"She's been helping me."

I tensed, not knowing how he might react. Did he think only Kamilla had been caring for Ashton?

But he nodded to her slowly. "Good. You do seem recovered. I will expect you at dinner tonight."

"Dinner? Oh, Rowan…I don't think I can—"

His voice hardened. "If she has been helping you, then you are recovered enough to come down to dinner. If not, perhaps someone else should come and stay. Lady Miranda, perhaps?"

Ashton's gaze dropped. "No. Not Miranda. I'll be at dinner."

"Good."

How I hated him. Threatening her with removing me and sending Lord Sauvage's wife? He always knew how to best manipulate Ashton.

Rising, he cast me one more glance before leaving the apartments. I fought back a shudder. Marriage with him would be no stroll through a meadow. That much was certain.

I carried the tea tray to Ashton. "Would you like a full cup or just a half?"

* * * *

As everyone gathered that night in the great hall to drink wine and mill about before dinner, the evening took on a surreal quality. A number of the nobles present actually offered Rowan and Ashton condolences on the loss of their mother.

And Rowan accepted graciously…as if he'd not run a dagger through her throat.

Apparently, everyone was going to pretend that Genève's death was an avoidable tragedy. I wondered if Rowan had relented over allowing her to be buried in the family crypt. I understood the point of the argument. As there was proof of Genève's culpability, Rowan had been found justified, but…as there had been no formal trial or verdict, officially, she'd not been sentenced with treason and therefore should be placed in the crypt.

Tonight, I wore a gown of dove-gray velvet. I'd not been seen in this yet. Not all women could wear light gray, but it made the colors of my hair and eyes more vivid.

Ashton wore a sky-blue silk, and I could see she was trying to please Rowan by staying with him and holding his arm. Word had spread of her running at him in the stable and hitting him even as he carried her out.

Captain Caron really did need to speak to his guards about future discretion. They might be loyal patriots, but a few of them had loose tongues.

Scanning around, I looked for the captain, but he wasn't on duty in the hall tonight.

Lord Paquet's wife, Elizabeth, greeted me first. "Lady Olivia. How lovely you look."

I thanked her and smiled as others moved to greet me. Everyone treated me as the future queen.

Though Rowan did not acknowledge me, the undercurrent of support I felt was strong. Both Lords Moreau and Sauvage bowed as if I were already wearing a crown.

When trays of steaming food were carried through the archways, Rowan and Ashton walked to the first table. She looked over and motioned to me to follow. The king sat in his chair in the center with Ashton at his right and Lord du Guay to his left. I sat to Ashton's right. It would have looked more appropriate for the two of us to switch places, but there was no way I could gracefully suggest it.

Ashton was quiet for all three courses, but she seemed well enough, and she ate a few bites of nearly everything. Several times, Rowan turned to encourage her to eat.

Lady Elizabeth sat to my right, and she chattered all through dinner. I managed to make interested noises, as I wondered how soon the council would make a more serious move to pressure the king into sealing our betrothal.

At the end of the meal, Rowan stood, and I expected him to ask Ashton to leave with him—for their usual games of chess.

But he merely stood until the hall fell silent, and all heads turned his way.

"Thank you," he said, and his voice carried to the archway. "And now, I wish for you all to rejoice with me at the news of my upcoming marriage."

What was he doing? Making a formal announcement of our betrothal? Ashton turned to give me a beaming smile.

"One week from tonight," Rowan went on, "I will join my life forever with the princess Ashton."

A sea of faces froze.

Ashton's smile faded, and she looked up at him as if she'd not heard correctly. I felt my cheeks flush red.

"Tomorrow," Rowan said, "I've called the merchants and city leaders to common court to make a public announcement. Once I have their good wishes, the council will convene to provide approval. It will be a small ceremony, but everyone here is invited."

Crooking his arm, he looked down to Ashton. "And now I would play chess."

She stared up at him, and for a few seconds, I thought she might refuse to take his arm. But though she dropped her gaze, she stood. Keeping her eyes on the floor, she let him lead her out of the hall.

I sat there, completely still, as voices erupted all around me. I knew why he'd done this. Rowan was no fool, and he'd carefully chosen a moment when there could be no questions and no discussion. But he could not have chosen a crueler method.

To shock Ashton in front of everyone.

To humiliate me in front of everyone.

"My dear...my dear..." the lady Elizabeth sputtered beside me. "I'm sure the king is playing a little joke. He will return and we will laugh."

I bit my tongue from responding to her silly—and false—reaction. If the king were to kill his own mother and then play a joke at a formal dinner two nights later, it would mean he was mad.

Rowan was not mad.

But he was determined to have his own way.

I wasn't finished yet. Tomorrow, he would announce his plan to the merchants and leaders of the city, and then he had to gain approval from the council.

Forcing a smile, I rose. "Yes, of course," I answered Elizabeth. "Would you please excuse me?"

A number of people were on their feet by now. Some were stunned by Rowan's announcement...but not the members of the council. I walked with my head high past all the glances thrown my way—as my status was now in question. The worst moment occurred when I passed Baron Augustine, and his face filled with pity.

Pity.

For some reason, I was grateful the captain had not been here tonight to witness this.

At the archway, I stopped.

The gaming room was down the north corridor, but Rowan and Ashton were at the mouth of the south corridor. Her back was against the wall. He wasn't touching her, but he stood directly in front of her with his arm blocking her escape.

Her body was tense, and her head was down.

As he had done before, he leaned in, speaking to her urgently.

After leaving the hall, she must have tried to make a run for her apartments, and he'd stopped her.

I couldn't hear Rowan, but Ashton shook her head once, and he frowned. I saw her mouth the word, "Please," and his frown deepened.

She said it again, and he finally stepped back to let her go. Ashton fled up the south corridor. As he turned, I stepped backward, so he wouldn't see me as he strode east toward his own rooms.

I couldn't bring myself to go back into the hall, but I also couldn't face going up to Ashton's apartments. Instead, I walked west, to my room.

* * * *

I sat alone, striving to devise ways that I might yet succeed here, but entertaining the possibility of failure.

What would that mean?

I trembled to think. When my father learned what had happened here, he would blame me entirely.

A soft knock sounded on my door.

I feared who it might be even before opening it, and was not surprised to see Ashton on the other side. Her arms were crossed and her expression was lost. I had seen that look on her face before.

We both stood for a long moment.

"I'm so sorry," she said quietly. "I'm so sorry for what he did tonight."

"You had no idea he'd make that announcement?" I asked. "He'd said nothing to you earlier?"

She shook her head. "No. But he means to do it, Olivia. How can he even...?" Her voice sounded so wretched that I wondered about one possible path.

"You've no wish to marry him?" I asked, "not even to be queen?"

"Marry him? He's my brother!"

Technically, he was not, but I didn't point this out. "Then refuse."

"I can't," she whispered. "That would hurt him."

My hopes fell. Ashton might fear Rowan, but she feared hurting him even more. I'd known this already.

A tear ran down the side of her face.

"I know this is unfair," she said. "But I don't have anyone else. Could I stay here with you tonight?"

To my shame, I felt a wave of pity. What was happening to me? I was a Géroux. She was the cause of all my trials, and all I could feel was pity.

Stepping back, I let her in.

Chapter Eighteen

True to his word, the following day, Rowan held a common court attended by the merchants, artisans, and city leaders of Partheney.

I forced myself to attend—as I had to know the impact of his announcement.

Few people here would know who I was, so I was able to blend in until Captain Caron spotted me. I wished he were not here. For reasons I couldn't explain, I didn't want him witnessing this. But he always attended common court.

His expression was taut as he moved to join me, so I assumed he'd heard about Rowan's announcement at dinner at last night.

Thankfully, he didn't offer me any words of sympathy as he took his place beside me and simply nodded. "My lady."

Then I was glad for his presence, and stepped closer to stand beneath his height.

Judging by the easy chatter and relaxed mood of the people around me, with the exception of the captain, no one in the hall had any idea of what Rowan would announce today.

Heads began turning as Rowan and Ashton entered the hall with six guards behind them. Rowan walked through the crowd with purpose. His large chair was up on the dais, with Ashton's smaller chair set halfway behind it. He motioned for her to sit, but he remained standing and faced the crowd. She sat with her eyes down, and her face was unreadable.

Rowan cut a striking figure in a red sleeveless tunic, with his dark hair waving down over the top of his collar. As always in court, the crown was on his head.

"My people," he began. As with last night, his voice carried through the hall. "I came here as the son of a king when I was twelve years of age.

King Eduard formally adopted me, and I became his son. I am his son."
He waved his hand back to Ashton. "Your princess has grown up at my
side, and she loves our people as I do, as many of you can attest by her
good works and labors to help those she can, and to ease their suffering."

Everyone listened and nodded in agreement.

"Of late," Rowan continued, "*I* have suffered at the thought of her being
married to a foreign king and being sent from the people she so loves.
Who among us can imagine life at Partheney without her gentle counsel
beside me? I am Eduard's son, but the princess and I share no line of
blood. Together, we could found a line of heirs and secure the future of the
kingdom. I have proposed an offer of marriage to her, and she has accepted."

If the crowd had been quiet before, complete silence fell now. I held a
long breath. This was the crux, the moment Genève had so feared, where
the people would either cringe away at the suggestion of incest…or worse,
they would not, and then question his right to rule.

"Who among us could part with our princess? Who could suffer her
loss when the answer is so clear?" he asked. "I *am* king, and I would see
the princess Ashton at my side in her rightful place as queen." Stepping
forward on the dais, he spoke directly to several men at the front of the
crowd. "Would you see Ashton as your queen?"

After an instant's hesitation, the men nodded. "Yes, my king."

Rowan stepped back and called out, "Queen Ashton!"

A low cheer went up that grew louder and louder.

I closed my eyes.

He had them.

They saw him as king…and they'd accepted Ashton as queen.

Close behind me, I felt the captain's strong presence. He didn't touch
me nor attempt to offer comfort, but neither did he cheer.

* * * *

The following two days passed in a fog.

Rowan refused to retract his order that Genève not be placed in the
family crypt. Her body was buried in a public grave without ceremony. I
thought this a mistake at a political and personal level. It embarrassed the
council, and it gave Ashton no chance to mourn properly or say good-bye
in a way that might allow her to begin to heal.

At dinner, the other nobles were polite to me, but no one remained in
my company for more than few moments, offering vapid words about the
weather or the wine or my gown.

My status was in question. I'd not lost yet, and there was a chance I might still become queen, so no one wished to offend me...but the chances were now slim. Rowan had won the people over, and he had their support at his back. This had been the main concern of the council all along. They had no opposition to Ashton. They only desired Rowan's crown to remain safely on his head.

On the third day after his announcement at dinner, he called a closed-door meeting of the council. This was my last chance for salvation, but I didn't hold out much hope, and I was not wrong. They were in session less than half an hour, and when they came out, the marriage had been approved.

I was now officially unwanted extra baggage, the third daughter of Hugh Géroux.

And I was afraid.

* * * *

Though on a purely intellectual level, Rowan was intelligent, even shrewd, in many ways he possessed a weak grasp of human nature.

If he'd only put off the wedding for several months, Ashton might have been able to reconcile herself better. If he had let her plan a wedding with the other noblewomen and given her time to grow accustomed to viewing him as her future husband, she might slowly have come to see him as a man...and not as her elder brother.

But he didn't.

As promised, he arranged an informal ceremony four days later—exactly one week from his initial announcement—and invited the council and any nobles in residence.

This included me, and I couldn't refuse or even feign illness without making myself the subject of pitying gossip. I had to attend and hold my head high. I even helped Kamilla arrange Ashton's hair. It all felt like a bad dream from which I could not wake.

At first, Rowan insisted Ashton wear a white gown passed down through her family. It came with a matching white ribbon to be tied around her throat. But she was so small that even Kamilla couldn't take the gown in enough without ruining it, so in the end, Ashton wore her peach silk.

The ceremony was brief.

Rowan and Ashton each spoke their vows and then signed the agreement. Lord Cloutier and Baron Augustine signed as witnesses. The noble wives tried to weep prettily and pretend it was a happy day, but everything was overshadowed by Genève's grisly death, her cold-blooded burial, and the fact that the bride looked like a lamb being led to slaughter.

The dinner after was an equally strained affair, and only Rowan appeared to enjoy himself. He fed Ashton small bites of food from his plate.

Captain Caron had been invited as a guest. Though he held no title, due to his station, he was a man who could walk comfortably in several worlds. Tonight, he dined at the second table, wearing a black tunic with silver thread. His hair was held back in a leather thong at the base of his neck. I'd never seen him in anything but a wool shirt and tabard.

My position here had altered radically…I also ate at the second table, placed well below him. Few people spoke to me.

I was nothing, a failure who would soon vanish back to the southeast.

Even before dessert had even been served, Rowan stood. His dark eyes glittered.

"My friends," he called. "It has been a joyful day. The musicians will be in shortly. Stay and dance and drink as late as you like." He looked down to Ashton. "But now, my bride and I will leave you…to retire."

As opposed to crooking his arm, he offered her his hand.

Slowly, she took it, and he drew her up. The fear in her eyes made me look away. I had no idea what she was about to face behind closed doors, and didn't want to think on it.

Smiles and congratulations followed them as they left the great hall, but it all sounded hollow.

Once they were gone, the smiles vanished.

As the musicians came in to set up, most people rose from their tables to stretch and drink wine while standing. Captain Caron crossed the hall partway to speak with Lord Sauvage.

I stood alone, but I heard Lord Cloutier's aging wife sigh as she watched the captain.

"A fine-looking man. It's such a pity he has no title," she said. "Otherwise, he'd do well for my granddaughter, Sophia."

Lady Miranda watched the captain dispassionately. "I've heard there's family money."

"Not enough to make up for a lack of title. My lord would never consider it."

It troubled me to hear them discussing Captain Caron as if he were some bull up for sale, but I held my tongue. My best option for safety at the moment was to remain invisible. And yet…I looked conspicuously isolated standing here.

The music began.

Captain Caron left Lord Sauvage and walked straight to me, holding out his hand. "My lady?"

Without hesitation, I joined him. He was the only man in the hall with whom I wanted to dance.

Out on the floor, he held my left hand in his and grasped my waist lightly as we stepped in time with the other dancers.

"A strange wedding," he said quietly.

This was probably the closest he'd ever come to criticizing Rowan, but I agreed with him. "Yes. Poor Ashton."

"You pity the princess?"

With him, honesty tended to spill out of my mouth. "Not as much as I pity myself."

I felt him stiffen a little in his steps. "Because it was not you who married the king?"

"No, because I dread what may happen to me now."

"What do you mean?"

"What do you think I mean? I've failed here, and my father will call me home."

Without warning, he stopped dancing and held me in place. I couldn't move.

"Are you afraid?" he asked.

The fear and despair inside me welled up, and I couldn't keep a brave front. "Yes."

Realizing that people were glancing our way, he moved us back into the flow of the other dancers.

"I can't do anything to help you," he said quietly, "but Ashton can, and she will. If you need protection, go to her."

My eyes focused on the blond hair of his close-trimmed beard. Could he be right? Would Ashton protect me? She couldn't seem to protect herself. But I had little else to try.

"I will. Thank you, Captain."

"Call me Micah."

I let myself become lost in the music and the skill of his steps. I danced with him until almost midnight and didn't care a whit what anyone thought.

* * * *

Midmorning of the next day, I stepped out into the courtyard for some air and saw Rowan speaking to Micah near the new stable.

I'd not expected to see Rowan up and about this early after his wedding night, but perhaps he had duties. More importantly, it meant he was not with Ashton.

Turning, I went back inside and made my way to the first of the south towers. I'd heard from Kamilla that the new couple had spent the night in Ashton's apartments. There I stood outside the door, not certain what I'd find inside.

Finally, I knocked. "Ashton, it's me."

"Come in," she called.

Upon entering, I found her still in her nightgown and silk dressing robe, but she sat at a table, sipping a cup of tea. Walking over, I made a quick examination. She looked well enough physically, but she was paler than normal, with a hint of that lost look in her eyes.

Subtle or euphemistic language seemed absurd. I was the one who'd brought her here the day Rowan ripped her gown and cut her mouth with his teeth.

"Are you all right?" I asked bluntly.

She didn't pretend to misunderstand me. "Yes. The king was not...unkind."

Well, that was something. But it struck me that this would probably be the strongest passion he'd ever receive from his wife, a quiet relief on her part that he'd not been brutal. He had no one to blame but himself.

If only he'd waited a few months.

Still, I had other worries, and sat down across from her.

"I'm glad you've come," she said. "You are the only one who would come to see that I was well."

"I did come out of concern for you, but also for myself."

The lost look left her eyes as she focused on me. "For yourself?"

"Do know Lord Arullian?"

She shuddered. "Yes. Mother didn't like to have him here any more often than necessary. She gave orders no serving girls were ever to be alone with him. His last wife's death was..." She trailed off, as if not knowing how to finish the sentence.

"He's asked for my hand," I said, "and my father threatened that he'd accept the proposal if I failed here. And I have failed here."

"Arullian?" she repeated. "No. Your father would not."

"He would. My father does not brook failure from his children."

"I am to blame."

In part, that might be true, but she'd not done anything to harm me. With the exception of Micah, she was my only friend here. "That doesn't matter now," I said. "What matters is that I not be called home."

Reaching out, she grasped my hand. "I won't let your father take you. I'll write him today and tell him that I need you here, and I'll suggest some favors may be traded. Do you know of anything he wants?"

I did not, as he told me little, but I was sure there must be something. "If there is, he will tell you."

"Good," she said. "Please don't fear. I will be queen, and I will protect you."

Chapter Nineteen

As with the wedding, Rowan wasted no time with Ashton's coronation, and it was carried out two weeks later.

This didn't give the other nobles of the kingdom time to plan or travel, and so only members of the council already in residence and their wives attended the ceremony. My father sent a letter with his regrets, but I didn't think he would have come even if enough time had been allowed—as he was embarrassed by my failure. Still, he did not call me home.

Whatever Ashton had written to him, for now, it appeared I was safe.

At the dinner on the night of the coronation, she came to me as everyone milled about drinking wine before the first course was served. Since her marriage to Rowan, I'd been sleeping in my own room. She'd resumed her work in the old stable, sometimes even going out to help deliver food and goods to the poor, so she and I had less time together in private.

"Olivia," she said quietly, pretending to take a sip of wine. "There will be some changes beginning tomorrow. I'll need to move into my mother's apartments. It's expected. I thought to offer you my current apartments…" She hesitated and glanced over at Rowan. "But I'm working on something more permanent to allow you to remain in Partheney."

"More permanent?"

"Don't ask me yet. I need more time, and for now, it may be wise to do nothing to bring you to the king's attention. Will you be comfortable in your room a while longer? I know it's not large."

I struggled to absorb all that she said and did not say. She was working on a way to allow me to remain here, but she didn't wish to call me to Rowan's attention? Why? I was no longer any threat to him.

Still, I'd sleep in the stable if it kept me from being called home.

"My room is fine. Can you not tell me more?"

"Not yet. Just trust me."

It was hard for me to trust. I liked all the facts at my fingertips. But I nodded.

* * * *

Several days passed. Seven members of the council announced they were packing to go home and see to their own estates until the next gathering. This showed their comfort, that they need not stay. Rowan's crown was secure, and Ashton was now queen.

I was on pins and needles, feeling like an extra appendage and looking for ways to pass the time. I helped Ashton in the old stable—sorting goods and food and loading wagons. I attended embroidery circles in her new quarters. I tried to pretend I belonged here.

Ashton once said, "I'm so sorry about your seating in the great hall. I'd have you sit beside me, but I don't want to bring you to Rowan's attention."

Did she fear that if Rowan actively noticed I was still here, he might send me away? When I asked her about this, she was evasive.

Five days following the coronation, I felt a need for fresh air and solitude, and so I took a walk in the courtyard, thinking to go down and visit my horse, Meesha. As I entered the stable, I stopped.

Micah stood a few paces away, cleaning a saddle.

"My lady?" he said in surprise.

Though I was usually comfortable with him, I suddenly felt like a girl invading his private space.

"Oh...forgive me. I just thought to check on Meesha."

He smiled. "Nothing to forgive. I was just thinking of you." He put down the cleaning cloth. "Come and see your horse."

He'd been thinking of me?

"I've feared you might be sent home," he said, as we walked between rows of stalls. "Has Ashton found a way to keep you here?"

"For now," I answered. "She says she's working on something for the future, but she won't tell me what."

We reached Meesha, and she put her head over the top of the stall so I could stroke her nose. "She looks well."

"Yes. I've seen to her exercise myself. She gets out every day."

"Thank you."

He tilted his head. "Have you eaten lunch?"

"Not yet."

"I'm off duty this afternoon and was about to take a walk out into the city. Come with me. I know a place that serves the best rolls and spiced tea in all of Partheney."

Had the floor behind him opened up, I could not have been more taken aback. He was asking me to go walking in the city, with him…unchaperoned?

But his eyes held a hint of challenge, and I'd not been outside the castle gates since my arrival. This entire place had begun to feel as stifling and smothering as a weight on my chest. Knowing I'd probably lost my wits for even considering his offer, I nodded.

"All right."

* * * *

Not long after, I didn't care about any repercussions.

The day was fine and warm, and Micah showed me a variety of shops and eateries out in the city. I'd never walked through a city before with no other purpose than to see the sights.

It was more enjoyable than I could describe.

It was…liberating.

Then he led me down a street of especially fine shops with colorful signs and awnings.

"There," he said, pointing to a shop with a bright yellow awning and numerous tables with chairs set up out front.

As we approached, my mouth began to water at the smell of freshly baked bread. Perhaps twenty people already sat at the tables, drinking mugs of tea or eating rolls and sausages.

Micah pulled out a chair at an empty table. "Come and sit, my lady."

I wished he would call me Olivia, but I said nothing.

Rather, I reveled in this new experience, of sitting with common people at a table outdoors. Several people called greetings to Micah and looked at me with open curiosity. With a slight thrill, I realized they'd have no idea who I was. Young noblewomen did not sit alone in public with soldiers in chain armor.

A large man with a mustache, wearing an apron, strode up to our table. "Captain. How are you this morning?" He glanced at me.

Micah didn't introduce me. "I'm well, Bertram. Could you bring us rolls, sausages, and spiced tea?"

With a nod, Bertram left, but he returned almost immediately with a tray, and my mouth watered again. The rolls were light brown and still steaming. I could smell the spice in the tea. Micah paid.

The life of the city pulsed around me, and white clouds floated overhead in a blue sky. I felt…free. Micah stretched out his long legs and ate three of the rolls.

A small white dog with long ears sat on the ground near a table occupied by several merchants. Upon spotting Micah, it came trotting over, wagging its tail and begging with a whine.

"This little one seems to know you," I said, smiling and breaking off a bite of my sausage for our visitor.

The dog took it carefully from my fingers.

"Yes, he knows me," Micah answered, stroking the dog's head.

One of the merchants looked over as if concerned the animal was bothering us, but Micah waved him off. "It's fine, Pierre. He's no trouble." Then Micah looked at me. "You like dogs?"

"Yes," I nodded, thinking back to my childhood with a fresh stab of loss.

"What is it?" he asked, concerned.

"It's nothing. It's just…"

And as we sat there, I found myself telling him all about my dog, Emma, from the time I was a young child to the night she died.

He listened.

* * * *

That evening, as I walked into the great hall before dinner, I was still awash in the glow of the afternoon, and my mind kept over going the sights I'd seen and things I'd told Micah—that I'd never told anyone else.

I was not paying much attention to the people around me until I saw Rowan and Ashton drawn off together near the hearth. He had hold of her arm. Her head was down, and he spoke angrily into her ear.

While the sight of this wasn't exactly new, I noticed something in her profile, perhaps a hint of anger. But she nodded several times as he spoke, until he let go of her arm.

A moment later, Lord Sauvage walked up to them and engaged Rowan in conversation. Ashton stepped back unnoticed, and then she saw me. After a quick glance at Rowan, who was distracted, she slipped away and came to me.

"What's wrong?" I asked.

"Nothing of much consequence. But the king is displeased with me. Several times this week, I have been wanted for one reason or another, and I've not been found in my apartments. Messengers have been sent to the old stable. There is much to be done in preparation for winter." She sighed.

"Today, a new tapestry that Rowan commissioned was finished, and he wanted my assistance in choosing where to hang it in his apartments."

"And?"

"I couldn't be found. I'd decided to go out with the wagons myself down to the docks for delivery. I know the fishermen's families better than Emilee. Micah was off duty, so I asked Lieutenant Arye to escort me."

"And Rowan is angry because you couldn't be found and you were down on the docks without Micah?"

She nodded. "I was perfectly safe, but he's insisting I give up much of my work and remain here inside the castle during the days."

This troubled me. Ashton been forced into both a marriage and a role not of her choosing, and now Rowan wanted her to give up the one task that was most important to her?

"Will you give it up?"

"No. I'll try to help him understand how important it is that I'm at the heart of this work. We need the nobles and the merchants, and a familiarity with those in need."

I was about to say more when Rowan noticed her gone.

Looking back at us, he crooked his arm. "Ashton."

She hurried back to him.

I was still worrying about her when I noticed Lady Miranda and Lady Elizabeth beside me, looking at me askance. Both their husbands had decided to remain in residence through autumn.

"My ladies," I said carefully.

Lady Miranda cleared her throat. Though just beginning to show her age, she looked magnificent tonight in purple satin. "My dear," she said. "Please don't think us unkind, but we thought to have a word."

Now I was on guard. This was the female equivalent to drawing daggers.

"Yes?" I answered.

Lady Elizabeth stepped closer. "Olivia, you were seen…coming back through the castle gates today, alone in the company of Captain Caron. Word has it you were gone all afternoon."

Word had it? Word certainly traveled fast.

"He asked to show me a bit of the city, and I agreed. I've not been outside nor seen any of our fair city since my arrival."

"That may be true," Lady Miranda said. "But surely you know the dangers of inciting gossip?" She leaned closer. "Your prospects here are limited now. It's possible the queen may be able to arrange an acceptable marriage for you, a second son at best, but she will not have even that option if you ruin yourself."

I felt a chill. An acceptable marriage? Is that what Ashton was attempting to arrange for me, a marriage to some nobleman's second son? Perhaps she saw this as the only way to keep me out of Arullian's hands. If she was the one who proposed the marriage, my father might not be able to refuse.

But I had no desire to spend my life with a man to whom I'd be expected to show constant gratitude…someone who had taken the king's leavings and given her a home and a minor position.

"I thank you," I said, curtsying, "for your counsel."

Then I walked away, wishing I did not have to stay for dinner. I wasn't hungry.

* * * *

Another month passed, and Ashton said nothing.

I felt as if I were caught in limbo, but each day, I was relieved when she did not announce that she'd found some second son who had agreed to marry me. But I'd also begun to worry more about her than about myself. Rowan did not relent in his belief that she must curb her time working with the poor, and she had taken to spending more time in the castle, but this weighed upon her, and I noticed that lost expression on her face more often.

Several times, I walked to the new stable to visit Meesha. Nearly every time I did this, Micah somehow noticed, and he would join me, but he didn't again ask me to walk with him into the city. Perhaps he knew I'd have to refuse.

Then, one afternoon, Ashton arranged an embroidery circle in her apartments, and she'd invited any noblewomen currently residing at the castle. Upon arriving, I noticed a difference in Ashton. She was animated, even smiling.

"Ashton?" I asked.

"Wait a bit," she whispered.

My curiosity grew.

Once all the ladies were seated with tea, Ashton sat on a couch and beamed at us. "I have news of a happy event." She touched her stomach.

She was with child.

A rush of emotions passed through me. I was glad for her, but a surge of pettiness also rose up—it should be me sitting on that couch, smiling and announcing the pending birth of the next royal heir.

Angrily, I pushed the thought away. She would want me to share in her joy.

Hurrying to her side, I grasped her hand.

"I'll need you when my time comes," she said.

"I will be there."

* * * *

Around this point, a routine began to develop. Rowan always dressed for dinner in his own rooms, and Ashton liked to have me in her apartments to help choose her gown or visit while Kamilla did her hair.

Though pregnancy agreed with her, she now clung to me a little more, as if in need of my strength. I hoped I still had strength to give. She would not speak of my future, and I felt I couldn't press her.

My father still had not called me home.

Autumn was upon us. One night, Ashton and I were in her apartments in the hour before dinner. I was already dressed, but decided to wear my hair down, and Kamilla left us to run to my room to fetch my silver clip.

Ashton and I were in her sitting room, and she was suffering a little from feeling queasy.

"Olivia, I'm not sure I should wear my blue silk tonight," she said. "Kamilla laid it out, but I think it's too tight. Would you go see if the red velvet has been pressed?"

Leaving her for a moment, I walked to the bedroom to check her wardrobe. I'd just begun to search for her red velvet gown when I heard the sound of the outer door opening, followed by Rowan's low voice. I couldn't make out his words.

But I stopped moving, for fear of making any sound.

He didn't know anything of my evening visits here, and Ashton had been adamant that we do nothing to call me to his attention.

I would remain in here and hope that he'd leave soon.

"What?" Ashton asked loudly, sounding aghast. "Rowan, you can't. He's wrong. Tell him no. Tell him you won't do it!"

She sounded so distressed that I moved silently to the bedroom doorway to better hear them, but I remained out of sight.

"He's not wrong," Rowan returned. "If we don't retaliate by force, we'll appear weak, and we'll open our borders for further attacks."

"He *is* wrong," she said. "Lord Sauvage thinks all solutions can be found at the point of a sword. But to invade Samourè? Have you thought about what that would mean? We'd need to raise taxes. Our people won't willingly go to war over an issue that could be easily solved, and if you can't convince them, you'll need to resort to conscriptions. Think on what bad feelings that will cause! Think of the innocent people of Samourè who will suffer. Think of our own men who will die needlessly."

I'd never once heard her argue with him, and I held my breath.

The sitting room went quiet, and then Rowan said, "I put in the order to raise taxes yesterday. We cannot appear as weak."

"You raised taxes on our people? Without even consulting me?"

His voice rose. "And how would I consult you? You weren't here! You were down in that stable doing the gods know what, probably lifting more than you should and risking our child! You care more for the children of poor fishermen than your own! If you stopped all that nonsense and attended to your duties here, you'd be more informed."

Rage swelled inside me. Before I could stop myself, I stepped from the doorway and out into the sitting room.

"How can you say that?" I demanded of him. "When you were the one who stood on that dais and won the merchants and city leaders over to your side by reminding them of Ashton's good works? You regaled them with reminders of her compassion for the poor and how they could not bear to lose her." All the pent-up fear and anger from the past months came out. "Now you chastise her for it? What a hypocrite you are."

Ashton stared at me, stunned.

But Rowan's eyes narrowed.

"What are you doing here?" he asked quietly.

My anger faded as I began to realize what I'd just done. "I came to help the queen dress for dinner."

"No," he said, "I mean, what are you still doing here at the castle? It's long past time you went home."

"Olivia," Ashton said, "Would you please go and see what is keeping Kamilla with your hair clip?"

Both frightened of Rowan and angry with myself, I fled her apartments.

* * * *

That night, I didn't go down to dinner. I asked Kamilla to bring a tray to my room.

When it arrived, I couldn't eat.

What had I been thinking? Ashton had worked so hard to keep me out of notice, and I'd stepped from her bedroom, shouting at Rowan and calling him a hypocrite.

But he'd made me so angry. His disregard of Ashton's counsel was beyond bearing—as was his accusation that she cared not for their child. How could he say such things to her? And yet...my foolish actions would not help her, and now I'd jeopardized my own safety. He'd most likely write to my father in the morning.

I had no idea how to save myself.

The door cracked, and Kamilla peered in. "My lady? The queen has sent a note."

A note?

Hurrying to the door, I took a folded piece of paper from her hand and opened it. It read:

> *Olivia,*
> *Come to my apartments tomorrow. Be sure to wait until midmorning, after the king has left.*
> *Please don't fear, and sleep well tonight.*

I read the note several times. What did it mean?

* * * *

Midmorning of the following day, I made my way to Ashton's apartments with a mix of dread and hope. My performance last night had probably forced her hand, and she was about to tell me which young and insignificant noble son had reluctantly agreed to accept the king's castoff.

I had no one but myself to blame.

After knocking lightly on the door, I cracked it. "Ashton."

"Come in."

I found her alone, but she looked weary, so tired, that for the first time she seemed older than her nineteen years.

"What's happened?" I asked instantly.

"Happened? Nothing. But I have welcome news for you."

I braced myself as she walked to her tea table, upon which lay several large pieces of faded paper.

"I've been working on some arrangements," she said, "but all is settled now." She lifted the largest document. "My aunt, my father's sister, never married. She owned a small manor at the northwest edge of the city, near the sea. When she died five years ago, she left the house and property to me. I have signed it over to you."

My heart slowed. "A manor? With property?"

"Yes, and you'll need an income to support a household. At first, I thought to arrange a stipend, but...stipends can be stopped." She lifted the second document. "I own a fief about twenty leagues south of the city.

My grandmother left it to me, and I've also signed it over to you. There is a vassal in place, but you'll receive most of the rents and a portion of the taxes. It's not much, but it will keep you in gowns and cover basic expenses and salaries for a few servants."

I couldn't believe what she was saying.

"Ashton...are you sure? These properties belong to you."

"I don't need them, and be warned. The manor house has not been occupied these five years. I've no idea of its state of disrepair."

I couldn't have cared less about its state of disrepair. She was handing me my freedom.

But why did she look so strained, so weary? And if both properties were hers, why had it taken so long for her to make these arrangements?

A nagging thought occurred. "Rowan has agreed to this?"

Even if the properties were hers, he was still her lord and husband. He'd need to agree.

She hesitated. "Yes. He has agreed. We spoke...at length on the matter and came to an agreement."

"An agreement? Do you mean a bargain?"

"Yes." She turned away. "But do not think on it."

I stepped directly in front of her. "What did you do, Ashton? What did you promise him?"

"I've relinquished leadership of my charity work to Emilee Martine. She'll now oversee the collection, sorting, and distribution, and I will spend my days here at the castle, so that I am accessible to the king."

"No! You can't let him demand that."

What a selfish creature he was. He'd agreed to my safety at the price of the only piece of her life over which he'd had no control.

"It's done." She held out both documents. "And the truth is, you cannot refuse to take these."

My heart ached for her, and my hatred for him grew.

But she was right. I could not refuse.

Chapter Twenty

The manor was so far out on the northwest edge of the city that it was beyond walking distance.

Two days later, Micah saddled Meesha and his roan stallion, and he took me to see it for the first time. It was both more and less than I expected. To my joy, the house was large, three stories with generous front windows. There were rose gardens and apple trees—long untended.

But once inside, I thought on Ashton's warning about disrepair. The glass in three windows was broken, with shards spread across the floors. The carpets, curtains, and couches were moth-eaten. Parts of the staircase's banister had fallen. We found a family of raccoons living in the kitchen—and decided not to trouble them just yet.

However, Micah's enthusiasm could not be contained.

When I'd first told him what Ashton had provided for me, his face lit up like a beacon. Now, he moved swiftly from room to room.

"It's not as bad as it looks," he said. "The roof is intact, and that's most important. A carpenter can replace that banister. Some of the furniture can be repaired. Once the house has been thoroughly cleaned, though, you'll need new carpets and curtains."

"And how will I afford all of that?" I asked.

"How much is your income?"

"I'm not certain, but Ashton implied it would be barely enough to support me."

He looked around again. "Let's go see the upstairs."

As we ascended, he offered his hand and warned, "Don't touch what's left of the banister."

Taking his hand, I let him lead me up. Only then did I realize that I'd once again placed myself in a compromising situation: completely alone with him while going to inspect the upstairs bedrooms. But somehow, today, it didn't matter. I need not worry so much for my reputation.

"Oh dear," I said, walking into the first bedroom. The mattress of the bed appeared to be rotting.

Micah walked over and opened the moth-eaten curtains. Then he opened the window.

"I'm not saying it won't be a task," he said. "But this could be a fine house again."

His mood was infectious. After all, I'd never shied away from a challenge. "Yes, it could."

He glanced back. "And you could be happy here?"

Through the open window, fresh sea air filled the musty room, and I smiled. "I could be very happy."

* * * *

It took almost a month to ready the house enough so that it might be at least livable for me. Ashton loaned me the money to hire workers and char maids. I would repay her as soon as my first rents came in. The rugs were discarded, as were the curtains. The family of raccoons was relocated into the nearby forest.

But during this time, the castle was abuzz.

Spurred on by Lord Sauvage, Rowan raised taxes again, and then he raised an army. As Ashton had predicted, the people did not support an unnecessary war. Rowan did nothing to win their support or give them a reason to rally. A few border raids—for which compensation had been offered—did not warrant the risk and upheaval of an invasion. Conscriptions soon followed.

Shortly before the men were scheduled to depart, Ashton and I were alone in her apartments, carding and spinning wool. She was beginning to show, and we'd let out a few of her gowns.

"Rowan says he may be gone several months," she said.

She didn't sound sorry.

"Do you still love him?" I asked. Of late, she and I had grown increasingly open with each other.

"Yes, of course. I'll always love him, but he's so changed since our marriage. I miss my brother."

She failed to understand he was exactly the same person. Her image of Rowan as her brother was a fantasy, an illusion, and now she was trapped with the reality. I didn't point this out. It wouldn't have helped, and in spite of my complete opposition to this invasion of Samourè, I was thankful that Ashton would have a break from Rowan, possibly lasting for months. A few months without his oppressive company would do her much good.

However, a few moments later, he came in from the corridor and entered the sitting room, stopping at the sight of me. He'd agreed to Ashton's bargain for his own sake, but he would never forgive me for the words I'd spoken to him in this room.

"Is everything well?" Ashton asked him.

He nodded. "Yes, but Lord Sauvage has proposed a change, and I've agreed."

"What change?"

"He's offered to lead the army into Samourè and has suggested I remain here." His gaze dropped to her stomach. "He's capable of leading, and it might be best for me to stay at this time."

With her eyes down, she nodded.

Ashton would get no break from him.

He was no coward and didn't fear battle. Rather, he'd seemed eager for it. But he glared again at me before walking over to sit beside her at her spinning wheel, and I pressed down a suspicion that he couldn't stand the thought of her enjoying several months in the company of people other than himself.

* * * *

I moved into my house.

The first income from my rents arrived, and I hired a cook and a housemaid. Only one of the mattresses upstairs was still usable, so I purchased two small beds and set up quarters for the women. I filled the larder adequately, if not well.

The effort of filling hours in a day was over.

For now, I was busy from dawn to dark. The house had been cleaned and had undergone some repairs, but I still owed Ashton money, and so I set about making the house a home as best I could on my own. There was much to be done.

Micah helped when he was off duty, sometimes bringing wine or sugared almonds to share with me. At present, the stable was a shambles, and I couldn't afford to hire a groom, so he offered to keep Meesha up at the barracks until something could be arranged for her here.

The first dark moment came when a letter arrived from my father. Reading between the lines, I knew he was furious. Me living at the castle as the queen's intimate friend could be useful to him, but me living in my own home as an independent woman brought him nothing.

He wrote that I needed to settle my affairs here, and he would be sending Captain Reynaud and a contingent in a week to bring me home.

When Micah visited the next day, I had him take me up to the castle on his horse, and I showed the letter to Ashton.

"Write back and inform him you will remain in your house," she said. "Tell him if he sends guard to fetch you, Micah and the royal guards will stop them. I'll have the letter sent by a swift rider and provide money for him to switch horses. It will reach your father in a matter of days."

"If I do that, he'll disown me."

"Does that matter now?"

It did. If I was no longer Lady Olivia Géroux, daughter of Hugh Géroux, I was unsure of my identity. But I valued my life here and my home here more.

I wrote back and did exactly as Ashton suggested. She had the letter sent.

Two weeks later, I was home in the afternoon, attempting to polish the wormhole-ridden dining room table when an answer from my father arrived.

I went to the front door myself, took the letter, and walked back to the dining room. Slowly, I opened the letter.

It contained a formal document finalizing my disownment and disinheritance. I'd known this was coming, but I couldn't help feeling the blow. I had no family and no inheritance. I had no surname. And yet I was free.

Nan, the young housemaid I'd hired, came through the dining room doorway. "My lady. You have a visitor from the castle."

A visitor? I was not up to pleasant chatter…or worse, a social call from someone like Lady Miranda.

"Show them in," I said dully.

She left, and soon the sound of long strides echoed from the hallway.

Micah strode in without his armor or tabard, wearing a simple wool shirt. "It's only me," he said cheerfully. "I don't know why she felt a need to announce me. I'm off duty and thought I'd start working on the stable."

As he was the only one I wanted to see, his unexpected arrival left me undone, and I couldn't hide my warring emotions.

His cheerful countenance vanished. "What is it?"

"I've been disowned. I'm no longer a Géroux. Now I am just…Olivia."

He stared, and his breathing quickened. "As selfish as it sounds, that news is beyond welcome to me."

"Welcome? Why?"

"Because it brings us closer to the same level for what I want."

I pretended not to understand him. "And what is it you want?"

In three strides, he closed the distance between us and took my face in his hands. "Marry me."

* * * *

Rowan despised me, but he loved Micah, and Micah was the type to rarely ask for anything. So, when Micah asked permission for us to marry, Rowan granted it instantly.

I thought it ironic when our wedding day proved far happier than that of the royal couple.

Rowan offered to hold it in the great hall, but this would have been awkward on a number of levels. Now that I'd been disowned, the other nobles couldn't attend out of respect for my father, and they would not even know how to interact with me.

In addition, Micah and I wanted to be married in the house that would be our own. Preparing for the celebration proved somewhat challenging, however. I had no formal dinnerware, and no matter how much I polished the table, I couldn't hide the wormholes.

I splurged on a white tablecloth.

I'd found a set of etched wooden plates in an old cabinet and polished them. Micah borrowed tin goblets from the barracks—which mortified me—but he insisted on paying for all the food and wine, and I didn't argue. The cook I'd hired was skilled, and I knew we'd not be embarrassed by the wedding dinner.

Nan and I cut dozens of late-season roses, and the house was filled with flowers.

I pondered what dress to wear.

But Micah spoke up right away. "That green velvet with the white underskirt. And leave your hair down."

I smiled.

Our guest list included Rowan, Ashton, several merchant friends of Micah's, and his seven closest friends in the royal guard. I knew I shouldn't ask any of the nobles, but Baron Augustine was in residence. In the end, I sent a note to him, and was so glad when he accepted.

Rowan wouldn't allow Ashton to ride her own horse in her condition, but neither would he keep her away, and they made a lovely picture when they arrived in the late afternoon on his dark horse. He held her carefully in the saddle in front of himself, guarding her safety and the safety of their child. Baron Augustine rode behind them, and all the invited guards brought up the rear.

Micah and I stood out front of the house to greet them.

Ashton beamed down at me as Micah jumped forward to lift her off the horse. She was growing a little heavier with child.

"Oh, Olivia," she said. "I am so glad to be here. What a joyous day, and I've not seen the house since I was a girl."

I was excited to show it to her and we went inside, leaving the men to their own greetings.

Once all the guests had arrived, we gathered in the main sitting room. A city elder performed the ceremony. Micah promised to love me all of my life. When he spoke, I believed him.

Rowan and Lieutenant Arye signed as witnesses.

The dinner afterward was loud and cheerful, at which Rowan laughed openly with Micah and the other royal guards. I'd long suspected Rowan was more comfortable with soldiers than with other nobles. I'd never seen him so relaxed as in this setting. No one even noticed the plates were made from wood or the goblets from tin.

Ashton sat near a merchant's wife named Emilee Martine, and they chatted away like old friends. Ashton, too, seemed happy, and she smiled down the table several times at Rowan.

Micah had been generous with the dinner. We served a salmon course, followed by a beef course, along with gravy, roasted potatoes, glazed carrots, fresh bread, and mince pies. He bought ale and a cask of good wine.

For the guards, the meal was especially pleasant, as they rarely dined in such a manner.

I felt this was a good start to our new life.

Near midnight, Rowan announced it was time to ride back to the castle, and everyone headed outside for good-byes. Under the moon, Ashton grasped both my hands.

"Olivia, thank you so much. This was...I wish it did not have to end."

Though she smiled, a flicker of mania, mixed with anxiety, passed through her eyes, and her hands somehow felt brittle to me, as if she might break apart. She glanced at Rowan mounting his horse. Sadness washed through me as I realized this evening had been a respite for her. She did not want to go back to her life at the castle. If I could, I would have kept her here with me.

"Ready, my queen?" Micah asked.

She nodded, but didn't let go of my hands right away.

"We'll have you back soon," I promised.

"And you'll come to see me?" she returned.

"Yes."

Rowan scooted back in his saddle, and Micah carefully lifted Ashton up to settle her in front. Baron Augustine kissed my cheek before mounting his horse, and I was glad he'd come. The guards called thanks and good-byes.

Then the entire party rode out, and I was left alone with Micah. Normally, the newly wedded couple would have been sent to bed by now, but as we'd hosted this party, we could not have left our guests.

Micah turned to look at the front of the house. He'd not yet slept here, and I knew this must feel strange to him. He'd been living in a barracks his entire life.

Taking his arm, I led him back inside. "Now, we begin our life together here."

"And since the house is home to both of us now, the first thing we'll do is restore it properly and buy new carpets and curtains...and commission a new dining table."

I smiled, thinking him teasing me. "And how will we afford that?"

Inside the sitting room, he stopped. "You know you've not married a pauper?"

"A captain's stipend may not stretch far enough for new carpets and a dining table."

He raised one eyebrow. "My father bought a partnership in a silver mine, and it's done well. When he died, I inherited his shares. I may not have lands or rents, but I'll wager I have more ready wealth than half the men on the noble council. I've had no use for money at the barracks. You can buy anything for the house you like."

I still thought he might be teasing me.

"In truth?" I asked.

"You didn't know?" He sounded skeptical. "It's no secret, and has been much discussed among local mothers hunting husbands for their daughters."

Suddenly, I remembered a comment overheard from Lady Miranda, but at the time, I'd been distracted and had forgotten it right away.

"No. I didn't know," I answered.

"Then you married me for myself?"

Refusing to feed his vanity, I answered. "Either that, or because you offered to repair my stable."

He laughed, but we stood near the foot of the stairs, and his good humor faded. He suddenly appeared almost nervous.

"Olivia. It's been a long and busy day. If you are tired...If you would rather not...If you would rather wait to..."

What a good man he was. I'd seen him look at me with open desire for months, and now that I was finally his, he put my feelings before his own. Standing on tiptoes, I touched my mouth to his.

"I am not tired," I whispered.

With a sharp intake of breath, he leaned down to kiss me back.

* * * *

The following months were the happiest in my memory.

True to his word, Micah spared no expense in allowing me to furnish the house. We bought new mattresses, fine carpets, and white lace curtains. We had the shutters replaced. We commissioned new couches and a new dining table.

We bought dishes and pewter goblets.

Micah hired a carpenter to repair the stable so he could keep our horses at home, as he needed to ride to the castle and back every day.

He never once made me feel as if I was spending *his* money. Rather, he expressed gratitude to me for sharing this fine house, and he treated me as if I'd done him some great service by marrying him. I spent my nights in his arms, marveling at the joy two people could find in each other. He opened his soul to me in the darkness.

"I loved you the first time I saw you," he whispered, "standing on that hill with your eyes blazing. I never dreamed you'd choose to marry me."

I felt loved. I felt wanted.

His duties as commander of the guards took a good deal of his time, and each day was different for him, so we could not live by a set schedule, as other married couples. Some days, he had entire afternoons off, and some days, when large numbers of nobles were visiting the castle with their own guards, he did not get home until midnight. Twice in those first months, he sent me a message that he'd need to sleep in his room at the barracks and would not be home at all.

I never minded this. I'd known that castle security was his responsibility when I married him.

When possible, we dined together at our new table.

His favorite dish was baked salmon, and he also liked steamed mussels with butter and parsley.

One night, he came home well past dark but still early enough for us to eat together. Our cook prepared several of his favorite foods, including steamed mussels. He seemed distracted, and barely noticed his dinner.

"Is anything wrong?" I asked.

He hesitated, as if not certain he could answer, and I grew worried.

"Is it Ashton?" I asked. The question made me feel remiss. I'd not visited her at the castle. There was so much to be done here.

"What? No." He set down his fork. "Lord Sauvage has been sending short reports on the invasion of Samourè, simply stating that all is going according to schedule. But today, a report arrived from Colonel Marlowe. He says thousands of Samourè citizens have been slaughtered or displaced, and in response, King Amandine has raised a sizable army. We've suffered heavy losses."

I thought of our conscripted men lying dead in a foreign land. I thought of innocent Samourè families suffering for Lord Sauvage's bloody "show of strength."

"What will Rowan do?" I asked.

"I don't know. I hope he offers a treaty and tries to end this." He took a bite of bread. "But I feel guilty because it all seems so far away, and even after reading those reports with Rowan tonight, all I could think was to get home to you."

I understood what he meant. It all seemed far away for me too.

I was no longer Lady Olivia Géroux, daughter of Hugh Géroux. I was Mistress Olivia Caron, wife of the commander of the royal guard.

And I'd never felt so at peace.

Chapter Twenty-One

Winter was just passing into early spring when a pounding on the front door awakened Micah and me in the middle of the night. We both hurried from our bed, pulling on clothes, and stumbled out into the hallway. Nan came from her room with a startled expression, clutching at her night-robe.

Micah held out one hand.

"It's all right, Nan. I'll see to this."

He left us and took the stairs down two at a time. I heard low voices, and then he came running back up.

"Ashton's time has come, and she's asking for you."

By my counting, she was several weeks early. I'd promised to be there for her.

"I'll make ready," I said. "Can you saddle the horses?"

* * * *

Micah got me to the castle swiftly. He thought it best if he remained at the barracks, and I ran for the south tower.

Ashton was in her bed with a midwife and Kamilla in attendance. Her black hair was damp, and her face was wet with perspiration. Rushing in, I grasped her hand.

"I'm here."

"Olivia," she said weakly. "I knew you'd come."

"Of course I would come." I looked to the midwife. "When did this start?"

"Not long after dinner."

"And you just sent for me now?"

"She's early. We thought it might be a false labor."

I was no expert in childbirth, but this was no false labor. Picking up a cloth and bowl of water, I dabbed at Ashton's head. "I won't leave you."

She fought not to cry out as another pain hit her.

Hours passed, and dawn was nearly upon us. The midwife checked her, and she seemed no closer to pushing. I worried Ashton might be too weakened and exhausted to push when the time came.

"What is wrong?" I asked the midwife. "Why is this taking so long?"

"There's nothing wrong. This is her first birth. It will take time."

At a convulsion of pain, Ashton cried out.

"I'm going to fetch her some brandy," I said, getting up and hurrying for the door.

Upon stepping outside, I stopped cold. Rowan stood there, just outside the door. He looked terrible, and for the first time, I could not help but pity him. Men, not even kings, were allowed into a birthing chamber. He was forced to stand out here and listen, with no idea what was happening inside.

"Olivia," he said in a rasping voice. "I just heard her cry out."

"It's all right," I tried to reassure him. "The midwife says this is normal for a first birth."

"But it's gone on so long. She won't die? Tell me she won't die."

I'd never touched Rowan before, but I reached out and touched his arm. "Of course she won't, but she needs a little brandy for the pain. Would you go and get it?"

I suspected he needed something to do, and I was right.

"Yes," he answered readily. "I'll go now."

"Just knock on the door when you come back. I'll come out."

* * * *

By midmorning, Ashton was finally ready to push. By that point, she could no longer sit up, and I had to hold her.

The midwife was ready to deliver the baby, and Kamilla had brought clean water and blankets. Ashton was trying, but she was having difficulty.

"You must push," I ordered. "Push!"

"I can't," she whispered.

"Feel my arms around you. Draw on my strength. Push!"

She bore down hard, and her baby came into the world.

The midwife held the child inside a blanket as it drew its first breath and began to cry.

"A boy, my queen," she said.

"Oh, Ashton," I said. "You have a son."

Tears flowed from her eyes. "Let me see him. Let me hold him."

The midwife cut the cord and tied it. Ashton was so weak that we helped her to hold him, but her joy was clear. "He is beautiful."

The child was indeed perfect, perhaps small for having been born early, but he boasted a head of dark hair.

Ashton looked up at me. "Is Rowan outside the door?"

"Yes."

"Would you go and tell him?"

He would not be allowed inside just yet, but I hurried to do as she asked, and I cracked the door. At the sight of me, he rushed up.

"You have a healthy son," I said.

"What of Ashton? Is she well? Is she bleeding?"

"No more than expected."

"Let me in."

"Not yet, my king. Give us a few moments more."

For an instant, I thought he might push past me, but he relented and I closed the door.

Walking back into the bedroom, I said, "We should be quick. He won't wait long."

For generations, noblemen had been kept away from the realities of birth. I was not entirely certain of the reasons, but it was rule none of us would break. Here, Kamilla was of the most use. While the midwife cleaned and readied the child, Kamilla manage to get the blood-soaked sheets off the bed without disturbing Ashton too much. Clean sheets were put on the bed, and the bloody ones hidden away until they could later be taken to the laundry.

Ashton's nightgown was changed. Her hair was combed.

All traces of the birth were removed, and Ashton was propped up on two pillows. Kamilla handed her the child, who was wrapped in a clean blanket.

"All right, my lady," Kamilla said to me. "The king may enter."

I was no longer "my lady," but I didn't bother to correct her. Instead, I went to door of the sitting room and opened it, nodding to Rowan.

He swept inside and strode to the bedroom.

At the sight of Ashton, propped up on pillows, with her black hair all around her, he closed his eyes briefly in relief. Then he went to her side.

"You are well?" he asked. "You will recover?"

She was exhausted, but managed a smile. "Look at him, Rowan. He is so beautiful. Might we name him Eduard?"

But Rowan didn't even glance at the child. Instead, he turned to the midwife. "The queen is well? There'll be no childbed fever?"

"The queen is well, my king," answered the midwife carefully. "I believe so."

"Might we call him Eduard?" Ashton asked again.

"What?" Rowan said. "Oh, yes. If you wish."

I was dumbfounded, as was Kamilla. One of the first duties of a king was to provide an heir, and Rowan now stood over a healthy son. Any other man would have been rejoicing. For him, the child seemed almost an afterthought. But I remembered that he'd had no sleep, and he'd been pacing all night outside the door. He, too, must be over-weary and strained, and he wasn't thinking straight. Soon, he would celebrate with Ashton over the birth of their son.

Leaning close to Kamilla, I whispered. "The captain waited at the barracks, but he will bursting for news by now. I'll go down and tell him."

"Of course, my lady."

* * * *

I took a room at the castle, in the same south tower, so I could stay and keep company with Ashton in her recovery. The birth had left her weak, but I brought her bread soaked in beef broth, and she insisted on nursing Eduard herself.

She delighted in him and could not seem to hold him enough. I think he gave her strength as much as the broth.

"Do you think his eyes will stay blue, Olivia?" she asked me.

"I don't know," I laughed. "Most babies are born with blue eyes. They will either grow lighter like yours or go dark brown like Rowan's."

Every noblewoman in residence came to visit, and the happiness caused by Eduard's birth was so great that none of them bothered to snub me or pretend I hadn't been raised as one of them. Even Miranda took Eduard from my arms so that she might hold him, and the smile she offered in thanks was genuine.

The only moments of discomfort occurred whenever Rowan came to visit. I didn't understand him. He never once held Eduard or shared joy with Ashton. He came to check on her recovery and to inquire when she might be well again.

Once, when he arrived, she was nursing the baby, and he stopped in his tracks at the sight.

"What are you doing?" he asked.

For the most part, Ashton had decided to pretend all was well and that Rowan was behaving like a normal father.

"Feeding our son." She smiled.

He did not smile back. "Yourself? Should you not arrange a wet nurse?"

"No. It's best in the early days for the mother to nurse."

"The early days? Very well…but you must soon hire a wet nurse."

His frown deepened, and I could no longer deny the truth. He was jealous of his own son.

I remained at the castle for a week.

One other important event occurred during those days. Near the end of the week, Rowan came to us and announced that he'd signed a treaty with King Amandine, and the war with Samourè was over. Unfortunately, the list of dead on both sides was long, and we would have a number of crippled and maimed men coming home. He was unsure how to help them, as all the extra taxes had already been spent on food, weapons, and supplies for the army.

In the end, Amandine promised to stop the border raids himself—which is what he'd suggested in the first place—and Rowan did not press him for financial reparations, as we had devastated the southern border of his kingdom. So, besides providing ourselves with a reputation for our brutal show of strength, we'd gained nothing.

Rowan would never admit it, but I think he regretted having allowed himself to be swayed by Lord Sauvage.

I tried not to think on it. For now, I gave all my attention to Ashton and Eduard. He was a sweet child, and holding him caused me to wish for my own child. As of yet, I showed no signs that Micah and I might soon have happy news ourselves.

Eight evenings following Eduard's birth, Rowan arrived in Ashton's rooms about an hour before dinner would be served. He brought a young woman with him.

"This is Marta," he said. "A wet nurse I've hired for the child."

Ashton was sitting on a couch, holding Eduard. "A wet nurse?"

"I believe you are recovered enough to join me at dinner," he said, "and for chess afterward."

"You wish me to dress for dinner and come down?" she asked, as if she was not hearing him correctly. "What about Eduard? I would prefer to stay here with him."

Rowan's expression flattened. "If he distracts you here and he is too much trouble, perhaps he should be moved to the nursery."

All the pity I'd felt for Rowan on the night of Eduard's birth vanished, and my old hatred rose up. He wanted Ashton on his arm at dinner, and he wanted her to resume their games of chess. He'd just threatened to have Eduard taken from her rooms and placed into the nursery if she did not agree.

"I'll send for Kamilla," she answered quietly. "I'll be down before the first course is served."

"Good." He nodded and looked at me. "You are invited to dinner if you care to stay."

I did not care to stay. I could no longer help Ashton, and I didn't wish to see any more of this tragedy playing itself out.

"No. But thank you, my king," I said. "I should rejoin my husband and see about affairs in my own house now." I turned to Ashton. "But I'll return to see you in a few days."

It seemed she might argue at my sudden announcement of departure, but she didn't.

"Don't stay away too long," she said, and her voice sounded small.

I left the apartments and walked as swiftly as I could down the stairwell and through the castle to the courtyard. I wanted Micah. I wanted to go home.

He was not in sight, but darkness had fallen, and I soon spotted him beneath the burning braziers down at the gates. Again, I walked quickly, to find him giving instructions about the watch rotation.

My arrival surprised him. "Olivia."

"I'd like to go home."

He could always read me well. "I'm done for tonight. You wait here, and I'll get the horses."

* * * *

The following day, Micah left early, and I tried to focus on all the duties I'd neglected over the past week. I didn't want to think about Ashton up at the castle, about Rowan using her own son to threaten her.

Our cook was a pleasant woman named Claire, and when I went to the kitchen to discuss the weekly menus, I realized it was bread-baking day.

"Might I help?" I asked.

"If you like, mistress."

We passed the morning making bread together and talking of small things. The activity helped keep my worries and fears at bay. In the early afternoon, Nan came to join us. She'd been cleaning rooms upstairs.

The three of us shared a light meal of cheese, ham, and pickles.

We'd just finished when I heard the sound of the front door opening. I'd not expected Micah home this early.

"Wife!" he called playfully. "Where are you hiding?"

All three of us smiled. Micah's moods were always infectious.

"We're in the kitchen," I called back, like some uncouth girl of the streets.

"Close your eyes," he called. "And keep them closed. I have a gift for you."

A gift? Micah allowed me to spend any money I wished, but he was not the type of husband to buy gifts.

I closed my eyes.

As the sound of his bootsteps entered the kitchen, both Claire and Nan gasped.

"Keep your eyes closed," Micah said, "and crouch down."

What was he up to?

Still, I crouched, and heard a light scrabbling sound. Something touched my hand, and I opened my eyes to the sight of a puppy just before she wriggled up into my lap. She was a small spaniel with soft ears and soulful eyes.

"Oh, Micah."

He and I couldn't speak of Ashton, as that would require me criticizing Rowan, but he'd seen my pain and tried to do me a kindness. He'd remembered my story about Emma.

"Do you like her?" he asked.

"She's lovely," I answered, gathering the wriggling puppy in my arms. Nan and Claire came to pet her.

"I thought we might stay with names beginning with the letter E," Micah said. "What do you think of Esmeralda?"

"Esmeralda?"

"Essie for short."

I stroked her ears, and she licked my face. "Essie."

* * * *

A month passed.

I'd ridden up to the castle several times, but I hadn't stayed long. So far, Ashton had managed to keep Eduard in her apartments, but Rowan always exacted a price, and I knew this could not go on.

But one morning when I woke up, I remembered it was common court day, and I decided to go and see Ashton up in the dais, whispering advice in Rowan's ear.

Somehow, I thought the sight might remind me of days past, back when Genève held some control over Rowan, before he'd manipulated his marriage, and Ashton's face had been bright with life.

Micah was already gone from our bed. He often slipped from our bed and headed off to work early.

I wondered how he might feel about me riding up through the city without protection, but we'd never discussed this, so he couldn't complain.

After dressing quickly, I saddled Meesha myself and rode through the city.

When I arrived at the castle gates, Lieutenant Arye greeted me.

"Is the captain already inside?" I asked.

"Yes. Court is just beginning."

"Can you stable Meesha for me?"

He lifted me down and took her reins. After thanking him, I headed across the courtyard and into the castle.

Up the corridor, the round entry chamber was empty, and I quietly stepped through the archway into the great hall. It was crowded.

My eyes moved to the dais.

Rowan sat in his large chair, and Jarvis stood to the right as always. The six guards stood behind in attendance.

But Ashton's chair was missing. She wasn't there.

Rowan's expression was tense as he listened to a young woman standing on the floor before him. She was thin, and her dress was threadbare. She carried a baby in her arms.

"My king," she said, "I cannot pay next month's taxes when they come due. My husband was taken for the army, and he was killed in Samourè. We've had no income since he left."

Shifting in his chair, Rowan nodded. "My condolences on the death of your husband. You will receive an extension until next summer. It is hopeful things will have improved for you by then."

She thanked him, but the faces in the crowd were as tense as his.

The next case was a middle-aged widow who'd lost her son in Samourè and was also asking for an extension. My gaze scanned the crowd. Most of the people here were thin women in threadbare clothing, and I guessed many of them had lost men. Rowan could not excuse their taxes or the kingdom could not function, but he'd bled them dry over the winter to pay for his war, and now there were few men to earn money.

Spotting Micah on the far side of the hall, I made my way over. He blinked at the sight of me.

"Did you ride up alone?" he whispered.

"I was fine. Where is Ashton?"

Though I think he wanted to continue our discussion of me riding through the city alone, he said, "Rowan said she's not well." He looked worried.

"I'll go up and see her."

He nodded.

* * * *

Upstairs, in the south tower, I knocked on her door, but no one answered. Pausing only briefly, I reached down and opened the door.

Inside, Ashton sat at her tea table, staring into space. She still wore her nightgown and dressing robe. Her hair was uncombed.

The cradle on the floor beside her was empty.

With an ill feeling, I entered the room and approached her.

"Ashton?"

She looked at me. "Olivia?"

There was bad cut on the left side of her mouth, but the blood had dried.

"What happened?" I asked.

Her eyes were so lost.

"What do you mean?" she asked.

"Where's Eduard?"

She looked away, staring into space again. "The nursery. I'm not allowed to see him for a while. Last night, Rowan insisted he be moved to the nursery, and I...I argued. I should not have argued with Rowan."

"Did he strike you?"

"Strike me? No, he would never. But afterward, he came to my bed, and he was angry, and he..."

When she didn't finish the sentence, I was grateful. I did not want to know any more.

I stayed with her the rest of the day. I tried to make her eat something, and I read her more stories. An hour before dinner, Kamilla came in. She stopped when she saw me.

"The king may be up shortly," she said. "But I don't think he'll expect the queen to come down for dinner."

Understanding her meaning, I stood. Rowan would not want the other nobles to see Ashton like this, especially not with the cut on her mouth.

"I must go home, but I'll return soon," I told Ashton. "We'll go and see Eduard. I promise."

She gazed into empty space. "Yes. Soon."

Turning, I fled the room and went down the back stairs. I had no wish to run into Rowan.

Once outside, I went to the barracks and found Micah. He watched me cautiously.

"How fares the queen?" he asked.

I wanted him to tell him that she suffered at the hands of her husband, and that he'd taken her child, and that she was disappearing inside herself. But it would pain Micah on several levels to hear such things…and there was nothing he could do to stop it.

"A mild indisposition," I said.

Relief flooded his face. He knew more of the truth than he let on, but he could not speak of it, and he was grateful to me.

"Are you ready to go home?" he asked.

I was more than ready.

As we rode home side by side, I thought on all my blessings: my kind and loving husband, my warm home by the sea, my safe and happy life. I tried with all my heart to focus on those things.

But I could not stop thinking of Ashton.

The Choice

Chapter Twenty-Two

The world around me vanished, and I found myself standing again in the alcove of the castle, staring into the three-paneled mirror.

I ached for Ashton. I longed for Micah.

Now, there were three images of the dark-haired woman as she gazed out at me from all three panels.

"Which action?" the woman asked. "You must choose."

Images and emotions surged through me until I couldn't think clearly.

"Which of the paths will you follow?" she asked. "Hesitation…instant resolution…independent action?" She paused. "Queen…chancellor…wife?"

Her statement of the choices let me focus, and my mind flowed backward to the life I'd lived as queen, married to man without love. And yet, I was queen, with power in Partheney, and my beautiful son, Henri. I could see his face as clearly as if I held him in my arms.

But Ashton was dead, and Micah merely the loyal captain of my guard.

And Samourè suffered under Rowan's revenge.

The images rolled forward to my life as chancellor at Ashton's side. Without Rowan, she'd risen to her role as queen, fighting the council and protecting the people from men like Lord Sauvage. How I loved her. How I'd fed my strength into her and trusted in her wisdom. We ruled the kingdom together.

I could still feel Micah's mouth on mine, the hunger in his kiss as we stole away to hide in his barracks room. I remembered every word he'd said to me, how we'd risked ourselves in our need for each other.

But I'd had to give him up. Reliving the moment broke my heart, and, here in the alcove, tears streamed down my face.

Micah.

Images rolled forward to the third life, the indescribable happiness as his wife. The joy of creating our home. The sound of his laugh. The warmth of his body in our bed at night.

But Ashton was crushed beneath Rowan's smothering love. No matter how much she gave him, he wanted more…and more, until he even took her child and left her as a shadow.

Ashton.

My mind raced. Did I know the future? What if I chose the third action, but with my knowledge I was able to convince her not to marry Rowan? I could tell her what would happen. I would make her believe me. Could I save her and still marry Micah?

But…what of the people of Samourè? What of our own people? Could I change those events?

The dark-haired woman in the mirror watched me.

"Once I choose," I asked, "will I still remember what I've seen? Can I alter events because of what I have seen here?"

She shook her head. "These are the possible paths, and you have been given the gift to see and to choose. But once you have chosen, all that you have seen will be gone."

I closed my eyes in pain. I would remember nothing.

"Choose for yourself," she said. "This is a gift."

But I couldn't choose. I loved two people, and I'd not give up one for the other.

A thought struck me.

"Wait," I said. "When the second choice ended, not even a year had passed. Might Ashton later come into enough power that she'd not need me to help battle the council? Might I one day be free to go openly to Micah?"

"You have seen what you have seen," she answered. "There is nothing more I can tell you. Which of the paths will you follow? Hesitation…instant resolution…independent action? Queen…chancellor…wife?"

I closed my eyes, breathing hard. I couldn't leave Ashton to Rowan, not for anything. I would have to take a great risk.

"Chancellor," I whispered and opened my eyes.

She nodded, standing now only in the center panel. "The second choice."

The air before me wavered, and the mirror vanished.

* * * *

I was in a corridor, outside an alcove, listening to the plans of a murderer and an assassin.

"Doesn't make any difference to me, so long as I get paid," said the man called Soren. "But you need not fear. I'll get it done."

I felt disoriented, and touched one side of my head, but when Soren turned to leave, I flew into motion, dashing to the nearest alcove to hide from sight.

He walked past me.

A few moments later, so did Genève.

An assassin was about to seek out Ashton in the stable and kill her. I was desperate for the crown. But not at this price, not at Ashton's life, and I had to save her. From where I stood now, the kitchens weren't far.

Without an instant of hesitation, I ran.

Upon reaching the archway to the kitchens, I looked ahead to a door and hurried through it. Once out in the courtyard, I cast about for any help, but the only guards in sight were all the way out at the castle gates.

Running toward the old stable myself, I resolved to do anything necessary to save Ashton. Just as I reached the door, I turned my head in time to see Rowan leading a horse out of the new stable, and I called out.

"Rowan...!"

The End

Don't miss the next book in the Dark Glass series,
A Girl of White Winter, **coming in August 2018.**

Chapter One

While I was growing up, I never realized how carefully the Lady Giselle hid me from the eyes of men. She did not do this from jealousy or selfishness, but to protect me…as my position in the household was not easy to define.

On an evening in early autumn, as she sat in a chair before me, I piled her dark hair atop her head and fastened it with silver clips. In her late forties, she was still lovely, and I always helped her dress for dinner.

Tonight, she wore a green velvet gown with a full skirt and long sleeves.

"Would you like your diamond pendant?" I asked.

Her mind was elsewhere. "Mmmmmm?"

She'd seemed unsettled since midafternoon, and I knew she was worried about the outcome of tonight's dinner gathering.

"Your diamond pendant?" I asked again.

This evening was important, and she would wish to look her best.

Nodding, she said, "Yes, my dear."

But as I went to fetch it, she reached out and stopped me. "Kara…his lordship has requested that you join us for dinner. The Capellos did not bring their wives or sisters, as this is a business gathering, and his lordship fears the numbers will appear too skewed at the table." She paused. "Once you finish dressing me, we'll need to find you a gown. He wants you to be decorative."

I tensed. "Must I?"

She nodded again, this time more tightly. "Yes. It is his lordship's wish."

Though it was common for me to join the family for dinner, over the past summer, I had turned eighteen, and I'd not been invited to join a formal dinner with guests in nearly three years. Lady Giselle kept me hidden, even from most of the manor guards. Again, though, at that time, I didn't realize what she was doing and didn't learn the truth until it was too late.

"Which gown?" I asked, nervous at the thought of dining with strangers.

"Your white silk, I think."

* * * *

That night, as Giselle and I walked into the great hall, my stomach tightened when I saw what appeared to be a sea of men milling around before dinner. In truth, only five of the men would be joining us at the table. The rest were merely guards of either our house or the Capellos'.

The group of five had gathered near the hearth.

The lord of our house, Jean de Marco, stood with his and Lady Giselle's two sons: Geoffrey and Lucas, who were both older than me by a few years. Lord Jean was a large man, and only recently had some of his muscle begun to sag a little. Glancing in our direction, he offered his wife a nod, but did not acknowledge my presence.

He had no love for me.

The other two men were strangers to me. One appeared late middle-aged and the other was in his early thirties.

A table stretched out in the center of the hall, laden with goblets, fine pewter plates, and a centerpiece of the last of our autumn roses.

Beside me, Lady Giselle drew a long breath as her face transformed into a welcoming smile. She took my arm, and we swept into the vast room.

"Gentlemen," she said, approaching the group of five. "Forgive our tardy arrival."

This was a polite but expected comment. Women of her station never arrived at a formal dinner before her guests. It was the lord's duty to greet them.

Both strangers turned to offer a greeting, but at the sight of me, the words froze on their lips, and they stared.

I was not taken aback, as this was a normal response from anyone seeing me for the first time. My lady assured me that it was due to my unusual coloring. I was small, slender, and pale-skinned, but my hair was so blond that she called it "silver" and my eyes so crystalline blue that they seemed to glow against the pale background. Once, Lord Jean had shivered as he studied me and said, "She looks like a winter morning."

I had long wished for dark hair and brown eyes.

Lady Giselle was accustomed to men going speechless at the sight of me, and she pretended not to notice their half-opened mouths. "May I present our ward, Kara."

Lord Jean flinched slightly at the term "ward," but I was the only one who noticed.

Turning to me, Giselle motioned to the men with a graceful hand. "Kara, this is Lord Trey Capello and his son, Royce."

Lord Trey must have been past fifty, but he was slender and striking, with light brown hair and a goatee. He recovered himself quickly, kissing first her hand and then mine.

"My ladies," he said. "We'll be blessed with your company at dinner."

Somehow, he sounded sincere, and I began to relax a little. Perhaps, I would be required to only nod and smile and not answer any difficult questions about my identity.

But Royce did not recover so quickly and continued to stare, running his eyes over my face and silver-blond hair. He bore little resemblance to his father, taller and more muscular with sandy blond hair and a clean-shaven face.

I hoped he would not try to engage me in conversation, as I was not nearly so skilled as my lady and had little experience in talking to men.

"Shall I ring for dinner so that we might sit?" Giselle asked.

Lord Jean nodded to her, and we gathered at the table. To my relief, I was seated between Geoffrey and Lucas. I didn't know them well, but they had long grown accustomed to my appearance, and neither would expect me to talk.

Unfortunately, Royce was seated directly across the table and although he'd stopped staring, he continued glancing in my direction.

A number of servants entered the hall carrying trays of food and decanters of wine.

Wine was poured, and the fish course was served. I was not fond of red wine but tried to sip politely.

"You understand I wish to buy the entire two hundred acres?" Lord Jean asked after swallowing a bite of trout.

This was the reason for the Capellos' visit. For nearly three centuries, the noble de Marco family had boasted one of the most renowned vineyards in the nation of Samourè. They grew white and red grapes, but of late, demand for white wine had been waning, and Lord Jean had long coveted a large piece of undeveloped land just off our southern border—and on the Capellos' northern border. Both its soil and its positioning were perfect for growing the purple grapes of burgundy wine.

I'd learned all this information from my lady. To date, the Capellos had never responded to any of Lord Jean's offers, but…it appeared the land belonged to Royce and not to his father, and now, Royce might be willing to sell.

Lady Giselle impressed upon me the importance of this meeting.

Lord Jean could not accept failure in these negotiations.

His question about the two hundred acres hung in the air. Royce didn't answer, but he was again staring at me.

"My son?" Lord Trey asked.

Royce turned his head to look down the table at Lord Jean. "Let us talk of business over breakfast. The ride was long today, and for tonight, I would rather dine and speak of less weighty matters."

His voice was deep and possessed a serious quality that suggested he rarely made jokes. I knew that he and his father would be spending at least one night with us, as their own manor was a full day's ride south.

Lord Jean's jaw twitched, but he nodded. "As you wish." Then he looked to Lady Giselle. "Time for the next course, I think."

* * * *

Somehow, I made it through dinner and dessert without being required to enter the conversation. I made certain to pay polite attention to all that was said in regards to crops and taxes and other matters men tended to discuss over dinner, and I smiled whenever Lucas or Lord Trey said something amusing—for they were the only men in the group disposed toward humor.

Finally, at the end, I breathed in quiet relief that the women would be excused so the men might switch to a stronger port wine and play cards.

Lady Giselle was a woman of flawless timing, and at the precise moment, she rose. I stood quickly.

"Gentlemen," she said, "it has been a pleasure. Kara and I will leave you to your amusements, and I shall see you at breakfast."

All the men stood in respect, and the two of us turned to leave, heading for the archway. I looked forward to a quiet night with her of reading aloud to each other or playing at chess or cards or working on our embroidery or hearing her thoughts on how Lord Jean might approach Royce in this land deal.

"My lady?" Mistress Duval, our housekeeper, came to the archway just as we reached it. "Forgive me, but the cook fears we don't have enough eggs for the breakfast that was planned. Could you come and approve a new menu?"

"Of course."

Lady Giselle was a woman who oversaw every detail of the running of her household. Normally, breakfast menus did not require approval, but we all knew the importance of this meeting. Everything from the guest rooms to the food had to be perfect.

Turning to me, Giselle said, "My dear. You go up, and I'll meet you directly."

"Yes, my lady."

She turned and swept down the east corridor for the kitchens. I headed for the west stairwell, so that I might ascend to her private apartments where she would soon meet me.

I had walked only about six steps when a voice sounded from behind.

"Wait."

The voice was deep and possessed of a serious quality.

Turning, my stomach again tightened at the sight of Royce walking toward me. Desperately, I looked down the east corridor, but my lady was gone, and I was alone with Royce. He strode to me with purpose and stopped. Facing him, my eyes were level with his collarbones, which were visible through the V-neck of his tunic. I did not look up at his face.

"Who are you?" he asked bluntly.

Despair flooded through me. I would not escape the evening without answering questions.

"Lady Giselle's ward," I whispered.

"That's not an answer. If she had a ward from one of the noble families, it would be common knowledge. You'd have been seen at court." He paused and if possible, his tone hardened. "Who was your father?"

I could not raise my eyes from his collarbones any more than I could answer his question because the truth was a family secret.

I knew the story well.

Almost nineteen years ago, Lady Giselle's brother, Jacques, had visited these vineyards. Giselle adored her handsome brother, who was charming and reckless—or so she described him to me.

At the same time, she had a beautiful lady's maid, named Coraline, of whom she had grown fond.

Upon his visit, Jacques seduced the maid, and as soon as he learned she was with child, he fled. For a marriage to a wealthy wool merchant's daughter had already been arranged for him.

When Lord Jean learned of Coraline's condition, he ordered that she be dismissed, but for the first time, Giselle went against him, begging that Coraline be allowed to remain. Such state of affairs was unheard of...to keep a pregnant woman as a lady's maid.

In the end, Giselle won, for she seldom asked him for anything, and in his heart, Lord Jean liked to please her.

I was born.

At first, out of guilt, my father sent Coraline some money, but he never visited or took any action to see me and remained at his home with his new wife. When I was two years old, he drank too much wine and took up a challenge to ride one of his horses in a race.

In his drunken state, he fell off over a jump and was killed.

When I was five, a fever passed through our lands, and some of our household died, including my mother.

I had no parents, and I was alone.

Lord Jean might not have noticed my existence had I been given to the kitchen women and raised as a servant. But Lady Giselle had only given birth to sons, and she had come to love me. She insisted I be raised as her ward, calling me her "niece" in private.

Again, Lord Jean protested, seeing me as the bastard child of a lady's maid, certainly not worthy of the title of ward in the house of de Marco. But again, Giselle won. I grew up as her companion, not exactly a niece, but neither was I a servant. I had duties for her, but I ate with the family and wore the fine clothing of a noble.

All was well until I turned fifteen, and the house guards began watching me enter a room. Of course they did not dare speak to me, but this was a forerunning of things to come. I was allowed to join dinners when we had guests, but then, during a visit from the Larues, the second son of Lord Alex Larue stared at me over the table. A week later, he asked Lord Jean for my hand in marriage—with no questions regarding my birth. Lord Jean thought it an astonishing offer and wanted to accept, but Lady Giselle pleaded that at fifteen, I was too young.

After that, she stopped including me at dinner when we had guests.

She kept me to herself, and I loved our quiet time together. She promised she would keep me safe.

And now…three years later, I was in a corridor, alone with a strange nobleman who continued demanding answers.

"Who was your father?" Royce repeated.

No matter that Giselle called me her niece in private, I would never expose her beloved brother as a seducer of women or a man who abandoned unwanted children.

So I whispered, "I do not know."

Before I knew what was happening, he grasped my chin and forced me to look up at him. Though his grip did not hurt, he allowed me to feel some of the strength in his hand. His eyes were a shade of light brown.

"What do you mean you don't know? If you're the de Marcos' ward, how is that possible?" He didn't sound angry, only confused. "Who was your mother?"

Wanting him to let me go, I tried to meet his gaze and answered, "Lady Giselle's maid."

He let go and stepped back.

I hadn't told him the whole truth, but enough to give him an understanding. No matter what Giselle called me, I was the illegitimate child of a servant.

I was no one, not worth his attention.

Whirling, I hurried for the west stairwell.

* * * *

The next morning, Lady Giselle sent word, informing me I would be expected at breakfast, but I was not concerned. By now, Royce had told his father of my low status, and they would not notice me. Besides, the men would be focused on the land deal, not upon any women at the table.

I wore my hair down and donned a muslin dress of sky blue.

My own private room was near to Lady Giselle's apartments, and as I reached her door, I found it open, suggesting she had already gone down without my help in dressing for the day.

"My lady?" I asked from the doorway.

Silence told me she was not there.

Quickly, I made my way to the stairwell and descended to the main floor. Upon arriving at the great hall, I found everyone from last night had already gathered—with the exception of Lucas and Geoffrey. Would they not be attending? Perhaps they were not necessary for the business dealings this morning.

Then why had I been asked?

Royce stood apart with his arms crossed, and he appeared to be watching the archway as I entered. At the sight of me, he went still and gave me the same fixed stare from last night. He took in my long silver-blond hair and light blue gown. Only this morning, I was beginning to recognize the expression on his face; it looked like hunger.

"She's here," he said. "We can begin."

Two things about these statements puzzled me. First, was he the one who'd requested my presence this morning? Why? And second...

breakfast had not even been served yet. Did he wish to conduct the business dealing before eating?

Lord Jean seemed equally nonplussed, but he gestured to the table. "By all means."

I could see that he did not care when or how these dealings took place, so long as he acquired the land.

Walking over, I greeted my lady and sat beside her. Lord Trey and Royce sat across from us, and Lord Jean took his place at the head.

As of yet, we'd not even been served tea.

Lord Jean began immediately. "I'm willing to pay two thousand in silver for the land. That's more than what it's worth and a fair offer."

Royce studied him with a level gaze. "I'm willing to take fifteen hundred." Then he motioned to me with his head. "But I want the girl."

I went cold.

Lord Trey turned to his son in open surprise.

Lord Jean frowned.

Lady Giselle stiffened, and she spoke first. "Sir," she said to Royce. "I don't understand. You cannot be asking for Kara's hand as you already have a wife. You were married eight years ago, and to the best of my knowledge, the lady Lorraine still lives."

Royce turned his cold eyes upon her. "You need not remind me of my marital status."

Lord Jean's frown deepened. "Then what are you asking?"

Royce leaned back in his chair. "I want the girl."

At this, all polite pretense vanished from my lady's voice. "As what? Your mistress? You'll set her up in some cottage near your manor until you grow tired of her? I think not!"

They all spoke as if I weren't there.

Lord Trey raised one hand to her and addressed his son. "This girl? You're certain?"

Royce nodded, but the brief exchange only increased the confusion in Lord Jean's expression.

Lord Trey sighed. "What my son suggests is not so shocking as it first sounds. We are more...modern at the Capello estate. Your ward would hold a position of honor, and she would reside with us, in her own apartments, at the manor. She would have a place in the family."

"As his mistress?" my lady demanded. "No."

"Giselle!" Lord Jean barked, as if trying to take control of the conversation.

Royce shrugged. "The girl is of no birth. She cannot remain your ward forever, and this is a good offer."

I remained frozen, but beside me, I could hear my lady's quick breaths.
"Kara is the daughter of my brother," she said slowly. "She is my blood."
All three men were taken aback, but I knew Lord Jean's response was one of embarrassment. This truth had never been spoken outside her rooms.

For just an instant, Royce's face flickered, and then he shook his head. "It is of no matter. She is of no name and no house."

My lady's hand clenched into a fist, but again, Lord Jean broke in, this time speaking directly to Lord Trey. "My lord...you can see the attachment my wife has for the girl. Surely, some other arrangement can be made in exchange for the land. I would offer twenty-five hundred sliver pieces."

Royce leaned forward in his chair, addressing Lord Jean. "There will be no further bargaining here. I will take fifteen hundred in silver for the land. But if you don't agree to my terms, I won't sell to you. And since I find myself in need of funds, I will sell the land to someone else." He paused to let the effect of his threat sink in. Then he repeated slowly, "I want the girl."

A long moment of silence followed, and then Lord Jean looked to Lady Giselle. "Get her packed."

My lady shot to her feet. "No!" Reaching out, she took my hand and pulled me up. "We will be in my apartments until these gentlemen leave."

Needing no urging from her, I gripped her hand and we fled from the hall.

* * * *

Once she and I were alone in her apartments, her anger began to fade and I could see fear in her eyes.

The sight of this was more terrifying than anything that had transpired in the past moments.

"Don't let them take me," I said.

But before she could answer, the door to her apartments opened, and Lord Jean stood on the other side with two of our house guards behind him. Upon seeing the guards, Giselle went pale.

As Lord Jean stepped inside the room, she shouted at him. "This is your fault! You were the one who insisted she be at the table last night to create a distraction and put them off their game."

His expression was difficult to read. I'd never once heard her speak to him in any other tone than polite deference. He appeared both angry and uncomfortable.

"They have promised me she'll be treated well," he said.

"Promised?" she cried. "What good is that? You know nothing of Royce Capello. For all you know, he keeps a riding crop under his bed."

Lord Jean took a step back. "Don't be vulgar."

"Vulgar? Me? You stand there and say that when you are giving our girl away to be some nobleman's whore!"

His discomfort increased, but so did his anger. "She is not our girl."

I stood pressed against a wall, and she suddenly went slack in despair. "Please, my lord. Don't do this. Don't take her from me. I could not bear it."

At this, he wavered. I could see it, and hope rose inside me. He loved her. He cared for her feelings.

But then, his expression hardened again. "I have no choice. I've paid the fifteen hundred, and the deed will be sent. A maid is packing Kara's things now, and the Capellos are making ready to leave." Striding over, he gripped my upper arm but spoke only to her. "You will remain here until they are gone. I'll leave men to watch over you."

With that, he dragged me forward. I struggled to pull away, but I don't think he noticed.

When we reached the door, my lady spoke from behind us.

"I will never forgive you for this, Jean. Do you understand what that means? I won't forgive you."

It was his turn to go pale, and again, he wavered.

Then he dragged me out the door.

* * * *

Down in the courtyard, I saw my trunk being lifted into the back of a wagon. A maid from the house came to me and wrapped a cloak around my shoulders, but I was too numb to respond or thank her.

I could not believe what was happening.

Lord Trey's and Royce's horses were saddled, and their six guards were making ready to leave. One of our guards led a white mare from the stables...with a sidesaddle.

The sight of this made me fear I would faint.

At the look on my face, Royce frowned. "What's wrong?"

Lord Jean's brows knitted and then smoothed. "Oh, Kara has never been on... She's never ridden a horse."

Royce blinked twice. "How is that possible?"

Shifting his weight between his feet, Lord Jean answered. "Because she has never been off the manor grounds. She's rarely been outside the house. You must understand that my lady has kept her...sheltered."

Silence followed, and even in my frightened state, I sensed there was a good deal taking place beneath this conversation. I simply did not know what.

"You could have her ride in the wagon beside your driver?" Lord Jean suggested.

"No," Royce answered. "I will lead her horse."

Turning, he gripped my waist and lifted me as if I weighed nothing, setting me into the saddle. Then he mounted his own horse and drew up beside me, lifting the reins over my mount's head and gripping them in his left hand.

As opposed to reassuring me, this act only made me feel more trapped.

I cast a pleading look at Lord Jean, but he turned away. My horse lurched forward, and I gripped her mane. Within moments, I found myself outside the gates of our manor for the first time in my life, and in the company of strangers.

I was not even allowed to tell Lady Giselle good-bye.

ABOUT THE AUTHOR

Barb Hendee is the *New York Times* bestselling author of The Mist-Torn Witches series. She is the co-author (with husband J.C.) of the Noble Dead Saga. She holds a master's degree in composition/rhetoric from the University of Idaho and currently teaches writing for Umpqua Community College. She and J.C. live in a quirky two-level townhouse just south of Portland, Oregon. Barb Hendee can be reached at www.barbhendee.org, or www.twitter.com/barbhendeeorg, or www.facebook.com/BarbHendee.org.

Printed in the United States
by Baker & Taylor Publisher Services